"Amy, I'm your birth mother."

Amy blinked once, shaking her head, looking less than pleased, mostly stunned.

"I realized," Sophie continued, "when you began talking to me downtown, when you told me your father's name–and yours. I didn't come back to Ouray intending to meet you or intrude on your life. It just... happened...that you and I met–and then saw each other again. But I don't feel it's right to deceive you any longer."

Amy seemed dumbfounded. She still didn't speak.

"Your dad and I were best friends all through high school, during the summers. We both came here each year with our parents."

"Does my dad know you're telling me this?" Amy demanded.

"We've talked about it." Sophie had imagined many reactions in Amy, reactions to this news. She had not imagined rage.

Dear Reader,

Being a romance author means being a student of all kinds of love–love of family, of friends, of the human spirit, of life, of that which is so intimate it remains private, hidden: our deepest beliefs, our strongest and most enduring passions, our vision, our trust. Though I've called this story, *How To Get Married*, it is a celebration of friendship and trust as much as romance and commitment. In many ways, friendship is the gold standard of love; we can't choose our family, but we choose our friends. It is a gift when one's lover and partner is the one friend we would pick again and again.

My life has been blessed by many remarkable friendships. As a writer, I'm hungry to learn about people, what affects their feelings, what is important to each person. But the intense and fluid bond of friendship, the warmth that erupts in spontaneous laughter, the familiarity of dear touch, the comfort that allows barriers to drop so that we can be ourselves, trusting that we are accepted and loved and safe, that the beloved will not violate us, gives birth to a love that can't be spoken or truly painted.

Sophie Creed is a woman who has been violated by someone she trusted. The result is a holistic loss of trust. It takes friendship–not a friendship that denies responsibility or says "I won't do it again," but a friendship devoid of violation, a friendship with someone who has never harmed her, who categorically *won't* do so–to restore her trust and faith in love…and to allow her to feel and be worthy of trust in return.

I wish you all the gifts of friendship in its most enduring forms.

Sincerely,

Margot Early

How To Get Married

Margot Early

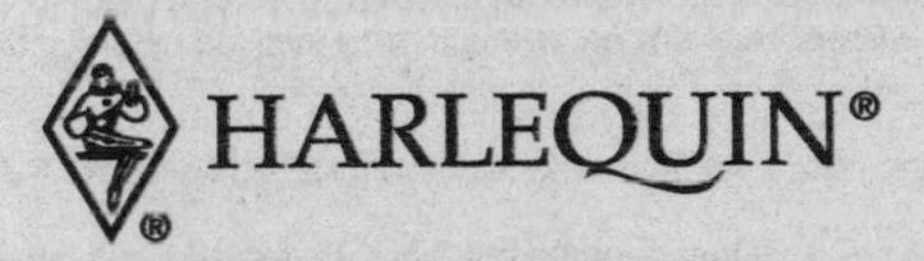

TORONTO • NEW YORK • LONDON
AMSTERDAM • PARIS • SYDNEY • HAMBURG
STOCKHOLM • ATHENS • TOKYO • MILAN • MADRID
PRAGUE • WARSAW • BUDAPEST • AUCKLAND

ISBN 0-373-71333-9

HOW TO GET MARRIED

This edition published by arrangement with Harlequin Books S.A.

www.eHarlequin.com

Printed in U.S.A.

Books by Margot Early

HARLEQUIN SUPERROMANCE

625–THE THIRD CHRISTMAS
668–THE KEEPER
694–WAITING FOR YOU
711–MR. FAMILY
724–NICK'S KIND OF WOMAN
743–THE TRUTH ABOUT COWBOYS
766–WHO'S AFRAID OF THE MISTLETOE?
802–YOU WERE ON MY MIND
855–TALKING ABOUT MY BABY
878–THERE IS A SEASON
912–FOREVER AND A BABY
1092–THE GIFT OF CHRISTMAS
"Epiphany"
1297–25 YEARS
"Wade in the Water"

HARLEQUIN SINGLE TITLE

FOR MY DAUGHTER
"Soul Kitchen"

For Gregory

CHAPTER ONE

Ouray, Colorado
Friday
Memorial Day Weekend

THE DISORIENTATION WAS BACK. Well, not back. It had never left, simply became worse when any loud sound intruded on her world. And music—music was not the same. Sophie could hardly bear to listen now or try to sing because it terrified her. It terrified her that crystal clear had changed to an underwater-like whining, to distortion, to an unsilence that made one ear worse than useless, disallowing enjoyment of the other's perfection.

A virus had done it, a virus others had caught as well, but it hadn't wrecked *their* ears. The doctors had said her hearing might improve with time, that many people did eventually get better on their own.

Two long courses of prednisone that had kept her insomniac, alternately terrified that her gift was lost and manically convinced that her *genius*, like Beethoven's, could transcend this. Months of oxygen therapy. Acupuncture. Sessions with a Lakota medicine man and then with a shaman from the Andes. Anything, anything, to help.

One perfect ear, and one ear with severe hearing loss and twelve percent speech discrimination. She'd nearly been hit by cars twice—or would have been. But the dogs both knew. Somehow they knew, and Cinders had shoved herself between the car and Sophie, pushing her mistress clear, while a car horn blared, painful, making the world rock. Loki had developed the habit, suddenly, of crowding Sophie's left thigh, as though anticipating the kind of trouble Cinders had averted.

Sophie had come back to Ouray, telling herself there were fewer cars here and less noise. She'd stay at her parents' summer place, the home they'd bought long ago for a retirement that had finally arrived. Sophie had brought her own home, too, her custom-built wayfaring wagon, styled after an English gypsy wagon—for when her parents arrived in June, just in case. Just in case they drove her crazy—and the reverse, of course. Ouray seemed unchanged from when she'd visited for three weeks each summer growing up.

It was summer now. The mountains were steadfast, rising steeply on each side of town, charming Victorian homes nestled at the valley's narrow head. And there were plenty of cars, not a parking space to be found on Main Street, definitely not for a rig like hers, a truck hauling a gypsy wagon.

And there was too much noise.

What if it doesn't get better? What if I always hear like this?

Braking the Tundra for some tourists trying to cross Main Street, she glanced behind her at Loki, front paws hanging over the back seat of the dual cab, dark brown eyes intelligent and concerned. Cinders had the bed on the floor behind the passenger seat.

I'll still have my dogs.

She laughed, half-hysterically.

After everything. After backbreaking work, after

sacrifices—one sacrifice too keen to be counted—after fighting and winning, was she now to lose it all?

So—back to the scene of the crime. Back here again.

It had happened long ago, but she would never stop thinking about it, never stop remembering, never stop wondering what her life would have been like, where that child, fourteen this summer, was now.

Sophie Creed, thirty-two, was attractive—some said beautiful—successful and talented, a musician whose hearing was suddenly compromised.

She should go to the market before she arrived at the house. She could have gotten groceries in Montrose but hadn't wanted to face a big store. It wasn't that she'd be recognized. That seldom happened. It was just the sound—the noise. The doctors had said she'd become accustomed.

Sophie didn't *want* to get used to it. She wanted her hearing back.

She sang. Every day she still sang. And danced. And played the harmonica and her violin. Bearing it. But music brought tears because sound that had been clear and perfect was now distorted.

She had passed the market when she saw a delivery truck leaving a place on the right, on the lower side, the west side, of the wide, sharply tilted street. Surely she could pull over there for long enough to run into the store. Sophie switched on her turn signal, waited, parked carefully along the curb. She'd put the dogs in the truck bed. They'd be happier waiting there.

Someone had told her she could train one or both of them as hearing dogs. As far as Sophie was concerned, they'd already begun that job, were already doing it. Both knew. Loki, the sable shepherd she'd gotten from the humane society, seemed to realize her plight. But Cinders, a long-haired sable she'd bought three years earlier from a breeder whose grail was Westminster—Cinders acted.

As she loaded them into the back of the truck, Sophie admired their muscles, their lustrous coats, the tall set of their ears. Sound roared in her own ears, and she jumped as a car passed. The cacophony in her bad left ear was so overwhelming that she couldn't, in that moment, hear properly out of her right. And she couldn't hear where the sound had originated, had no directional orientation.

She jumped when she saw someone just beside her.

"Sorry," the girl apologized. She was a young teenager, dark-haired, with very fair skin, a few freckles, glasses and braces. "I just…your dogs."

Sophie said, "What?" Another car passed, and she started. "I'm sorry. I have a hearing problem right now." She'd had it for five months. Some people got better; some didn't. A hearing aid wouldn't help but would only make it more difficult to hear from her good ear. Plugging the left ear didn't really help, either.

And that was for normal functioning.

But she was a musician.

"Your dogs are beautiful. I wanted to see them. My dad…dogs."

"You can pet them." Sophie tried not to jump as another vehicle passed.

The girl offered a closed hand to Cinders for the bitch to sniff. Loki hung back, reserved. His appearance was obviously European—blocky-headed, sturdy, powerful, extraordinarily male. He and Cinders looked like two different breeds, beautiful in different ways. Cinders had good hips. Loki's were fair.

Sophie studied the girl. She had excellent posture, seemed self-possessed, with some regal characteristic beyond dignity that acknowledged neither nearsightedness nor braces. Her hair shone smooth, almost black with just a hint of dark red. Behind her glasses, her eyes were brown. Her coloring was not unlike Sophie's, fair, with a good complexion.

And Sophie, tired of contact lens problems at gigs, had undergone laser surgery on her eyes four years before. "Do you live here?" she asked, to be polite. An eighteen-wheeler, down off Red Mountain Pass, rumbled by, and Sophie tried not to cringe. *I have to get away from this noise.*

The girl nodded. "We train protection…I said. Also bomb, drug…that kind of thing. Mostly…obedience now. Aggression problems. My dad used to be… Then he…"

No hesitation in the words, but Sophie's hearing missed some. She watched the teenager's lips, collecting and failing to collect information. "Did you grow up here?" Not caring, being polite.

"We lived in Denver…eight. Then, my dad…retired…K-9… But he grew up here—well, kind of. His parents helped raise me. My mom died when I was a baby."

The skin on the back of Sophie's neck hummed, electric, her whole body sharply aware. She knew. Not in words. In her bones. She didn't yet know *what* she knew, but every part of her was knowledge. "Who is your father?"

"William Ludlow. I'm Amy."

That was what she knew.

The other thing she knew, seeing the girl's brown eyes that were the same shape as her own, with the same slightly lush, slightly curling, sable lashes, was that Amy Ludlow's mother had not died when Amy was a baby.

Amy's mother was Sophie Creed.

DEAD?

That had not been part of the agreement, the solemn agreement she'd made with William Ludlow not long after her eighteenth birthday. It seemed unlikely to her, almost unbelievable, that skinny black-haired William Ludlow with his clear brown eyes, with his heavy black brows, had become a cop. He had been a writer; his interests were languages and math. He'd been to school all over the world, spent time in Papua New Guinea, Indonesia, Irian Jaya, places like that. His father was an ethnolinguist, specializing in the languages of New Guinea. When Sophie met William, he'd been familiar with seven or eight languages (three of them dead) besides English, *plus* some tribal dialects absolutely useless unless one were to travel to these places, where people practiced customs Sophie had found both horrifying and fascinating. And he'd had a plan. Whenever anyone asked him what he was going to be, his answer was always the same. *An ethnologist and author.*

He'd wanted to study other cultures, whether Hasidic Jews in New York or indigenous peoples of the Arctic.

How could he have become a cop?

She hadn't asked Amy.

He'd chosen their daughter's name, and Sophie hadn't argued, hadn't much cared.

William had told Amy that her natural mother was dead.

No. That was not part of the agreement.

Pulling the truck and wagon to the curb outside her parents' four-square Victorian, Sophie tried to shrug it off. What, after all, had she expected of him? Her father was a minister—her parents' life was about God—but when she'd revealed that she was pregnant, William had become even more traditional than she was. He'd mentioned—once—her *abandoning* Amy, which had rubbed Sophie more than a little wrong. She'd been adopted herself, had never believed herself abandoned and never felt a burning desire to look for her birth parents. Besides, William's parents were going to help him with the baby.

But next her status as an adopted child slash birth mother had come up for review. William had suggested—again, only once—that she'd felt compelled to give up Amy to justify her own birth mother's having relinquished her.

Sophie hadn't told Amy her name. But Amy had said where to find Mount Sneffels K-9. The property was off the Camp Bird road, on the way up to Yankee Boy Basin, she'd said.

We breed them, too, but we don't have any litters right now. So many people are bringing dogs for us to train. We have German shepherds, though, and Dutch shepherds, and a Dogue de Bordeaux. Our German shepherds come from Czechoslavakia, and one of our studs is a black sable. Your dark sable reminds me of him.

Or so Sophie thought she'd said.

Would she take Amy up on her invitation to visit Mount Sneffels K-9?

Ever since she'd relinquished her infant daughter, walked away from her for reasons of foresight and maturity, she'd known that if she really wanted, she could find William Ludlow and contact him again and meet the daughter she'd let go. But she'd never planned to do it. She'd planned *not* to contact Amy.

Amy had been born in Glenwood Springs. During her pregnancy, Sophie had lived in nearby Carbondale with William. She hadn't wanted the people of Ouray to know she was pregnant. If they didn't know, they couldn't tell the child the identity of her birth mother.

Later she'd typed up something for William to give Amy, a description of herself, of her health issues as she knew them, of her talents and dreams. That, she had reasoned, would allow Amy to develop a healthy identity.

Had William even shared the information she'd left for their daughter?

She trembled in the afternoon shadows—shade cast by the mountains that clutched the town. She unloaded the dogs and took them up to the house, unlocked the door.

Did her parents know? William and Amy had obviously been in Ouray for some time. Wasn't it likely that her parents had run into one or both of them? And they'd always liked William, despite their disapproval of sexual activity outside marriage.

Sophie loved the Ouray house. On her brief, infrequent trips to Ouray since leaving home, she had helped her parents with what she called the house's "salvage style." Even the front door, with its Arts and Crafts stained glass, had been rescued from a condemned building in Salt Lake City. Sophie had come across the door during some rare downtime on tour. And in the foyer sat two Gothic Revival chairs she and her mother had refinished and reupholstered, working together, trying to make their work as like each other's as possible.

Sophie had been looking forward to seeing her parents. But what if they knew William was in Ouray? The last Sophie had heard, William and Amy had moved away.

Sophie's own parents were not interfering people. Their hands-off approach, Sophie often thought, had helped make their adoption of her so successful. Of course, they'd all been through therapy—Sophie and her parents. But Dan and Amanda Creed were simply very balanced people who had wanted to adopt. And, actually, they'd known enough about her background that they'd wanted to adopt *her* in particular.

Damn William. Telling Amy that her birth mother had died seemed part and parcel of his irrational reaction to the whole pregnancy so long ago. She'd been the one with the religious parents, but he'd said matter-of-factly, *We should get married.*

She'd pointed out that they were only eighteen.

Now that she was thirty-two and had seen a few relationships, his sudden show of conservatism troubled her more than it had then. In her experience, the traditional men were the men who wanted to own her. They started out saying they were just trying to take care of her. But it always seemed to turn into something else. Still, she had agreed that William, with his parents' help, could raise Amy. It was a bit late to start complaining that he was too *traditional.*

He had violated their agreement. That was the only issue.

As Loki sniffed the Gothic chairs with too much interest, Sophie growled at him. He was a challenge, all right. Unneutered until a couple of college students got him at the age of two, taken to a no-kill shelter when they moved to a place that didn't allow dogs, he'd first set about marking Sophie's house and trying to establish dominance over her. He still wanted to scent-mark in strange buildings, especially where dogs had lived, and keeping him convinced that she led the pack was a full-time occupation.

Now he gave her a white-tooth smile, a grin against black face, dark body. When she gazed sternly back, he averted his gaze and followed Cinders, who had gone to sniff the hall tree.

"No sniff."

Going up to Mount Sneffels K-9 and seeing William might lead to Amy knowing who she was. And Amy had seemed *fine*. Romantic clothing. Flared jeans and platform shoes and a poet's shirt. She'd worn a tarnished silver crucifix on a silver chain interrupted with tiny pearls.

She was fine. Sophie's father was fond of saying, *If it ain't broke, don't fix it.*

At the moment, the phrase was all Sophie could hear.

William had lied; so what? The important thing was that Amy was happy, developing into a healthy adult. At least, this appeared to be true.

Not only that, Sophie had been granted the privilege of seeing for herself that her daughter was thriving.

Everything is perfect just as it is.

Maybe she wouldn't even bother to ask her parents if they'd known William and Amy were in Ouray.

She'd made several trips up to her room, had backed the gypsy wagon into a spot on the far side of her parents' gravel driveway and begun to make herself some dinner before she remembered her hearing loss.

AMY LUDLOW DID NOT LIKE her father's fiancée. Crystal was often compared to Jennifer Aniston. She spoke Persian-Farsi and several other languages, having worked for the CIA for six years. She'd been in a long relationship with an extremely wealthy man who had treated her exquisitely. She did not fit in. Not in Ouray. Not in Amy's life. Not in her father's. The two had met in Phoenix at a law-enforcement conference where her dad was speaking to K-9 officers on animal behavior. Crystal had been there speaking on circumstances in which law enforcement and intelligence overlap. Amy understood that Crystal had made a fortune giving the same talk over and over since 9/11.

Why was he marrying her?

Well, the fact that she was fantastically gorgeous had to play a part.

Amy longed to go away. Ouray was boring. There was nothing to do. When she was older, she wanted to go somewhere as a foreign exchange student. On the Internet, she'd already found some programs for doing work in Central America. There were groups that took kids her age, which put paid to her father's insistence that she was too young.

If she could just get away…

But Crystal will always be part of our lives now.

Amy thought she *should* like Crystal. Crystal seemed to really care about having Amy as a stepdaughter.

But she'd also tried to get Amy to talk about her mother, and Amy didn't want to talk about that.

It happened again when Amy went out to the training facility, the barn with recycled metal siding, to find her father. He and Roy Bales, an old-timer who often acted as an agitator—getting the protection dogs to attack him—were doing bite work with an American bulldog, so Amy moved silently away so as not to distract the dog.

"Hi, Amy. Are they busy in there?" Crystal appeared as Amy closed the barn's side door.

"Yes. Bite work. The chrome Hummer's dog." Amy identified most clients—the protection dog clients, especially—by what they drove. She'd once pointed out to her dad that he couldn't have chosen any career that attracted more weirdos.

He had said, *Never talk that way about dogs.* Tongue in cheek. Knowing perfectly well what she meant.

They got along seamlessly, and they didn't need Crystal Rowe.

"Amy, I had an idea."

Amy wanted to say, *Here's an idea. Why don't you leave me alone?* Even Crystal's beautiful matching white velour sweatsuit annoyed her. This was Ouray. Where did she think she was?

"Why don't we write to your mother's parents and ask them for a picture of her?"

Amy didn't know why she resisted this course, except that she knew her father wouldn't help. He didn't like to talk about her mother, and it was obvious why. Though they'd been young, he'd really loved her. Amy's mother's parents were seriously Christian, very religious, he'd said, a minister and his wife. They weren't happy about the pregnancy and devastated by what had followed—their daughter had died of a postpartum infection.

Her name was Tomaira.

He had described her. Brown hair, brown eyes, a heart-shaped face, small and skinny and cute.

What her father had given her of her mother, his description, was what she had...all she had.

"Why don't you stay out of it?" Amy hadn't meant to say that, to respond so angrily, but her mouth kept going. "It's really none of your business."

Crystal straightened, looking both stunned and unafraid. Amy had the feeling that this was something she was used to—angry females. Jealous females. She was a physically beautiful woman and had undoubtedly learned to deal with rivals. No doubt, she saw Amy that way.

Because no matter what, Amy thought, *my father will always love me more than he loves you.*

Except. Except that Crystal wanted a baby. *We're try-*

ing, Amy had heard her tell a girlfriend at Jacques', the café in Ouray beneath the refurbished Victorian Mont-Michel Hotel. Good grief—trying *and* talking about it in public in Ouray, where there were no secrets. Amy was surprised it hadn't been in the newspaper.

If her father had a child with Crystal, he would certainly love the baby as much as he loved Amy. *I'd love the baby, too.*

But what did her dad see in this woman beyond good genes?

Crystal said, "I'm trying to be your friend. If you can't recognize that, I'm sorry for you."

Wounded.

In a snotty way.

"I thought," Crystal added, "that you'd like a picture of your mother. I keep telling William he should get one for you."

Amy *did* want a picture of her mother, had always wanted one. But for some reason, her father didn't think it was a priority. Or didn't want her to have a photo.

Amy had imagined *many* reasons for that, including that her mother was unattractive. They hadn't been married; they'd been very young. If Amy had been adopted, she wouldn't have a picture of her birth mother, either. At least her father had been able to tell her a few stories about her mom. And he had described her.

He had said, *For a while, she was my best friend.*

Amy believed it, believed it because of the thoughtful way he spoke, usually staring at some spot near him, but seeing something else. Seeing the past.

"It was nice of you to try to do what you thought I'd like," Amy said with effort. "But it doesn't matter. Really. It's just a personal thing, and I'd rather not talk about it." *With you.*

Never, never to Crystal, would she say aloud any

of the possible reasons her father had never showed her any picture of her mother. *She was old enough to be my grandmother, she was a famous murderer, she was nothing like he's ever told me, she's not really dead, she's a nun,* and on and on.

Crystal would patronize her, and Amy did not need to be patronized. She *knew* things. It was a trait she'd had as long as she could remember. Like when one of her teachers had died in a car crash, Amy had dreamed about it and known it was true before being told at school in the morning. And what had happened in Denver, the reason her father had left the force—that, too, she had known before she'd known. The possibility of becoming a professional psychic of any variety struck her as undignified, but she was certain that her future vocation, whatever it was, would be compatible with this double-edged gift she had of *knowing.*

"Okay. I was just trying to help. Both you and your dad."

Amy ignored this. Neither of them needed Crystal's help. The two of them had been doing fine before this woman came along.

"Okay." Crystal brightened. "So let's do something fun. Want to go to Durango or somewhere and find you something special to wear to the wedding?"

I really don't want there to be a wedding. I don't want you to marry him at all.

Truthfully, she wouldn't have hated Crystal if Crystal was going to be a stepmother to one of her friends. She would tell the friend, *She's okay. Really. It could be worse.*

But there were little things that bothered her.

She was watching TV with Crystal one night, and a female character on the show had been making fun of her elderly lover. Crystal had laughed.

Crystal had probably had everything, everything in her life, quite easy.

Amy had, too, in some ways. Not in others.

Others included the reason her dad was no longer a cop.

He wouldn't tell Crystal *that.* He had promised he never would, but Amy didn't want to ask him. She didn't like to think about it because it made her feel sick with shame and very strange. Sometimes she wondered if she'd dreamed it.

But she knew she hadn't because it had been with her, as fact, for too long to be a dream.

"We don't have to go right away," Crystal said when Amy didn't answer. "I just thought it would be fun. Also, we could get you a few summer outfits."

I don't need new clothes, and I don't want them.

Amy wasn't threatened by Crystal. Just as she *knew* certain other things, she knew that Crystal wouldn't be part of her and William's life in the long run. He might marry her, yes, but it wouldn't last. Crystal was not the love of William's life. Amy didn't know who was or if such a person existed, but it wasn't Crystal. She suspected it had been her mother.

Amy decided to be candid. In her experience, this was the way to go. Even annoying, too-perfect Crystal should be able to understand if Amy was completely frank. Amy had begun to create a character based on Crystal in the graphic novel she was developing. Cartoons and animation were her favorite things. Art, in some form, was definitely her future. The Crystal character was called Miss B. Miss B. fingered her jewelry while she talked about the early tragedies in her life—a strict and domineering stepfather, stepsisters whom her parents preferred to her….

Candor. "You don't have to take me shopping, Crystal. You don't have to be my friend."

"I know."

How had a woman with such a soft, young voice ended up working for the CIA?

"But I thought it would be fun," Crystal said again. "We're like each other, Amy. You—well, I bet you feel the way I did when my mother remarried."

It was a great opportunity. Why not? Why not say what was on her mind? "You mean, you wondered how she could pick someone so immature, shallow and spoiled?"

The moment the words were out, Amy wished them unspoken. Hurt flashed over Crystal's face, and her blue eyes were watery.

No point in apologizing. How could an apology possibly seem sincere after what she'd just said? Yet how could she *not* take it back?

"I didn't mean that," she said quickly.

Crystal pressed her lips together very tightly, then relaxed them. "I think you probably did, but thanks anyhow." She hugged herself, hugged the perfect body, looking vulnerable and invulnerable at once. She turned away, elegant and still quite fragile, and Amy couldn't think of a single way to use what had just happened in her graphic novel. She was too ashamed of what she'd said, and she knew why she'd said it.

Crystal was right. Not about understanding how Amy felt about her dad's remarrying. Other things.

It *was* weird that Amy had no picture of her own mother when she lived with her father, who had known her mother, presumably pretty well. Not a single snapshot? What about her dad's parents? Why had she never asked them if they had a photo? There was nothing shameful about her background. She lived with her father. Her mother, he assured her, had loved her.

Why didn't she quite believe it?

Why didn't she even know exactly *what* she didn't believe?

Whatever it was, she had a feeling Crystal didn't believe it either. But Crystal had been too sensitive to say so, at least to Amy.

WILLIAM FED KLAUS and refilled the Dutch shepherd's water bowl, then stepped out and secured the door of his kennel. Mentally, he reviewed his schedule for the coming week. Trip to Grand Junction Tuesday to pick up his new Czechoslovakian bitch at the airport. Crystal had said, *You're going to breed dogs again?*

He had asked, *Why did you say it like that?*

I just thought—you've talked about doing something different.

She had a point. He'd never meant to spend his life doing this.

Of course, he'd never meant to spend his life as a cop, either. He'd chosen law enforcement because it had seemed straightforward to him in a way that little of life was. There'd been more to it. Having been close to someone who was on the receiving end of crime, whose life and personality had been so changed by that crime... He'd wanted to somehow stop that from happening to someone else—or see perpetrators punished. But law enforcement hadn't been what he'd expected. He'd liked it, liked the personal skills he'd learned on the job. It was the K-9 program, however, that had led him to what now seemed his destiny.

Now, dogs were his life. Lately, he felt more and more comfortable with the idea of staying in Ouray even after Amy graduated from high school.

He supposed that when he'd first met Crystal, he'd talked to her about traveling, about pursuing ambitions he'd held when he was younger, before he'd become a father. Over time, he had begun to tell himself that he was still a scholar, that he always would be, and he was content in his quiet world.

But the real answer was that his ambitions had changed. He'd fallen in love with dogs and the world of animal behavior. He contributed regularly to the most important training journals, had written two books on canine development, learning and behavior that had become standard texts in the field and was working on the third volume in the series. But Ouray was a stopping point for Crystal. She'd said so in many ways.

It's not what you'd call culturally diverse, is it?

Not particularly. Nor racially diverse.

And speaking of culture, there's not much of that either, is there?

William had found himself inches from saying, *If you don't like it, why don't you leave?*

Now the wedding date was set. August eighth.

Even though three weeks ago, he'd told her he needed a break from their relationship.

Crystal seemed to have ignored that—as well as his not sleeping with her, not wanting to sleep with her.

No—not ignored. She was trying to please him and trying to please Amy, and he sensed desperation in her niceness.

He didn't want to feel contemptuous of her, and he was beginning to feel that way. Contemptuous *and* pitying. For an ex-cop training dogs in a small town, he could be arrogant, he supposed. Or so Amy said. Once, before introducing him to her favorite teacher, his daughter had hissed at him, *And Dad, try not to be snotty. Not everyone was raised in a global village, you know.*

Crystal was smart; it was one of the things that had attracted him to her. She was also surprisingly thoughtful and compassionate for someone so pretty.

But she didn't love dogs, and she wasn't completely comfortable around them. Some small part of William suspected that her eagerness to marry him concealed a silent determination to marry him *and* shape him into who she wanted him to be. He knew instinctively that nobody got married and remained unchanged by the experience. But that was different from getting married with an agenda for remaking one's new spouse.

"William."

It was her. She'd been in and out of the barn three times while he was working with Klaus, and he hadn't appreciated the distraction.

Also, he hadn't asked her to come over. Yet she'd arrived and made herself at home.

This is going to be her home.

His house was constructed on the same theme used later for the barn. Recycled materials, corrugated metal treated to appear weathered, siding treated in the same way. He'd bought the land from his parents.

Crystal said, "I thought I'd make lasagna for us."

It wasn't the kind of plan he could gracefully discourage.

Except by breaking the engagement.

By breaking her heart.

At least, he thought that was what would happen. If he'd believed she *wouldn't* be heartbroken, he'd have ended the engagement already, because hearts should be broken with broken troths.

Would his be?

Maybe.

He stopped in front of her, took off his glasses, polished them on his T-shirt, and put them back on. "Crystal, when I said I needed some space, I really meant that."

She didn't avoid what he was saying. Instead, her

blue eyes searched his face, looking for unspoken truths. "You're having doubts."

"Yes, I'm having doubts!" he exclaimed. "I have a fourteen-year-old daughter and my own business. I've never been married, and I'm not sure I want to be." He was blinking too fast and knew what that meant—*lying, Ludlow.* He *did* want to be married—if it was right.

Crystal had come along *seeming* right without necessarily *feeling* right to him.

"Why don't we spend a little time together," she asked, "instead of your running away from me? I don't think you can sort out whether or not you want to marry me by being alone. We could drive up into the mountains. You could bring your violin. You haven't played for me for a long time."

He remembered a long-ago moment, a girl shouting at him, *Oh, yeah, marrying you and having this baby. The way* you *like playing second fiddle to anyone at all?*

The memory almost made him smile.

But he never smiled when he thought about Sophie Creed. She had been a hurricane of selfishness, and he was sure she still was, wherever she was. At least Crystal wasn't like that.

He always *would* be first with her.

That thought did make him smile, and abruptly he put his nearest arm around her and steered her down the slope toward the house. "You can tell me," he said, "which vegetables to chop."

"No, I'll cook, and you can play music for me. Then, afterward," she said, "I'll try giving commands to Sigurd, and you can tell me how I'm doing. He's just so *big*. How does Amy do it? Your daughter is so amazing, William."

Just cold feet. He knew it now, knew it with great relief. Crystal was a nice person, she'd be a great stepmother for Amy and everything was going to be okay.

Crystal was capable.

Crystal could help Amy through the things he and his daughter could never talk about.

All but one of those things.

CHAPTER TWO

AS CRYSTAL LAID OUT ingredients for lasagna, Amy did the unexpected. She walked into the kitchen and offered to help.

"Thanks!" Crystal exclaimed, and gave Amy a quick hug which William watched with suspicion.

Were Crystal and Amy making peace after some conflict he hadn't witnessed and that they'd colluded in keeping from him?

"Your dad's going to give us some music."

When William was five, his parents had told him he needed to learn an instrument. They didn't care which one.

They had recently taken him to *Fiddler on the Roof* in Chicago, and he'd been intrigued by the idea of trying to play an instrument while balancing on top of a building. The choice had stuck. He'd had lessons almost everywhere they'd lived and been expected to practice whether there were lessons or not. He'd picked up some other instruments during his travels with his parents, but he still loved the violin. He owned an instrument too fine to be left unguarded and a couple of hundred-year-old bows.

The summer he was sixteen and part of the Youth Orchestra in Ouray, Sophie Creed, an annual and brief visiting student, had played first chair. And whined about it.

Playing Mozart now, William stole a look at Amy and Crystal in the kitchen and saw his daughter suddenly double over laughing at something Crystal had said.

Everything was going to be fine.

In fact, it would be very good.

He was unreasonable to tell himself that she didn't really *know* him, couldn't know him, because he hid so much of himself, unwilling to *be* known.

When they'd finished dinner, it wasn't yet dark. Instead of having Crystal give commands to Sigurd, his black sable Czechoslovakian male, earner of great stud fees, William suggested they walk both Sigurd and Tala, Amy's Dutch shepherd bitch, to town for ice cream. As they hiked down the unpaved road, passed often by Jeeps and SUVs coming or going from Yankee Boy Basin, Sigurd walked on a leash with Crystal. Aloud, she admired his head, his beautiful massiveness, his overall majesty, but William knew she wasn't at ease, wasn't really *enjoying* Sigurd.

Still, he could love her and marry her. The dogs, his dogs, must take commands from her, from every person in his household, but she needn't immerse herself in dogs. It would be better, in many ways, for her to have her own interests.

And she did.

He barely listened as Amy told him about a couple of pretty German shepherds she'd seen in Ouray that afternoon, then started going on about the owner's camper.

"No, Dad, it was a gypsy wagon. It was so cool, with wood and little windows with curtains. It had Wayfairer written on it, like the band, not the regular word. But just in little letters, like it was the name of the wagon."

Name of the wagon.

Later, he wondered if he had deliberately ignored something that should have alarmed him.

Because he was busy trying to enumerate, for himself, Crystal's interests.

The city. Opera, of all things; he liked that about her. Foreign policy.

We don't agree politically.

Of course, Crystal wasn't strongly political. She regarded intelligence-gathering as separate from—or perhaps transcending—party politics.

She had an interesting mind.

They crossed a bridge, then veered from the road and took the dogs down the Box Canyon Trail and on another trail that came out at an alley that eventually dumped into 4th Street.

The ice cream store was on the corner of Main and 4th.

Sigurd's ears had shot up. Sigurd had the best ear set of any dog he'd ever owned, erect, perfectly proportioned.

"Dad, that's her up there. I want you to see her dogs."

William considered relieving Crystal of Sigurd's leash. He didn't tolerate aggression in his dogs. Not toward people. Not toward other dogs. Many people didn't understand that *aggression* was an undesirable quality in any dog, including protection dogs. Sigurd had been imported with Schutzhund titles and had worked as a police dog in Czechoslovakia. But the dogs ahead on the sidewalk were an unknown quality.

Their handler seemed tiny—smaller than Amy. Her fluffy dark hair waved to several inches below her shoulders. She was slim, and William could see from the half block that separated them that she wore clogs or some kind of shoe with a little bit of heel, flared jeans, and a long-sleeved white shirt with a hood.

Later, he realized how strange it was that he'd noticed the woman before the dogs.

They were beautiful shepherds, as Amy had said. Sables, one long-haired, a "fault" that had never bothered him. A sound dog was a sound dog. Their owner had both on leads, and even at a distance, she seemed strangely jumpy, starting as a car passed in the road.

It was when she started that he knew her.

Fourteen years was not fourteen years, because he had seen her on the occasional concert poster, on promotional posters and displays at music stores. In his own daughter's CD collection. And when he heard that voice… Did he still *know* it, or did he only believe he knew it, remembered it? He never ignored her image, always studied her face with its dark eyes and dark eyebrows, a face not classically beautiful like Crystal's yet more arresting because it lacked Crystal's model-like elegance. Somewhere between heart-shaped and oval, still somehow the face of a very young person.

Wayfairer.

But Amy, who had said it was the name of the band, had not recognized Sophie Creed. She didn't know that Sophie Creed's middle name was Tomaira. Her parents had named her Sophia Tomaira. Tomaira, a word from a Venezuelan tribal dialect, from an area where their parish at the time had a sister church. The word meant *shaman.*

That was one way to start a female off in life thinking she was the center of the universe, a shaman of wisdom.

There had to be an excuse he could make now, some reason not to meet.

"Let's take the dogs down to the park," he said.

Amy gave Crystal a look that shared misery. "Dad,

I don't want to. I only said I'd come to the ice cream place with you. If you're going to the park, I'm going home. Besides, I want you to see these dogs. That dark sable is called Loki, and you should see his face. He looks like he could be Sigurd's brother."

There was no way he could walk up to Sophie now, not with Crystal and Amy and the dogs.

But Sophie had already met Amy.

Did you tell her your name?

The question came out, in a different form, before he could stop himself.

"Did you introduce yourselves?"

Amy and Crystal both shot such sharp looks at him that he felt his skin burn. They couldn't know. Neither of them could know.

But he supposed it had been an odd question.

And Crystal does know.

No. Crystal suspected. Something.

Why don't you have any pictures of Amy's mom? Not even a yearbook picture?

That was easy. They'd never gone to the same school.

In retrospect, telling Amy that her mother was dead hadn't been the smartest thing he'd ever done. Nonetheless, it had saved him from something he'd wanted to avoid. How could he tell his daughter that her mother had abandoned her? Or why?

She was a very talented musician, and she wanted to be free.

Free to be famous.

Amy said, "I don't know her name. Yeah, I told her about us. About what you do."

More caution was needed. He knew how to get what he wanted while revealing nothing. Perhaps it was a skill he'd learned in law enforcement—begun to learn even before that. Yes, he'd learned deceit early, as a survival strategy. The only way to protect one's soul from exposure was to keep it secret. To keep secrets in general. On some level, it was what his whole family was about; concealment, maintaining a façade, bound them, and he'd become good at keeping secrets. Too good, he knew, just as he knew that secrecy was a poor building block for marriage. "Did she recognize the name of our kennel?"

"You are so vain," said Crystal, shaking her head with a laugh.

"I don't know. She didn't say."

No one turned toward the park.

SOPHIE TIED Loki and Cinders in the courtyard of the ice cream place. "Sit." They sat. "Down."

Loki yawned and looked away.

Cinders lay down.

Sophie stared hard at Loki, and he yawned again, then complained as he slowly, grudgingly, bent his elbows.

"Good dogs. Stay."

A Humvee passed, with the distorted, echoing cacophony to which she doubted she would ever become accustomed, whatever anyone said.

She had been composing music in her head on the way over. "Leaf on the Water." About sound, about losing sound, losing love.

Thought I saw you, touched something else…

She'd set out wanting to write a song about her daughter. But she'd already done that—songs about the child she'd given away, the experience she'd bypassed, the star she'd caught and let go.

A Rolling Stones CD played in the ice cream store, and Sophie decided she was going to have to manage without hearing what the young man behind the counter said.

He said something when he saw her, probably asking if he could help her. A distorted version of "Get Off of My Cloud" overwhelmed the quack of his voice.

"Mmm—" She studied the flavors behind the glass in the counter. "Could I please have a small scoop of cinnamon ice cream on a sugar cone?"

He said something else. Not a question.

"I can't hear you. I'm sorry. My hearing is very bad." She had gotten used to saying many versions of this.

He leaned closer and repeated himself. She caught "one size," and looked up at the boards behind him.

She said, "Whatever," but he was staring past her, and made some remark in which "your dog" came through.

Sophie spun and heard, despite Mick Jagger and the chime of a door being opened, Loki's snarl.

Shit.

She shot through the door, banging past a pretty blond woman to—

Them.

"Loki, *wrrrong,*" she growled.

He was attempting to drag the heavy table and benches with umbrella overhead out of the courtyard to get at the black sable who stood alert on the sidewalk.

Damn, where was the Super Soaker when she needed it? Sometimes, *sometimes,* that helped curb Loki's aggression toward other dogs. She had also tried an electronic shock collar. On the highest setting, it annoyed Loki enough that he might sit down and scratch at his neck a bit. The marine air horn had been a great idea she'd gotten from reading a mystery novel, but she'd tried that only once since her hearing loss. The pain was not to be repeated.

She growled at Loki again, grabbing his leather collar. He was huge, ninety-five pounds, quite different from Cinders's slinky seventy-pound show-dog look.

Meanwhile, William Ludlow stood sedately beside the immaculately behaved black monster that had stirred such instantaneous hatred in Loki. It was William. Sure, people changed dramatically between eighteen and thirty-two—no, thirty-three; he would've had his birthday. But he was still leanly built, not terribly tall, maybe five-ten-and-a-half. Black hair, too long and streaked with premature gray, Aragorn-like, a lean craggy face, one of those eaglelike noses that keep a man from being pretty.

The last person you would ever expect to become a cop.

Yet she could tell, now, that he had been one. Something about the way he carried himself, the straight self-confidence.

Sophie could not afford to glare at him as she wanted to. She had to deal with her dog.

Cinders hadn't moved from her down-stay and looked up at Sophie for confirmation of how good she was.

"Loki, *down.*"

Loki bared his teeth at the black dog.

"*Wrrong.*" She used the growl she'd been taught in obedience class with him and her right hand to signal *Down.*

Amy, holding the lead of an animal that wasn't a German shepherd, that was some similar breed, said, "Dad, I can take…around…block."

The blonde had come out of the ice cream shop. Was she with them? Had she gone in looking for Loki's owner? She resembled Jennifer Aniston, so much that Sophie did a double take.

No. Just William's girlfriend.

Why that twinge of disappointment, of loss?

William had always liked girls, and they'd liked him. Sophie would bet that was still the case. The men she'd known who were mean toward women, who genuinely didn't like them, those men had been cruel from adolescence. Or so she suspected.

William wasn't mean.

Although he continued to hold the black dog's lead and made no move to take his probably *intact* male dog away. Loki was neutered, but the change had come late. William said, "They do look like each other, Amy." He spoke to Sophie for the first time. "My daughter told me how much your dog looks like Sigurd."

His voice was pitched in that range she could hear. Baritone.

Sophie didn't miss a word.

Her dog growled again. Sophie repeated the *down* command, verbally and with a hand signal, forcing him down.

He went down.

William appeared not to recognize her.

It made her want to launch herself at him. Or let Loki loose, except that she had a feeling the aloof black dog would come out on top.

William *did* recognize her. He must. But he'd told Amy that her birth mother was dead. Had he told the truth to the Jennifer Aniston look-alike?

The woman crouched beside the black dog and said, "Good boy, Sigurd," and stroked his back.

The dog did not lick her or even glance at her.

Sophie thought how great they all looked together. William, Amy and the woman who was gorgeous enough for the two of them.

Seeing them like that, Sophie hated William Ludlow.

It was probably because of the whole lie he'd inflicted on Amy. Maybe trying to convince her that this woman would've made the perfect mother.

I gave birth to her. I loved her, and I do love her. I just wasn't ready to be a parent.

But William, a man, had accepted the yoke of parenthood, and he'd been only a year and a half older than Sophie. And male.

She hadn't been ready for marriage, that was for sure.

She still, often, remembered what he'd said at the time. She remembered because she'd thought it was true, and she still thought it was true, or *should* be true.

We don't have to be in love. We have to decide to love each other. We're friends, and that's most of what being married is.

Maybe it worked that way for men.

Her mother's lot, however, had been and was to be a servant. Her father honored her for it, yes. But there was still too much waiting on an adult who was capable of looking after himself. Or so Sophie believed.

But lately, in the last few years, she'd begun to see that her mother *liked* waiting on her father.

Which convinced Sophie even more thoroughly that she was not marriage material. Almost as though she didn't know how to even *want* to be married. She absolutely could not subordinate herself to a man, and her adult relationships had been with one man after another who seemed to believe that was her role.

Well, she suspected William's cute companion did know how to get married.

Amy handed the dog's leash to her father and said, "Do you want me...while you get your ice cream?"

"I'm sure she doesn't," William said.

"What did you say?" Sophie asked Amy, angry that she couldn't hear her own daughter.

"I can sit with your dogs," Amy said, coming closer. "If you want to go get ice cream."

I'm deaf in one ear. I caught a virus. This happened. Sophie couldn't say it in front of William. He would think it served her right for abandoning their daughter. He'd said it just the once, but she was sure he'd never stopped thinking it.

What had always struck her, in her recollections of him, was how sober and mature he'd seemed at the time. When he'd said, *I'll raise her. I'll raise her, Sophie,* she'd known she could count on him, even as she knew that he wanted her to do it with him, that he believed it was the right thing and what she'd chosen was wrong.

Sometimes she even wondered if she'd walked away from Amy out of spite, out of anger, out of rebellion at the loss of freedom to which William had thought she should be consigned. And resigned.

Other times, she knew that wasn't the reason—and also knew music was only part of the reason.

"Thank you," Sophie answered, looking not at her daughter but at William, unable to keep the triumph from her eyes. *She told me. She told me that you told her I was dead.*

Amy said suddenly, "Are you Sophie Creed?"

Sophie heard that perfectly, perhaps because she knew the question so well.

She nodded.

"Oh, God, I *love* your music. I love your voice."

The blonde asked William, "What do you want, honey? Do you want me to go in and get the ice cream?"

He felt as if his face was in premature rigor mortis. He tried to make his mouth work, but *should* he let her go inside with Sophie? What if Sophie told Crystal?

Forget Crystal. Wait till she tells Amy.

"Uh—" he said, his eyes fixed not on Crystal but on Sophie.

"Are you in one of those teen bands?" Crystal asked her.

Sophie understood her perfectly, easily identifiable Chicago accent and all. *Oh, do you play the sappy sort of music that sixth-graders like?* Which showed how much this woman knew about the tastes of sixth-graders. Sophie exclaimed, "How sweet of you. No, I'm thirty-two."

She distinctly saw William trace the inside of his cheek with his tongue.

"My band is called the Wayfairers. We play folk, alternative and world—sometimes in combination."

"It sounds unfocused. I mean—diverse."

"She's won a Grammy, Crystal," Amy said impatiently.

"Nominated only," Sophie corrected her. Bitter thought. "I think I will get some ice cream. This is Loki, and that's Cinders being a good girl."

"She wrote that song you were telling Dad you like. 'Now, I Believe.'"

"Oh, I love that song! I want to have it at..."

Our wedding, Sophie finished for herself. Sometimes she wished she'd never written "Now, I Believe," although it had been the Grammy-nominated song. Articulating the feeling of believing in a soul mate—then discovering that soul mate, which of course was a lie. Primarily, Sophie wished she'd never written it because it seemed to have become a sort of wedding staple, which was not the image she wanted to project for the Wayfairers.

If the Wayfairers continues to be.... Something else she didn't want to think about—the stresses her hearing loss had put on the band. Personality conflicts that seemed to intensify rather than ease over time.

Actually, personality conflicts with her.

Lalasa's jealousy.

And, face it, Sophie's jealousy of Lalasa, her percussionist, whose beautiful head had been inflated by too much enthusiastic copy in *Rolling Stone.*

We're threatened by each other. We're band mates and should be on the same side, have the same goals. Instead, we're rivals.

"I'll make sure Loki doesn't pull over the table," Amy assured her.

"William trains…dogs," Crystal put forward.

A vehicle roared past.

"…problem dogs," Amy said to Crystal.

Sophie went back inside the ice cream shop, praying for no dog fights.

A moment later, the heat of the summer night wafted into the air-conditioned interior of the ice cream shop.

She drew a breath and glanced behind her, the twitch of a half smile in place for Crystal, with whom she didn't want to speak, whom it was nearly impossible to hear.

It wasn't Crystal.

William said, "So," and expelled a breath.

"So, I'm dead? Your daughter told me."

He blushed, then gestured toward the counter.

Sophie ignored the gesture.

The man behind the counter was speaking to her.

"Oh. Cinnamon," she said. "A single scoop on a sugar cone, please."

"What was I supposed to tell her?"

"The truth?"

The man seemed completely disinterested in their conversation. William must not know him, Sophie reasoned, or he'd fear their being overheard—and everything they said being repeated throughout Ouray. And to Amy.

"Don't worry," she told William, the liar. "She seems happy. I have better things to do than blow your cover—or whatever you call it. Does what's-her-name know?"

"Crystal."

"Her."

No answer.

"Sorry. I couldn't hear you," Sophie muttered, knowing very well that he'd been silent.

"Because I didn't say anything?" A two-can-be-snotty tone of voice.

"So she doesn't."

"It's nothing you need to concern yourself with."

Sophie considered. Should she concern herself?

All that concerned her at the moment was the demise of her career because of her hearing loss.

You can still sing. You can still play. It's not over.

But it was different. Sound was no joy—not the kinds of sounds she was hearing.

Please make it come back. God, please make my hearing right again.

With this thought, Sophie understood how little she had changed since she'd walked away from Amy fourteen years earlier. Music was still the most important thing in her life. Her calling meant more to her than the child she'd borne.

Which was why she could let Amy go on believing that her mother was dead.

Maybe that Crystal person is going to marry William and be a mother to Amy.

The idea made her shudder. *Couldn't you do better than her, William?*

But what did she know about Crystal, anyway? About any of them?

That Amy had good taste in dogs and listened to the Wayfairers.

That William lived a colossal lie and was attractive to gorgeous women—one of them, anyhow.

That Crystal was a bitch.

You don't know that, Sophie. Maybe she was sincere about the teen band question.

"You still don't care about her, do you?"

Sophie jumped. Stared. "If I didn't *care* about her, I would've told her that you've been telling her lies her whole life. I suppose you never even gave her what I typed up for her? Don't answer."

"One lie," William said, ignoring the question. "Or you could consider it a metaphorical truth."

"*I* couldn't consider it that, but I imagine *you* want to."

"He wants your money."

"What?"

She turned in the direction William had glanced. "Oh. How much?"

She couldn't hear him, but she could read the numbers on the cash register. She handed three dollars over the counter and took her ice cream cone, then looked at William.

He watched her oddly.

"What?"

"I guess even folk concerts can destroy your hearing."

"That's not what—" But she didn't want to tell him, didn't want him to realize how bad it was.

She peered out the glass at Amy and Crystal and the dogs.

"Well, bye," she said, heading for the door.

"You don't want to know her?"

Strange how she seemed to hear every single word he said—even when she'd rather not.

"I didn't know it was an option. Without—well—insinuating myself into your lives."

"Crystal's right. I could teach your dog to hold a down-stay."

"He *can* hold a down-stay."

Silence.

"My dogs are *immaculately* behaved."

"I saw."

The jerk.

"Weren't you going to become an ethnologist or something?" She thought he paled a bit, and wished she hadn't said it. He'd been willing to do what she had not—give up his dreams for their daughter. "She said you were a cop."

He nodded. "I was."

"So you're saying you could work with Loki and I could get to know Amy." Behind the ice cream counter, the man who'd helped her answered a cell phone. Actually, he and William didn't seem to know each other. Possibly he was just in Ouray for the summer. Perhaps William saw him as someone who didn't really belong to the community and therefore wouldn't tell all and sundry what they were saying about Amy.

"Actually, that isn't what I said."

"You said you could teach him to hold a down-stay."

"Just flaunting my excellence in my field."

"Well, that makes more sense. It would make no sense at all for you to train my dog. Seeing that I know a secret you want to keep from our daughter."

This time, William did glance at the ice cream man.

No, Sophie reasoned. He wouldn't want her to know Amy. But what he'd said had reminded her of a memory that came with a twinge both pleasant and sad. How they used to trade brags in the style of ancient warriors before battle, back and forth, back and forth, until one of them came up with a line that was so good, the other laughed—because that had been the contest. You couldn't laugh at what the other person was saying. The object, if Sophie had ever tried to articulate it, was to top the other person in making an extreme boast about something pathetic in its triviality.

A bunch of girls from Durango are coming over tonight to watch me toss litter into trash cans from four feet.

Gourmet chefs from five continents are assembling in my parents' kitchen right now to taste the water I boil.

It was a game from the past. Now, she suspected she carried too much venom. But she couldn't resist picking up the other end of that stick—the ritual insult. "You're afraid of Loki. I understand. It's really better if you don't work with him because he can always tell."

When she stepped outside, Loki immediately stood to greet her. Crystal waited near the curb with William's dogs, the black shepherd and the other shepherd-type dog. She shifted uneasily from one leg to the other. Sophie found it interesting that the black velour track suit wasn't covered with German shepherd guard hairs. *She doesn't like dogs.*

"Thank you, Amy. Loki, did I say to get up? *Down.*"

Loki sat and looked at Amy, then at the black dog. He stood again.

"Maybe I should just get them out of here," Sophie said, taking Loki's leash with her free hand. As she started to untie Cinders, Loki pulled to the end of his lead.

"He needs a prong collar," Amy said. "You should bring him to my dad."

"He has a prong collar. He's just not wearing it." Sophie drew him toward her awkwardly, bracing her body against Loki's pulling. He could erupt in snarls at any moment. She saw his lip curl and hunted for a place to put her ice cream cone.

Amy grabbed his leash. "You eat your ice cream. Loki, sit."

Incredibly, he sat.

Cinders got up from her down-stay without being released.

Sophie ignored her and started on her ice cream. "Thank you. Thank you very much. I should pay you a dog-sitting fee."

"Are you visiting Ouray? Just passing through?"

"Actually, I spent summers here growing up. I'm going to be staying for a bit."

Crystal sighed audibly.

Amy said, "Crystal, you can tie them up and put them in down-stays."

Awkwardly, Crystal tied the black dog, then the bitch, to the same parking sign. "Stay," she said.

"Tell them *'Down.'*"

"Down."

"Use their names," Amy coached. "Sigurd, *down.*"

The black dog hit the concrete.

"Now, you tell Tala."

"Tala, *down,*" Crystal said credibly.

Tala looked up at her and held out a paw.

Sophie laughed.

"God, she's cute," said Crystal, who looked as though she wanted nothing more than to get away from both dogs. "Oh, well."

"You have to make her do it. Use a hand signal. Tala, *down,*" Amy commanded.

Tala whined and wagged her tail.

Sophie felt certain that this dog knew exactly what she was being asked to do and was choosing to do something different.

Amy gave Tala the evil eye.

Tala looked up and down the street, checked what all

the other dogs were doing and slowly folded down beside Sigurd.

"She's pretty. What is she?" asked Sophie.

"Dutch shepherd. She's mine. We have other dogs, too. Our Cane Corso's away at stud right now, having a dirty weekend, as my dad sometimes says. He'll be back in a couple of days."

Sophie cracked a smile. She liked Amy. William must be proud.

"How do you practice with your band if you live here?" Amy asked.

Sophie hesitated.

"Amy—" Crystal, passing them, stopped. "Discretion."

"Sorry. That was nosy," Amy apologized.

"It's okay. I'm taking some time off." Five months already. *The rest of your life?*

"My dad's a good musician," said Amy. "I mean it. He plays the violin. Sometimes he plays with different quartets and symphonies in the area."

This didn't surprise Sophie at all. Something horrifying and competitive surged through her. What if William had become a better violinist than she was? It was possible. More than possible.

It shouldn't matter, but this was her Achilles heel. She suspected it had to do with walking away from Amy. Somehow, her past actions seemed more justifiable to her when she could conceive of herself as an excellent musician. Of course, she'd never be a virtuoso, but if William had actually learned to play better, while taking care of Amy…

Sophie absolutely hated the idea.

And she had to know.

When he emerged from the ice cream shop minutes later, with Crystal, Sophie said, "Boy, I'd like to find a trainer who *could* teach Loki to hold a down-stay."

CHAPTER THREE

WHEN SHE GOT BACK to the house, Sophie called her parents to tell them she'd arrived.

Well, that was supposed to be the idea.

"How's your ear?" her mother asked.

"I think it's the same." *And I can't bear to think about it.* "I might try another course of prednisone. Mom, Dad, did you know that William Ludlow is in Ouray?" *Did you know about Amy?* But she couldn't yet say her daughter's name to her parents.

Silence.

"Well," said her father.

"Y-es." Her mother drew it out.

"And Amy?"

"Well," said her father.

"Y-es. Yes. We knew."

Thank you for telling me. The words would have been acid. But before she asked, she'd believed she didn't care about their answers. "So, you've met Amy?"

"Well—yes." Her mother, this time, repeating the refrain for both of them. Sophie always thought of Dan and Amanda as a pair; sometimes it seemed to her that everything they did, conversation, movement, meals, took place in divine choreography. "Sophie, you told us you didn't want your daughter to know your identity. You've told us you didn't want to know what she was doing, how she was. It wasn't how *I* would've felt, but we've always tried to respect your wishes."

"Thank you." Everything her mother said was true.

She had excellent parents. They had told her everything they knew about her birth mother, who'd been a dancer going to a performing arts high school. It surprised Sophie that her birth mother had not had an abortion. Which was why William's talk of her *abandonment* of Amy had particularly offended her. She had *not* been abandoned. She had been carried and nurtured into the world.

So had Amy.

"We didn't know what would be best," her mother continued. "We *talked* of telling you, Sophie, but we didn't anticipate your coming back to Ouray. Then, when you said you were going to— Oh, I suppose we should've said something. Is it all right, dear?"

"Yes. Yes. But did you know that William told her that her birth mother is dead?"

Silence.

"No," her father said. "No, we didn't."

"That wasn't what you and he agreed on, was it?" Amanda asked.

"No. It wasn't."

Silence again. Her parents would not condemn William. They weren't like that, weren't judgmental. They'd been so successful in her father's various parishes because they *weren't* judges. They listened and thought.

Strange that William's parents, agnostic if not atheist, had been as smothering and controlling as the least-flattering stereotype of a reactionary religious household. While hers, whose life was spreading love and faith, were so emotionally healthy.

But that didn't mean she was. Less than a year earlier, her keyboard player had called her "the Kalithe-Destroyer of Intimate Relationships." Since he was a good friend and since his observation about the love partnerships in her life was appallingly accurate but most of all because he was superb on the keyboard, it had caused no professional rift.

William's parents.

She didn't know why she hadn't considered them till now. Where were they? They used to spend summers in Ouray, and they'd helped raise Amy. Or that had been the plan. Sophie had few misgivings; William and his brother had turned out all right. In spite of ...

Well, something was amiss. His mother had married with a great deal of family, Sophie knew that, and Moira Ludlow had always seemed to control the purse strings. In any case, a division had existed between his parents. Though the family had lived together abroad while William's father conducted field work, there appeared to have been inexplicable periods of separation, too. Bill Ludlow was a handsome and charming man; William had mentioned incidents that more than suggested dalliances abroad. Yet sometimes Sophie sensed something even darker in their family. A secret perhaps.

She asked, "What about his parents?"

"Oh, Ouray's their home now, I think. Moira's the director of the Chief Ouray Botanical Garden. There's a little shop and everything. He still travels quite a bit—does a lot of writing."

"How can there be a botanical garden here? The growing season's only about three seconds long."

"Well, now, it *is* more than that, Sophie. But they have a greenhouse you walk through—is that the right word, Dan? A solarium for the colder months. There are trees outside and walking tours and garden tours, of the houses in Ouray, that kind of thing. It's a retirement project for Moira and very educational for everyone else. Lots of information about what plants were used by the Utes and for what, you know."

"Where is this place? I haven't noticed it."

"Up behind the school. It's very nice. Quite large, too, and then the tours go up into the forest."

"I'll have to walk through."

"Yes. It should be relaxing."

Oh, yeah, like an outside gig in an electrical storm.

"We're planning to leave Tuesday," Amanda continued. "After the weekend traffic."

"Mmm. Well, be careful." It would be good to see them. She was the healthiest adopted person she knew. None of the usual nonsense about not fitting in. Good grief, her birth parents hadn't even been married—there was nothing to fit in *to.*

"How do Loki and Cinders get along with other dogs?"

Sophie had been ready to say goodbye. "Okay." Cinders, anyhow. "Why?"

"We have a new family member."

"You got a dog?" Sophie was stunned. Her parents had *never* been willing to have a dog when she was a child. Her mother, they'd said, would have to do all the work, Sophie would tire of the animal.... And so on.

"He's a Schipperke. His name is James."

For the apostle, undoubtedly.

"What's he like?"

"Adorable. Quite small. Actually they were used on canal boats in Holland for catching rats. We saw him work in this barn in Missouri where we got him."

"I can't wait to meet him." Her mother would have been the one to choose him. Well, maybe not. They probably decided together. Sophie smiled at the picture of her parents with a dog and thought, *Please like him, Loki.*

She and her parents said their goodbyes. She hadn't told them that she was thinking about allowing William Ludlow to train Loki. She wasn't sure. The whole thing seemed dicey. Clearly, William wasn't thrilled with the prospect, but maybe he'd been unable to find a credible reason to refuse—one that would seem believable to Amy. Maybe he feared that she'd wonder why he wouldn't train this particular dog. Only she and William knew the whole story, knew *everything*. And no one beyond his parents and hers knew that she was Amy's birth mother.

She didn't have to go. She could just not turn up. She'd made an appointment to come the next afternoon at two, but she didn't *have* to go.

By noon the next day, she was still having doubts. She passed some time performing one of her personal hearing tests. She checked her own hearing by picking up the telephone and listening with her bad ear, waiting to see if she could hear, even faintly, the recorded voice after she failed to dial.

Faintly. Faint, distant, unintelligible squawking.

Sophie hated when people assumed a hearing aid would help her. It wouldn't. It would only amplify the cacophony she heard with her left ear, further drowning out whatever sense she could make of the world with her right. It was Lalasa, of all people, who'd mentioned the issue of safety. A pot had boiled over on Sophie's stove while the timer buzzed, unheard. Sophie didn't even mention her trouble with traffic.

She wondered if Cinders could be trained to hear stove timers. *I could train her. Somehow. It can't be that hard.*

But I need to hear! I'm a musician.

She went to retrieve her violin from the other room, to practice. She unfolded a music stand near her parents' baby grand and searched in the seat of the piano bench for music. Classical. Classical.

In case William really had surpassed her.

SHE DROVE UP the Camp Bird Road behind a Humvee giving tours. Volcanic rock on one side—slabs had been sheared away to create the narrow road of gravel, dirt and rock—and a crevasse on the other, the path carved by the Uncompahgre River. Every year that she could remember, someone seemed to go off that road—once it had been motorcycles, dirt bikes or cars; now she supposed people drove off on ATVs, too.

How did Amy and William manage in the winter? As she wondered, the sign for Mount Sneffels K-9 appeared on her left. They weren't too far up the road.

Loki and Cinders sat in the back seat, listening, watching, smelling.

Why am I doing this?

Well, obviously Loki needed professional training. Since getting Cinders, her first dog, Sophie had become convinced that people who don't love their dogs enough to train them should get another kind of pet—one with polyester stuffing. She owed Loki more than he was getting.

But that was the least of her reasons for going to William.

It was a chance to know Amy.

But do I want to know Amy?

She hadn't—not until she'd met the fourteen-year-old her daughter had become.

She had never stopped caring about her. In some ways, it would've been better if Amy had been adopted by strangers. She'd always hated the idea that she, as birth mother, would be interpreted for her daughter through William Ludlow's eyes—not the most sympathetic gaze. Nonetheless, she'd thought often of that child, prayed for her, hoped and wished and desired the best for her, always believing that someone, anyone other than her, would be better able to provide that *best* for Amy.

She, as an ongoing influence in Amy's life, had never been part of those hopes, dreams or fantasies.

Yet, she *had* wanted to know her—maybe later. She'd wanted the mother-daughter connection—sometime.

But I'm not mother material.

How she knew that, she couldn't say. She was a musician; music was her life.

He was part of the music in your life.

She preferred not to remember that about William Ludlow. Singing together, practicing together, performing together. He had never cared about music the way she had. But he'd cared when they'd played and sung together. He'd cared about what they'd been *together.* Not for fame or fortune but because they'd made music.

Would he have followed her to her dreams if she'd agreed to help him raise Amy?

No.

He'd said so.

He'd said it was no life for a child.

He was one to talk. He'd seen his first tribal warfare in New Guinea when he was six; in similar settings, he'd grown used to the company of cannibals. Sophie had always wanted to know about the parts of his childhood he *hadn't* revealed. He used to shrug and say, *Things are different there. But people are people. They just have different customs.*

Really different.

THE HOUSE RIVETED HER at once. Adirondack-style, in both stone and wood, it rose two stories beside a larger barn, with an exterior of wood and antiqued corrugated metal. Extending from two sides of the barn were dog runs, made of chain link and concrete. Sophie rolled down her window and heard barking as she steered the Toyota down the winding driveway through Gambel oak. William must do something for money besides training dogs. She knew kennels that sold protection dogs could do very well. Was that the source of their money?

She half expected to find Amy not at home and William prepared to turn her away. He didn't want her to know Amy. If she were him, she *would* want Amy to know her natural mother. In fact, in his shoes, she'd try to make it happen. But she remembered too well William's attitude toward her the last time she'd seen him, the day Amy was born and she'd placed her daughter in his hands.

You're not going to nurse her, are you?

Even after fourteen years, the memory enraged her. Any man, any teenage boy, should've been able to *see* how hard it was for her to say goodbye to her child. She had sobbed after she'd let Amy go, and it had been all she could do not to take her back, not to go to William and agree to any plan.

Biology had spoken loudly that day and during the following months, months that had given her time to regret her decision, time to doubt.

Yet she'd *known* she was meant for something different—which meant that Amy had a different destiny as well.

She couldn't imagine William's attitude had changed. He'd been bitter at her walking away from their child. That bitterness must have increased as the years wore on, as he realized he'd given up his college years—and probably a college education—to raising a baby.

A Humvee sat parked behind a blue Forester next to a faded black Saab outside the house. William stood talking to a man climbing into the Hummer.

As the client backed out, Sophie pulled the Tundra into an empty spot.

William came to the driver's window.

Loki barked at him threateningly.

"Thank you, Loki." Sophie covered her left ear. His barking hurt, but she always thanked the dogs for an alarm bark and then told them to be quiet. She said, "Quiet." He sniffed at William, his huge—and in her opinion, adorable—nose quivering. "Where's Amy?'

"A friend's house."

Part One of her prediction was on the money. Now would he say he couldn't help her with Loki, after all?

Part Two wasn't going to happen. She wouldn't give it a chance.

Turning off the engine, she opened her door. "How much do you charge?"

Loki leaned forward from the back seat, sniffing the air. He gave another sharp bark.

"Obedience? Aggression problems?"

"Loki's not aggressive!"

"We can explore that theory later. A hundred dollars an hour for private training."

"What are you going to do? Give him psychotherapy?"

"No. Only his owner."

"Ha ha," she said.

"There's the issue of denial, for instance."

"What am I denying?"

"Your dog's aggression."

At least he wasn't sending her away.

It annoyed her to give William Ludlow a hundred dollars an hour to work with her dog—especially considering their difference of opinion about Loki's nature. It wasn't as though he scrapped with every dog he met.

Still, something about this disagreement, the ease of it, comforted her. It was familiar.

William had known her *before.* Before her world had changed. He was the tangible reminder that once things had been different, that once the world had looked different, had been different. Once she'd been innocent. Once she had *believed.*

She wouldn't again. Her opinions about men were too well formed. She'd decided that men had one of two agendas in relationships: for her to be their mothers or for them to overwhelm her life, taking control. At least, that was how her non-platonic adult relationships, such as they were, had felt to her.

But friendship existed. Sometimes it survived through miracles as well as trials. Amy was a miracle. William Ludlow changing his perception of Sophie as having abandoned her daughter was too much of a miracle to ask.

"Fine," she said. "A hundred dollars an hour. I assume we're not talking six hours."

"I certainly hope not."

In other words, he was eager to be rid of her. Exactly what she'd expected.

So, if this didn't involve a lot of training, she could afford it. She could learn techniques and practice them on her own.

Turning from William, she opened the back door to let Loki out. Catching his collar, she swiftly clipped on his leather leash.

"Does he run away?"

"Well, I don't let him. But yes. I mean, when we've been hiking, he sometimes goes tearing off and doesn't come when I call him."

If he'd had a clipboard, she thought, he would've made a tick on it. *Imperfect recall.*

Except that his entire unwavering focus seemed to be on her and her dog, measuring the relationship between the two of them.

"Let's go in my office."

The office was a tiny cabin in the style of the main house. It looked out on the kennels.

A heavy hardwood desk stood against one wall beside filing cabinets. In the center of the main room, around a woodstove, sat four lodgepole chairs with deep cushions.

"Have a seat."

There were clipboards, after all. He handed her one—with attached ballpoint pen—and took another for himself.

"Loki, *wrrrong,*" she growled, yanking on his lead as he lifted his leg against William's desk.

She told her dog to lie down, but Loki ignored her and sniffed the floor, then the table legs.

"Loki, *down,*" she repeated.

William never interrupted this kind of moment unless things got out of hand. This was evidence, evidence that the owner did *not* have control of his dog.

He pretended to ignore her struggle to get Loki first to sit, then to lie down. She succeeded more quickly than many of his clients.

Finally, she slipped off her sandals and crossed her legs. She still had the dancer's body he remembered. Straight posture, proudly carried head, nice breasts, slim hips and legs he knew would be slim and muscular. He didn't want to feel attracted to her—or even attracted to her appearance. She wasn't as pretty as Crystal. But he could look at her forever, never tiring of the arch of her black eyebrows, the striking difference between them and her lighter hair.

Passing her a black-and-white glossy handout, he said, "This is for you. It helps you identify what your dogs' facial expressions and postures mean." He tapped a photo on the left side of the page, of a German shepherd with lip curled back, ears up and slightly forward. "When Loki growled at Sigurd last night, he looked like this. That is classic aggression."

He waited for her to argue or to justify her dog's growling.

She began filling out his client questionaire.

He didn't bother to see how many boxes she was checking—boxes for health problems, boxes in the behavior problem section.

Loki stood again.

"Loki, down."

She didn't look up.

Loki looked at William.

"Loki, *down,*" she repeated, giving a quick jerk on his leash, which was attached to a standard training collar.

"Does he have a prong collar?"

"Yes. I can't find it. I mean, I had it while I was driving here." She struggled to drag the huge dog into a down.

"Are you moving here?"

"I don't know. No. I mean, no, I'm not doing anything different with my life. I just…needed to get away from the stress."

Something had happened. William was sure of it. When he was a child, a sorcerer in New Guinea had told him he had the sight. William didn't believe that, but he did believe that all people are intuitive. When he paid attention to his intuition he sometimes *appeared* to be more psychic than other people. Amy was the same way, but more so.

In fact, he suspected she knew he'd lied to her about her mother's being dead.

Amy would figure that if he'd told her that lie, it was because her mother had done something worse than being dead. She probably wondered what kind of mother could be worse than a dead mother. She was smart and complicated.

But keeping secrets, which occasionally led to lies, was how he coped. He'd been told it resulted from growing up with an overly intrusive mother. Yes, he still had secrets from Sophie. And from Crystal. He could imagine revealing those secrets to Sophie, but how would Crystal react to all he had to tell her? Sometimes, everything that Crystal was, everything she offered, seemed perfect for him and for Amy.

Other times, his intuition shouted that he shouldn't marry her.

And last night, as he'd drifted off to sleep—alone once again—he'd fantasized that Sophie could come into their lives and somehow help them recover from the situation that had made them leave Denver. He had imagined that Sophie—Sophie, who cared so little about Amy that she'd left her when Amy was hours old—could now ease the pain and disillusionment Amy must feel, that still must affect her life.

Of course it affected her life. How many fourteen-year-old girls spent an hour a day in yoga and meditation and read Simone de Beauvoir?

But Sophie would offer no help. How could he have pretended to himself that she would?

Well, it wasn't as though anything was *wrong*. Amy had friends. Her grades were excellent. And it was every father's dream to have a fourteen-year-old daughter who had never asked if she could go on a date, who seemed uninterested in boys, who seemed above them and above such trivial concerns as falling in love.

But something *was* wrong. Something under the surface.

He turned his attention to Loki.

When Sophie had finished filling out her form, she passed it to him with a check for a hundred dollars, made out to the business.

He skimmed the sheet. "You got him from a shelter. Tell me what you know about him. Do you know when he was neutered?"

She told him everything but never mentioned her hearing loss and how vulnerable it made her. Or how lonely she would be without her dogs. In any case, she was lucky; Loki was healthy.

She concluded, "I think he's from European lines."

"Probably." He skimmed her form, noting that Loki had been in fights with other dogs and started them "sometimes." "Will he fight a dog of either sex?"

"I'm not sure." Her voice was small, hesitant. "He's protective of me."

"Actually, you need to be protective of him. Let me explain." He told her about pack drive, that she needed to be the leader and that Loki needed to feel he was under her protection. Even a dog trained as a protection dog worked under the owner's control or was trained to do particular things in particular situations.

"I feed him. He walks on a leash unless we're out hiking. He *knows* I'm the leader."

"I think he does. But you could get the message across to him more consistently." He reviewed her sheet again. "You feed them twice a day. That's good. What's mealtime like?"

"I make them both stay down while I get dinner ready. They can't eat until I say 'Okay.'"

He lifted his eyebrows, impressed—and relieved. They could get through the training more quickly. *Maybe in an hour—before she has a chance to spend time with Amy?*

But Sophie wouldn't tell Amy that she was Amy's birth mother. She just wouldn't do it. Her attitude apparently hadn't changed in fourteen years. She still didn't want a child.

As far as Amy was concerned, her mother *was* dead, because Sophie wanted nothing to do with her.

Right?

Unfortunately, he didn't know *what* Sophie wanted.

Briefly, he gave her more ideas for establishing dominance over the dogs: insisting that they *Wait* before getting out of the truck and at doorways, daily thirty-minute downs at home, insisting that the dogs earn petting by going *Down* on command.

They went to the kennels, and he got Amy's dog, Tala, to help him. He demonstrated how to encourage positive eye contact. They practiced heeling, sits and downs.

The acoustics in the barn kept startling her, and she had to ask him to repeat himself three times.

The third time, he said, "How is your hearing?"

She blurted it out. "To be perfectly honest, I have severe hearing loss in my left ear with about twelve percent speech discrimination."

"Meaning that in a hearing test, your left ear understands twelve percent of words correctly."

"Yes. I hear distortion in that ear. It came from a virus." Before he could ask. "It's called sensorineural hearing loss. A fair number of people get it from viruses. I got sick, my hearing went weird, like I was underwater, and I picked up the phone one day and couldn't hear out of my left ear."

"How does that affect your music?"

I'm not sure I can do it anymore. She shrugged. "Sound really isn't the nice experience it used to be. Anyhow—" rushing on "—that's why I keep asking what you said."

He nodded, though his face had grown quiet and slightly troubled. "Is it going to get better?"

"That's the big question. It's unlikely to get much better after all this time. It's been almost half a year." She'd never said those words out loud before. "But, hey, Beethoven was deaf."

As though it didn't matter.

"Still. You don't need that." He shook his head.

He was sad for her. He wasn't pleased at all, gained no spiteful satisfaction from her hearing loss. She'd been wrong about William. Well, she'd been silly to expect such a hateful reaction from him, just because he'd accused her of abandoning Amy.

And since then told Amy she was dead.

He said, "Okay. Here's where it gets tough. Your corrections are good but they need to be faster—and stronger. Loki's growling at another dog, a prelude to a snarling no-holds-barred fight, is unacceptable, and you have to let him know." He took a prong collar from a rack on the wall of the barn, removed a link, and brought the collar to Loki. He put it on the shepherd. "I'll get Sigurd. Now, the second you see Loki so much as wrinkle his nose, do a *strong* correction and a sharp about-turn, taking him away. The second he relaxes, praise him lightly, happily and *briefly*. But keep talking with him if you want."

Surprisingly, it went exactly as William had instructed. Loki seemed slightly shocked at her sudden, loud growl, the quick snap of the collar and abrupt about-turn. They were twenty feet from where he'd growled when the whole incident seemed to slip off him. She said brightly, "Good boy, Loki. Let's go look at this part of the barn. What's over here?"

His ears went back, ever so slightly, and his jaw relaxed in a dog smile.

William put Sigurd in his kennel, and Sophie returned the prong collar to the rack and Loki to her car. Meeting her by the Tundra, William handed her a photocopied sheet listing techniques that would remind her dogs she was in charge. Going through doors first, eating before them, eye contact sessions twice a day, preventing neighborhood sniffing and marking, learn-to-earn petting and more.

"Do you think that'll work on the street?"

"Your big challenge is to read him every minute. But actually, the next test will be to bring him to class. You'll find that more affordable."

She'd taken Cinders to classes, but that was before her hearing loss. He didn't have to tell her the advantages of classes over private instruction. Loki would have to get along with other dogs, would understand that other dogs were asked to do what he was asked to do. He would learn to obey her *with* distractions.

"You have classes?"

"There's a woman who teaches in Montrose."

Suspicion crept through her. "You don't have classes?" she clarified.

He paused on the verge of lying, and knew she saw the lie forming within him. He said, "I might start some in a few weeks. I have to see how many people I have."

Sophie couldn't silence her curiosity. "Does Crystal work?"

"She's a public speaker. She used to work for the CIA, but the public speaking circuit is more lucrative."

Sophie could think of nothing more to say about

Crystal—and no way to ask the things she wanted to. How long he'd been seeing her. If Amy liked her. "How did you end up in law enforcement?"

"I just…got interested."

"In K-9 units?"

"Partly."

"Did you go to the police academy while Amy was a baby?"

"Yes. Then I went through K-9 training."

"Why did you quit being a cop?"

William hadn't expected the question so soon. Strange, in all his daydreams of Sophie somehow addressing that very situation with Amy, he hadn't imagined telling her about it. Because he couldn't tell her. He'd promised Amy he wouldn't tell anyone. His parents knew; they'd told his daughter that of course they believed her.

If Sophie had ever been a parent to Amy, he would've told her.

But under the circumstances he couldn't.

"My boss was caught in a sexual—well, a crime, actually. He lied his way out of it until the witness, as well as the victim, felt victimized and finally went along with his story. I know the witness, and I believed the witness. I couldn't stay. He resigned last year, under duress. There was another incident."

"Why didn't you join another department?"

Hesitation. "Well, we came back here to regroup and liked it."

Regroup, Sophie's mind echoed. *We came back here to…*

"Was Amy the witness?"

William cursed himself. And said nothing.

"What did she see exactly?"

"How could it matter to you?"

Right to the heart of the matter. How little he'd changed.

"It matters," she said coolly.

Their eyes met.

Understanding passed between them.

He said, "I've promised Amy I won't talk about this. Can I count on you to keep it to yourself?"

She considered. "Yes."

"I was working in Denver, and Amy and I went to a party. A barbecue. Lots of kids were there. Amy went in to an upstairs bathroom and saw my boss sodomizing the host's fifteen-year-old daughter. She went out and talked about it to one of her friends who was there, and later the friend's father heard her repeating it to someone else. Those parents told me."

Sophie stared at him.

"I asked Amy, and from what she said, the words she used, I have no doubt she was telling the truth. She was nine years old. It was highly unlikely that she'd make it up. She hadn't been exposed to anything like that. Anyhow, she subsequently recanted, said it wasn't true. I'm fairly certain that my boss frightened her. Back in those days, she'd be terrified if anyone even mentioned it. She had nightmares."

"Has she had counseling?"

"Some." He shrugged. "She didn't like it."

"I do care about her, William. I carried her for nine months and gave birth to her, and, though you may find it difficult to believe, I love her and always have, and I've never stopped thinking about her."

This was the bad dream William didn't want to experience. If it had been anyone else's situation, he would've said that of course the birth mother feels lifelong attachment to the child. But in the case of the mother of his child, it *couldn't* be true. He saw the irrationality of that conviction, yet felt powerless to change it.

She asked, "Do you still think it would've been best if I had decided, at the age of eighteen, to marry you so Amy would have the privilege of living with both parents?"

"I don't. It wouldn't have been."

She had learned to sense anger in men, but she didn't sense it from William. Rather, he was quite calmly making her angry and watching her attentively, like an anthropologist or psychiatrist preparing to take notes.

What was more, she'd asked him a question to which there were only two answers. Yes, she'd done the wrong thing by Amy out of selfishness. Or no, she wouldn't have been a positive addition to Amy's childhood.

"Why did you tell her I'd *died?* Why couldn't you tell her what I'd told you to tell her?"

"Do you think she would ever have stopped asking about your identity?"

It was a fair point. "But hasn't she anyhow?"

"Not really."

"You could've told her the truth."

"I swore I'd never tell her your identity. I swore to *you,* Sophie. And since your career was the most important thing in your life and you thought this could damage it—"

"That wasn't why I asked for anonymity, and you know it. It was a very complicated situation. You've always known just how complicated. And *I'm* adopted and have never met my birth mother. I wanted Amy to be able to bond with whatever woman you found, the same way I bonded with my parents."

"Well, my plan met that criteria. I gave her an accurate picture of you—actually, a flattering picture."

"A photograph?"

"No. Of course not. But she knows you're—well, she

knows that her mother was a talented musician. Beautiful and fun to be with."

So what objection could she have?

Only that he'd told a massive lie to their daughter.

She climbed into the Tundra.

Pulling out of the driveway, she passed a white Lexus pulling in with Crystal at the wheel.

CHAPTER FOUR

IN SOPHIE'S EXPERIENCE, lies and secrets had a life of their own. Did Amy believe that her mother was dead? Somehow, reviewing her brief encounters with her daughter, Sophie doubted it.

And what impact must it have had on Amy to reveal something true and then be frightened into saying it had been a story? What did that do to a child, to anyone?

Sophie thought of Galileo, tortured into declaring the earth to be the center of the universe, whispering at the last, *But it still moves.*

Over the next few days, Sophie practiced assiduously and spent an hour of each day songwriting. The only way to write good songs was to write a *lot* of songs. Then some were good enough to perform. She played her harmonicas and violin, sang, practiced the classical Indian dance that was her only hobby besides her dogs and had become part of her performance experience. Through it all, she told herself that everything sounded different only to her. She couldn't hear *herself* correctly out of her left ear, but she would adapt if she must. She would adjust.

So she was singing. She was playing music. What was to stop her from contacting the band, saying let's get some gigs, let's do a live CD, let's keep going?

She'd said she needed three months off. Three months in Ouray, a summer with her parents.

But did she really need that time, or did she just need to face the reality that music would never again sound the way it used to?

Because suddenly she wasn't sure she could stand even being in the same town with Amy without being acknowledged as her mother.

What good would it do to tell her the truth?

William maintained that Amy had been changed by the events in Denver, and Sophie could certainly see that. It was a big deal to know something as the truth and have other people say you lied. And Amy had witnessed a rape—the rape of a teenager by an adult in a position of trust.

The more Sophie thought about it, the more that fact disturbed her.

But Amy was obviously fine.

Sophie was simply curious about her daughter.

She wanted to see her bedroom.

She wanted to know her favorite subjects in school.

Did she like sports?

Did she play a musical instrument?

Sophie could have asked William these things. Why hadn't she?

Because he doesn't want me to know her. He's afraid of me already, afraid of my telling Amy the truth.

Of course, she couldn't be a *mother* to Amy. She wasn't the mothering sort and had understood that when she was eighteen. But she could be a friend.

In which case, it was better if Amy didn't know the truth.

Over the following days, Sophie ran with the dogs at least twice a day and sometimes took them downtown. On the walks and runs, she didn't let Loki sniff or scent-mark. On Memorial Day, a golden retriever on Sixth Avenue snarled at Loki, and a full-on fight ensued, which Sophie's traffic whistle failed to break up. A neighbor finally ran up with a hose to stop the fray.

Her parents' yard was fenced, the fence lined with flowers now in bloom, some of them creeping up the boards. In the yard, she practiced eye contact with each dog individually, sitting the dog in front of her and saying, "Watch me," then gazing into the dog's eyes, usually saying "I love you," and many variations on the same theme. If the dogs went through doors in front of her, she called them back. She followed the instructions William had given her to the letter, though she didn't see how any of them would stop her dog from getting into fights.

He did not call to check how Loki was doing.

She did not call to ask for another appointment.

Instead, she practiced classical Indian dance, a meditation for her and something that had always given her more confidence onstage. Yet now it, too, reminded her of how the quality of sound had changed.

On Tuesday night, her parents arrived.

As one of them touched the front doorknob, Cinders and Loki both began alarm-barking.

"Thank you," Sophie told them.

Loki continued barking.

"Loki, that's enough! Thank you."

She opened the door. "Oh, hi." She hugged her father, the closest, first, then her mother. "Oh, he's so cute. I love how he's shaped."

James stepped onto the threshold with uncommon dignity.

Then he sprang to the end of his leash and onto Loki's nose.

Sophie saw it happen.

James started it.

Snarls, growls.

Uncharacteristically, Cinders jumped in.

"LOKI! CINDERS!" She made her voice as close to a growl as she could but suspected she was simply shouting.

"James!" her mother cried.

Amanda was blond—naturally, though at sixty-eight she'd highlighted her hair. She was shorter than her daughter and not as strong.

Sophie dared to reach out with both hands and grab Loki's collar. She yanked him back, with James attached to his throat.

Her mother grabbed her dog, saying, "Down, James, down. Are you all right?" She picked up the Schipperke and examined him for wounds.

Sophie struggled with Loki, dragging him toward the stairs, telling him, "Time out." And "Cinders, time out."

Cinders followed willingly.

On the way up the stairs, Loki wagged his tail.

Without speaking again, Sophie put both dogs in their crates, heavy, collapsible wire cages that she covered with blankets and in which she always laid their beds. She'd had one lover who said he'd never put animals of his in "cages." Shortly after this revelation, Sophie had stopped seeing him. Crating her dogs was one of the most humane methods of imposing discipline.

In her bare feet, jeans and tank top, she returned downstairs and found her parents in the kitchen, her mother feeding and watering James.

Way to reinforce fighting, Mom.

"You look beautiful, Sophie," her mother said. "I'm so glad you're here. And the house is really nice. The flowers are gorgeous." In the vase on the table. "They're not ours, are they?"

"No. Not enough of ours are blooming yet. I got them at the farmer's market yesterday. James is cute."

"I'm sorry Loki doesn't like him."

Sophie controlled her reaction with difficulty. "Well, James jumped on him and bit his nose. You can't expect him to do nothing." Although she couldn't help wondering what William would have expected from one of his dogs in that circumstance.

Her mother had just taken a glass from the cabinet. She set it slowly on the counter and stared at Sophie. "Sophie, Loki *charged* him. That dog is huge."

"Then why did it happen *inside* the house? Loki didn't charge outside to eat James."

"James came inside, and Loki attacked him."

Both women turned to Dan Creed, who sat at the table, nibbling on one of the lemon-poppyseed cookies Sophie had made that afternoon. "I didn't see it," he said through a mouthful.

And he wouldn't have said what happened if he had, Sophie thought.

"Well, Loki's getting training," she said. "William helped me with him a bit. And I need to take him to classes. Maybe James should go to school, too."

Again, her father showed no reaction. Her mother, however, lifted her eyebrows at the mention of William.

Sophie didn't say, *It was a way to see Amy. But I didn't get to see her.* Because she'd always said she had no interest in seeing Amy.

"He's so well behaved," her mother said as the Schipperke jumped up on her.

At first, Sophie wasn't sure who she meant.

"You should see him heel," Amanda went on. "And he does tricks. He's smart like a border collie. And oh, how he can catch rats. We had him at work in our friend's barn. He must have dispatched fifteen of them."

"Easily," said Dan.

She was going to have to keep Loki separate from James all summer. *Damn it.* Her mother deserved a dog, this was her parents' house, and Loki *might* have growled at James even if James hadn't attacked him. But now…

"I bet we could take Loki and James to school at the same time," Sophie repeated. "There are classes in Montrose."

Because William didn't want her in his classes.

Because she'd said she didn't want to know Amy or want Amy to know her.

"Tell me about William," her mother said, sitting down at the table. "And you met Amy."

"You've met her?"

"Just seen her, really. We never know what to do."

"It does make it awkward that I'm supposed to be dead." She sounded churlish, but she wished her mother would just admit that James had started the fight. *She won't, though. Puppy love is blind.*

Any animal that size that attacked one of Loki's size deserved to be eliminated from the gene pool.

"Is he neutered?"

"Yes, yes. We don't want puppies."

Thank goodness. Sophie helped herself to a cookie and told her parents she'd been playing a lot of music and writing songs and added that she was adjusting to her hearing loss, which was somewhat true. Though she hadn't heard anything her parents had said or shouted during the dog fight, now that James wasn't yapping she could hear them pretty well if she turned her good ear toward whoever was speaking.

"Won't it affect how you hear your band, though?" her mother asked.

Dan threw his wife a look that could have meant warning or exasperation.

Sophie understood. Her parents must have agreed to bolster her hopes that her career wasn't all washed up.

Well, it wasn't, and she didn't need cheerleaders.

"Beethoven was deaf," her father pointed out.

"Right." Sophie gave a firm nod of agreement.

"Amy doesn't know who you are?" her mother asked, as though clarifying the matter.

"She knows I'm Sophie Creed. She listens to the Wayfairers."

"Well, isn't that something," said Dan.

"Well, she would, wouldn't she? You're very popular," Amanda put in. "You know, she looks a bit like you did at that age. I don't suppose she's noticed."

"Not having seen me at that age." Suddenly, Sophie was exhausted. Loki *did* need a trainer. *She* needed one. William was good; she had no doubt of that, but everything felt too complicated.

And she didn't like Crystal.

She didn't want Crystal to be Amy's mother, and there was nothing she could do about it. "I think I'll turn in. Will what's-his—James—sleep in your room? Can I let Loki and Cinders out in the yard in the morning?"

"Oh, of course. Especially if it's too much for you to walk them if your balance is off."

"My balance has never been affected by this hearing loss, and it's certainly not too much for me to walk them."

"You do look tired, dear. Go on up."

As Sophie stood, her mother rose from the table to embrace her. "I'm so glad you're here," Amanda said. "And I really hope everything's all right. I didn't anticipate your seeing William or Amy. We seldom run into them, and—well, as I said—we never know what to do. We leave them to themselves. We thought it's what you wanted. We weren't sure whether or not to mention that they were here. And we really didn't know he'd told Amy her mother was dead. I don't think he was being malicious. That's not his way."

No. It wasn't. Yet a certain bitterness—the metaphorical act of cutting Sophie out of the family picture—that *was* like William. "It's fine," Sophie assured her parents and made her way upstairs to her dogs, wondering about a life in which her daughter had been told she was motherless, a life in which she, her daughter's mother, agreed to support this story.

Before she reached the top of the stairs, she admitted to herself that she wanted Amy to know the truth.

BUT SHE HADN'T PLANNED that Amy would be told her mother's identity. That wasn't the agreement she and William had reached. He had abandoned their agreement, but that didn't mean she should.

She called the trainer in Montrose. The woman told Sophie, "I'd have to see him and evaluate him before agreeing to have him in class. But if it's fighting, you could go to William Ludlow. He's right there in Ouray. The other thing is, I'm not starting a new class until August, and it seems like you have an immediate problem."

Sophie called William and got his answering machine and reported what the trainer from Montrose had said.

He called her back an hour later. "You can bring him up now, if you want." He sounded resigned.

When she drove up to the cabin, he met her outside again.

"Is Amy home?" she asked.

"Yes. She's sulking."

"Why?"

"Because she wants to go to a dance workshop in Crested Butte next weekend, and I told her she can't."

"It seems pretty harmless. What kind of dance?"

"I couldn't tell you. It wasn't relevant. Amy likes all kinds."

"So what's the problem? Was she going with someone?"

"Brittany Nichols and her mother."

With Loki on lead, she followed William to the training barn. "What's the problem?" she asked a second time.

"She already said she'd go to Denver with Crystal to shop for wedding clothes."

Wedding clothes.

"Is someone getting married?"

"I am. And Crystal." He didn't look at her. "Let's get started."

Before they began, Sophie said, "My parents have gotten a Schipperke. He walked into the house last night, launched himself at Loki, grabbed his muzzle and wouldn't let go. It took all three of us to separate the dogs. Cinders got into it, too. My mother thinks he needs no training, but I'm telling you, he's a tyrant. James—that's the snarler—tells my mother what to do, and she does it *and* she thinks it's cute."

William's lips were uncommonly mobile, gorgeous in a slow smile of amusement, broadening to a grin.

"What?" Sophie demanded.

"I have a convert."

"I've always believed in dog training. My dogs *have* had classes. It was just hard to get to them regularly."

He nodded carelessly. "Did Loki snarl at him? What was Loki doing before the fight started?"

"Well, he barked. I don't know, he might've growled."

"Let's do our best to make sure your dog behaves immaculately. Maybe then your mother's won't prove such a problem. Let's start with the socialization exercise we tried the other day. We'll have him see Sigurd again, and then he can meet Thunder."

"Who's Thunder?"

"Our Cane Corso. The one who was away at stud."

Loki growled at Sigurd, and Sophie rebuked him and led him swiftly away, praising him only when he'd relaxed. The next time, William had her talk happily to Loki as they approached Sigurd and lead him away even before he growled, praising him happily.

Then William switched dogs.

As soon as he led Thunder into the training barn, Loki gave a low growl. Sophie told him, "*Wrrrong.*"

"Make him sit and lie down," William told her.

She did, with difficulty.

But as William brought Thunder nearer, Loki stood and resumed growling.

Sophie clamped her hand around his muzzle. "*Wrong.* No growl."

They practiced with the two dogs for an hour, until Loki could pass within ten feet of Thunder without growling.

"I guess it's progress," Sophie said when William returned from putting away the Cane Corso.

"You bet it is."

"Where do we go from here?" She decided to be candid. "I can't afford more private lessons at a hundred dollars an hour. And I don't think the Montrose woman will take him."

William looked as though he wanted to say something about the other dog trainer, but didn't.

"I'm starting a beginners' obedience class Thursday nights. A hundred and twenty dollars for ten weeks. You can bring Loki. I think we'll be able to deal with his aggression in that context."

"Thank you." With ten weeks of class, she'd be certain to see more of Amy.

"Obedience classes are important, especially for large breeds. Some insurance companies won't insure the homes of people who own German shepherds, rottweilers—"

She interrupted him. "You've turned out differently from the way I thought you would."

"Dog trainer? Dog writer?"

"You write about dogs?"

He explained.

"Well, that does make sense. I guess I never saw you being a cop. I never saw you doing this, either."

"Your point?"

"I'm just surprised." She had to say more. "And I never saw you marrying a spy—or a retired spy. Or whatever she is. She's gorgeous. I don't know her. I'm just surprised," she repeated.

"Why?"

"She looks like the kind of woman who irons her T-shirts." Sophie tried not to make it sound like an insult. And it wasn't an insult. Crystal looked neat, unruffled. "She's *very* pretty," she added quickly.

"But I grew up with headhunters and cannibals, and you expected me to choose someone more exotic."

Some current lay under those words. A current that referred to parts of his childhood she couldn't know. Couldn't know, Sophie reflected, because he wouldn't talk about it. She'd guessed more than once that his father might have a penchant for women from some of the cultural backgrounds he researched—just another facet of the infidelity she suspected there. But William was never keen to discuss any of it, and she'd never been comfortable pushing it.

"I suppose I meant something like that. It really

has nothing to do with how you grew up—just how I remember you."

"I have doubts."

She'd heard wrong. She knew he wouldn't have said he had doubts about his fiancée. If he had doubts, he'd put the wedding on hold and deal with his fiancée, not speak to someone else about the problem.

"What?" she asked.

"Time's up. So, I can expect you for class?"

"Yes. I don't suppose I could say hi to Amy."

"On what pretext?"

Sophie considered. "You could offer me a glass of water."

He pointed out a cooler with paper cups at the edge of the barn near the equipment rack.

"Or lend me a book."

"Or say that I'll see you in class."

"Sophie! I didn't know you were here."

They both started, even William. Neither had heard Amy enter the training barn, but she was so close to the door that she couldn't have been there long or heard what they were saying.

She wore flared black tights and a raspberry-colored leotard and had braided her straight dark hair in two neat plaits. Sophie was a master of all types of braids—French, herringbone, four-strand, rope. *It would be fun,* she thought, *to work on Amy's hair.*

"Hi, Loki," Amy said, joining them.

Loki stood up with a dog smile, looking for attention.

Sophie said, "Loki, sit."

He didn't.

"We're starting class Thursday," she told Amy.

"Lucky you, Loki. You get to go to school!" Amy exclaimed.

Loki gazed at her in delight while Sophie pushed down on his back until he sat.

"How's Cinders?" Amy asked. "Is she coming to class, too?"

"Loki's going to take all my concentration."

"I could handle her for you," Amy offered. "And you could practice with her at home between classes."

"Amy," William said quietly. "She can do that anyway."

Sophie said, "But it *would* be good for her to be with the other owners and dogs. I could pay you."

"In addition to the fee for another dog?" William broke in.

Amy glanced at him, clearly puzzled by the way he was trying to dissuade Sophie from having both dogs in class. "You wouldn't have to pay me anyhow," she told Sophie. "I'd be glad to. She's a sweet dog. She won't be any trouble."

"The class is full," William announced.

"Oh, Dad, you know there are always no-shows."

She needs to be told the truth—and soon.

Amy would feel even more betrayed if Sophie accepted this favor, let her handle Cinders, and then the girl discovered that Sophie was actually the mother she'd been told was dead.

"Just bring Cinders when you come to class," Amy said. "And if there are no-shows, she can get one of their spots."

"Thank you for offering to help," Sophie smiled sincerely. *Thank you for letting me be near you.*

As Amy returned to the house and William walked Sophie and Loki down to her vehicle, he said, "Your mother may as well bring the Schipperke, too. I'll enjoy taking your money."

Sophie ignored his tone, pretended he'd never tried

to discourage her from being near Amy, pretended she'd never noticed. "This morning they were talking about driving up to Silverton and visiting a friend there who has a rat. Not a pet. The undesirable kind. Trust me, if my mother's dog catches the rat, I'll never hear the end of it."

"Are you practicing while you're here?"

At first she thought he meant dog training. "Of course."

"It's probably hard to hear your band and stay in sync with them."

"I can play with other people," she snapped, defensive.

He lifted his eyebrows, as though surprised by her reaction. Or maybe doubting her answer. "I'm sure it's not as difficult," he said, "as playing with other strings."

How dared he imply that what she did with the Wayfairers was easy!

Of course, he just wanted to insult her. "I still play classical music," she said.

"Oh, I'm sure."

"And I've always been able to keep up with you, if you're implying something like that. Remember who was second fiddle. But I no longer play with amateurs." The statement was rude and untrue. She loved to have fun, to play with friends who weren't professional musicians. Perhaps she hoped to goad William into challenging her.

"That seems like a good way to keep improving."

A remark *so* typical of William.

"I'd play with you," she said tightly. The conversation was like musical challenges they'd shared in the past. She dared him now in the hope that he'd invite her to play with him, at his house. "But I assume you don't practice much now."

"Why would that be?"

"Or play with other people."

"Bring your fiddle when you come to class," he said. "We'll play afterward."

She wouldn't mention Amy. "Crystal won't mind? I mean," she added, "I know you two must be busy planning the wedding."

"I know what you meant."

Which wasn't what she'd said. She'd meant that Crystal could be jealous. But why should she be? Crystal had no idea that she was Amy's birth mother. Even if she did know, that was no reason for jealousy. Giving birth to her daughter, walking away from the child, the months of depression and uncertainty that had followed—all of that had erased for Sophie any trace of the teenage love she'd had for William, any romantic feeling at all. In truth, every encounter she'd had with any man since then had been shaped by the fact that she'd relinquished Amy. No—by more than that. Men were not important to her in the way she was to them; she doubted they ever would be. In the unlikely event she ever married, the reasons and the attraction she felt for the man involved would be complex.

More complex, she suspected, than William's reasons for marrying the Jennifer Aniston look-alike.

She let Loki in the back seat, shut his door and climbed into the front. She couldn't stop herself. "Does Crystal play an instrument?"

"Why do you ask?"

"She's going to be Amy's stepmother."

"As I said, why do you ask?"

The jerk. "I do care about Amy," she began, not for the first time.

"Don't bother," he said. "She's gotten along without that for years. To answer your question, Crystal doesn't play an instrument."

"Then she must like dogs," said Sophie, who knew perfectly well that Crystal *didn't* like dogs, that she might actively *dislike* them.

William didn't answer, just waved politely—too politely—and turned back toward the house.

The truly relevant question occurred to her then.

Did Crystal like *Amy?*

HIS MOTHER CALLED that evening as she did every night. William had come to accept this and to understand that his mother's need to remain central in his life had more to do with his father, who'd let her down—more than once. The way he played the role of husband dropped a dark veil over the whole family, leaving his two sons inadequate for never seeking justice for their mother. In this world, Moira Ludlow, wronged wife, involved herself with her adult children, clinging to them and sometimes interfering. "Well, honey, I just want you to remember what that woman did to you and Amy," she cautioned William. "I don't know why you're even training her dogs."

"I'm a dog trainer, and they need to be trained," William answered as he stirred the cream of broccoli soup on the stove, then put the lid back on to let it simmer.

"I can't imagine why you want anything to do with her. You realize that she might blurt out the truth about Amy? She might tell Amy just for her own ends."

William thought about this, as he had many times since first seeing Sophie again on the sidewalk downtown. "Which would be?"

"Oh, she's probably very insecure if she's lost some of her hearing like you said. Being Amy's birth mother is the one thing no one can really take away from her. She probably realizes now what a silly choice she made, pursuing fame and abandoning her child, not to mention you. I mean, your father and I have had many chances to give up on each other. But we've worked it out for our children."

William didn't appreciate the information.

"It's the kind of sacrifice a person has to make to understand that it's the *only* right choice," she continued.

He bit his tongue. Too well, he remembered childhood scenes from New Guinea, he and Jonathan helpless witnesses to his mother's screams of fury at their father, who was, she felt, excessively friendly with the native women. Jonathan, at age four, had pointed out, *But they're his other wives!*

Not happy times to remember. The strange thing was, his parents had remained married and enjoyed some degree of contentment.

Maybe his mother was right. Surely for him, taking care of his daughter had been the only correct choice.

But would it have been for Sophie? He'd ceased to believe so—yet did believe that she must have known *many* periods of doubt and mourning for what she'd set aside. Not him—Amy.

"What's it going to do to your relationship with Amy," she asked calmly, "if she tells her the truth? And what does Crystal think about all this?"

"Actually, she doesn't know." He heard how it sounded.

"Know what? That Amy's mother isn't dead? Or that she's Sophie Creed?"

"Either."

"Well, maybe that's for the best. I can't tell you that. But is this wedding going to come off? Because I don't mind telling you, we're investing some time and money in being around here for that weekend."

Again, William weighed the pros and cons of his proximity to his mother. His father, when he was in town, which he was more and more often, was a better grandfather than he'd been a father—no problem there. His mother? Well, he, William, was her favorite son, as he had stood up for her to his father. And he had relied on her to help raise his daughter. But Crystal had said plenty about his mother calling every night to ask what they were having for dinner and, most of the time, to talk through the preparations, and William agreed she had a point.

Tell her I'm here, Crystal had said.

William had put the calls on speaker phone so she could participate in the conversations.

He was very glad he wasn't on speaker phone now, considering his mother's fixation on Amy's situation and on Sophie's possibly revealing the truth and catching him in his lie.

"The wedding's going to come off," he said, with less and less conviction that it would.

"Well. Just don't jeopardize your relationship with Crystal. Your dad says the same thing."

William decided not to comment on the source of that advice.

"I've never trusted that woman and I never will. Someone who could walk away from her own child like that. Well. How's the soup coming?"

"Actually, I need to focus on it." They said their goodbyes, and William breathed. He didn't need his mother's warning. It took no effort to work up an argument for not trusting Sophie. Her hearing loss must be shaking up her life. And she could easily shake up his—and Amy's.

CHAPTER FIVE

"WE—WELL, it started with Lalasa. But it's every band member, Sophie. And nobody meant to tell you over the phone."

"I'm not sure anyone meant to tell me at all," she snapped to Fiona, the band manager. "Could you please tell me again *every band member's* reason? Because I can't believe it."

"Lalasa," Fiona said in a slightly flat voice, "cited personality differences."

Naturally.

"Gavin wants to produce other bands."

"He wants to produce other bands? He's a bass player!"

"He perceives himself as something more than that," Fiona said quietly. "And Lalasa feels that the band performs and produces more songs that you've written than songs by and for her."

Sophie had known that as certainly as if Lalasa had already told her. She hadn't needed her manager to say it. "She's a percussionist. How can you write a song for a drummer?"

"Sophie, you know how unfair that is."

Because Lalasa had sung for the band. She danced. She wrote songs, and they were good. She played non-percussion instruments from India, which helped give the Wayfairers their distinctive sound. And she was

Sophie's oldest friend in the band. They had danced together, Lalasa teaching her Indian sacred dance, Bharata Natya, which had become part of her own life, and of their performance together.

What Fiona was telling her was nothing unexpected, nor as abrupt as it seemed. The Wayfairers had been itching to go their separate ways before she lost her hearing. All the Wayfairers except Sophie.

"Robbie?" she asked.

"Wants to do more solo work. In short, they feel the band is really 'Sophie Creed and the Wayfairers.' Your hearing loss gave them all a chance to ask themselves, 'What would I do if?' And face it, it's not the first time they've asked that question."

"This is about the 'W' word, isn't it?"

"It's not about weddings. They know you don't like weddings, either, and the band doesn't do weddings."

"Yes, but it's because of that song."

"It is not because of that song. It's a great song. People love that song."

"The band hates it."

"This isn't about a particular song."

"You think I brought this on myself, don't you?" Sophie demanded. She was talking on her parents' phone because her cell didn't work in the house. Her parents and James had gone for a walk. The day before, James had indeed caught the rat in Silverton, and the feat had been the talk of the kitchen table ever since.

Loki, who had been lying nearby with Cinders, now sat up and began to whine. Knowing he was reacting to her emotions, Sophie tried to breathe more slowly, tried deliberately to relax.

"You certainly didn't ask to get a virus that would cost you your hearing," Fiona said.

"But you think I'm hard to get along with."

"Look, everyone has issues." Fiona clearly didn't want to voice what she thought. "Maybe you just need to talk to someone. It's not like you're out a career if you don't have band. You're a great musician."

"But I can't get along with people."

"You said that."

"You think it."

"I think— I think you can be—maybe—excessively blunt."

"She can't sing, Fiona. You know it. Her songs are good enough, but her voice is mediocre."

"I just think saying 'You're unprofessional,' perhaps wasn't the most effective way to deal with her wanting to sing, especially as she *has* sung for the band."

"What else?"

"I don't want to have this conversation, Sophie."

"They say I'm a prima donna, don't they?"

"Sophie, I'm not doing this. There's no going back."

"Why not? Has someone made other plans—already?"

"They've *all* made other plans. Already."

"Think of The Doors, and what they put up with in Jim Morrison. Did any of The Doors quit the band because he was an alcoholic who sometimes wasn't even *onstage?*"

"Sophie, I think that's part of the problem."

"What?"

The manager sighed. "Let's just stop. We don't have to do this."

"What?"

"They don't feel about you," Fiona said carefully, "the way The Doors felt about Jim Morrison."

She didn't have to say what she didn't say, because Sophie understood perfectly.

The band members were quitting because she, Sophie Creed, just wasn't good enough to put up with.

And with her hearing compromised, she could only get worse.

"YOU'VE REACHED Mount Sneffels K-9. Canine Good Citizen classes start tonight, Thursday, at seven p.m. We're located at 3876 Camp Bird Road, three point four miles from Highway 550. Please leave a message after the beep."

"William, it's Sophie. I'm going to have to miss class tonight. I'm not feeling well. I'll come next Thursday, if that's all right."

A clatter and a beep. "Sophie?"

Amy.

"Yes."

"It's fine if you come next time. But I'm sorry you're not coming tonight."

I'm missing the chance, Sophie thought, *to play music with William.* And to see Amy.

But she no longer had the heart for that practice session between old friends and competitors. How could she face them, *tell them,* that she'd just been deserted by the musicians with whom she'd played, so successfully, for the past four years?

"If you feel better, come anyhow," Amy said. "If you don't, you should come up here soon and get your homework sheet. Or if you're feeling really bad, we can bring it to you."

Oh, William would love that.

She heard the interest in Amy's voice, the wanting to know her.

The Wayfairers' splitting up *wasn't* the end of the world. Fiona was right. Her career wasn't over.

But I can't hear, and I was never that good in the first place. That's why they're all leaving—because I'm not good enough.

Resentfully, she remembered Gavin in particular. Gavin with his shaved-head reactionary *strangeness.* So lonely and friendless that he'd come over to her house at night uninvited, strip down to his long johns, pull out a book he'd brought and make himself at home.

What did you do with a person like that, especially when he was a member of the band?

Gavin quit because he's in love with me, and I'm not in love with him. And he thinks he's a therapist, and he's not.

"You know—I think I might feel okay later," Sophie said. "By the time class starts. And your dad invited me over to play music with him."

"He *did?* He didn't tell me!"

"Do you play an instrument?"

"The clarinet."

"Then you can play with us." Sophie smiled, not just at the thought of playing music with her daughter but also because William would be furious.

Suddenly, for the first time, her band's quitting seemed to have benevolent purpose. To allow her to pick up some lost jigsaw pieces of the puzzle of her life.

WILLIAM DIDN'T WANT to speak to Crystal. What was she doing here before this class? He'd told her he needed space.

But she maintained that space wouldn't tell him whether or not they should get married. In that, she was probably right.

She didn't play an instrument and didn't like dogs. Sophie hadn't asked *What do you have in common?* but the question didn't need to be asked aloud.

Now Crystal was here and Sophie was coming over to play music with him—and Amy.

Crystal was not going to like it. Sophie had read that

one right, but at the moment the need to prove that he could play better than she could had triumphed over his common sense.

Even though Crystal wouldn't like it, she'd pretend to.

She does like dogs.

Really.

Some.

But there was no missing the disinterest of her glance toward Thunder, who lay off lead beside him near the outdoor kennels where he was watering the summer flowers.

"Got a dog for me to train?" he asked.

Crystal hugged him around the neck and kissed him fondly and possessively. "I just thought I'd watch and see if I could learn anything." Tires crunched over the gravel in the drive. "Oh, look, it's your friend with the German shepherds."

"Amy's going to handle one of them in this class." He turned to go in to the barn, and Crystal followed.

She said, "She doesn't live in town, does she? The woman with the dogs? I thought she was in a band or something."

William didn't bother to point out that even in Ouray there were bands; he knew what Crystal meant. "I don't know," he said. "She's going to be here for the class." *That's all I know.* But those words wouldn't come. Because that definitely wasn't all he knew.

Amy entered the barn from the door closest to the house, behind him. "Hi, Crystal." Her voice was flat, empty of emotion. Powerful in its lack of enthusiasm yet lack of ambivalence.

The Delphic sibyls, William thought, had probably had voices like that.

"Was that Sophie's truck pulling up outside?" Amy

asked in the voice of an eager teenager instead of a prognosticator of dire events. "Oh, here she is. Hey, Sophie!"

William's heart pounded. He became conscious of the sound of his own breath and knew immediately that he'd made a terrible mistake. Amy and Sophie must not be in the ring together with other eyes upon them. They must not be seen side by side.

He lifted his eyes.

They didn't look that much alike. Sophie's hair was thick and curly, burnished with dark, dark auburn. They both had brown eyes, though Amy's glasses hid hers.

A man with a particularly noisy schnauzer entered the barn. Behind him was an elderly woman with a yellow Lab William figured was genetically ADHD.

Amy took Cinders's lead from Sophie, and together they entered the ring. Loki looked up from sniffing the floor to glance at the schnauzer, then went back to scents.

"They look cute together," said Crystal.

She didn't mean Amy and Cinders. "Our dogs are better-looking." He turned to the clients entering the barn. "Everyone please fill out a registration form if you haven't already," he told them, walking away from Crystal.

In the practice ring, surrounded by criss-crossed wicker gates, Sophie sat down in one of the folding chairs arranged near the gate and made Loki sit, then lie down, beside her. Surprisingly, he stayed. The long down William had suggested she practice each night had begun to pay off. As Amy took the seat beside her, Sophie studied the objectives for the class hung on a chart-holder on one wall. "Never, never, will Loki be able to pass another dog without major posturing," she muttered. "Never, no way."

"Think positive," Amy said. "You'd be surprised. We had this one bitch in here who wanted to scrap with every dog she saw."

"I guess he'll get a lot better in ten weeks."

"It's great you're going to be here that long."

"Actually, I'm going to live here." She had decided in the same breath that she'd decided to come to class tonight. If her band's quitting represented an opening for her to know her daughter, then she would remain in the town where her daughter lived.

Sophie eyed Crystal, who stood across the ring watching her and Amy astutely. Of course, William would have asked her over. Or did she live here?

She would be watching and listening when they played music.

I'm not good enough. My band quit because I'm not that good.

In response to Sophie's announcement that she now lived in Ouray, Amy stared at her, neither pleased nor displeased. Simply incredulous. "*Why?* I mean, there's nothing here for anyone with a life."

Sophie remembered being eighteen and thinking the same thing.

It had taken her until this moment to realize that a life was built *inside* and that what she'd built in the years since she'd left Amy and William she had built from outside her instead.

No, that's not true.

Because performing live, feeling the enthusiasm of the crowd, was everything. People calling out requests for favorite songs, all of that. Yes, it came from outside her, but there was an exchange. She channeled something to her audience, and together they all became something bigger. The classical Indian dance that was so much a part of both her and Lalasa's worlds helped her become even more of a finely tuned instrument.

She couldn't think of that now. She had to focus on her dog and what he was doing. "Loki, sit."

THEY STARTED with a romance by Schumann. It wasn't easy, and Sophie was impressed with Amy's skill on the clarinet. William's playing was better than she remembered, crisper and more songlike, too.

He would have the first chair now.

Crystal stood near the bar, a wineglass in hand, smiling appreciatively.

As the last note faded away, Crystal said, "You two look like you've been playing together for years."

"Sound like," Amy corrected.

"No, I meant they look like it. Your little tussle over turning the page."

Sophie said nothing. This was dangerous territory. Why was Crystal bringing that up? She was right. *We weren't careful.*

Sophie said, "Can you two play 'Black Is the Color'?"

Amy tried the first notes of the love ballad experimentally.

"Sing with us, Crystal," Sophie encouraged, to distract William's fiancée from the direction of her thoughts, from thoughts Sophie could almost read. *She knows. She knows. Seeing Amy and me together, she knows.*

With compromised hearing, singing was marginally easier than playing with others.

"Black is the color of my true love's hair. His lips are like some roses fair...."

Crystal came over to stand beside Sophie, beside her good ear, and sing with her. Her voice was a nice soprano.

There's an instrument for you, William.

"I love my love, and this he knows. I love the ground whereon he goes...."

Sophie no longer trusted her own voice, which cut out in her head, disappearing from her left ear as her bad hearing tried to trick her. She was afraid she would weep if she continued to sing, more afraid to stop, most afraid to fake it. Was she off-key? If she was, these people would know.

"I go to the hills...."

As the song concluded to the tender last strain of William's violin, Crystal sighed and gave Sophie an impromptu hug. "Oh, thank you. This is so much fun. I have no musical talent, and you're a celebrity."

"You have a nice voice."

"Oh, thanks. I don't use it."

"You should. I think you're marrying into a musical family here."

"That's for certain," Crystal agreed. "Is this your first trip to Ouray?"

"No. My parents have a house here." Guarding every word, saying as little as possible, changing the topic, Sophie had no doubt that Crystal guessed the truth behind William's lie about Amy's mother being *dead.* Well, probably not the whole truth, but she wasn't a stupid woman and probably resented being told such a story.

Well, that was for them to work out.

But it raised an interesting question. Would Crystal agree with Sophie that Amy should be told the truth? Possibly William's CIA bride could be an ally.

Crystal, however, seemed content to have a break from music. Any conversation would suffice. "Sophie, are you sure you won't have a glass of wine?"

"Oh, why not?" *My life is in such shambles, anyway.*

Amy and William put down their instruments as Sophie followed Crystal to the kitchen counter, where Crystal poured her a glass of merlot.

"I only ever have one," Crystal said. "I'm a lightweight, but also drinking can really make you look old. Don't you think?"

"I do."

"You look like you work out. I mean, you must, being a performing artist."

Sophie shrugged. "I run, play with the dogs. Bharata Natya is my favorite, well, *physical* thing."

"What's that?"

"Classical Indian dance. Well, that's the short answer."

"What's the long answer?" asked Amy, wandering over to join them.

"The long answer is very long. But basically, like most sacred dance in India, Bharata Natya follows the outlines and rules laid down in an ancient text called the *Natya Shastra.* Many people perceive the forms and postures of the dance as symbolic of truth. Properly performed, it's meant to be a way for God to manifest Himself and uplift human consciousness from the mundane to the divine."

"Can you do some for us?" Amy asked.

"Well, I do incorporate it in performances. More accurately, it influences what I do onstage. It's the basis for other forms of dance I use."

"Can Dad play something and you dance?"

Sophie shrugged.

William lifted his violin and bow. "What do you want?"

"You used to—" Sophie stopped herself and felt her face go read. "A person used to be able to just—" she stammered to hide her mistake. There was no way to say something that would have meaning and effectively hide her blunder, that she knew anything at all about William Ludlow and what he used to do. "There's a tango I love. Albeniz. You probably don't—"

"Now you're talking," he said. He lifted his instrument, and she knew that he remembered the piece she wanted, remembered and understood.

But he, too, had given them away.

"This isn't the real thing, mind you," Sophie told Amy and a now-frowning Crystal. "Bharata Natya is performed in stages, to strict timing—*Jatis,* phrases made up of long and short syllables. But I'm used to improvising with the band."

As she'd said, it wasn't the real thing—and yet it was, in emotional content. She chose a form usually danced late in the dance, describing elaborately the nature of God. But for her it also became the nature of human life, which is made beautiful by pain and suffering, by the tenacity of the spirit, by change and growth, birth and death.

William's eyes were on her, and she felt the air on her bare shoulders and on her midriff where her camisole hiked up.

She felt his wanting from across the room.

It wasn't what she'd expected.

Yet must have wanted. Must have, because it hit her like lightning, the wanting back.

She stopped dancing, breathless, stunned as Maria von Trapp in the midst of dancing with the Captain in *The Sound of Music,* stunned to find herself in love and a man in love with her.

But I'm not in love with William. Nor he with me.

"I'd like to learn to dance that way," Amy said.

"I'm not a teacher. Even Lalasa, who taught me, isn't strictly a teacher, though she is a professional. And it's a vast art. But I could show you some movements."

Crystal yawned and stretched. "I could do with a walk. Why don't you two dance, and William and I can take the dogs out for a bit."

It was a suggestion no one could decline.

"WILLIAM, DID YOU know her before?"

It was dark, but the dark was no cover. He had opted to take only one dog—Sigurd—on this walk up the deserted Camp Bird Road. "Who?"

"Sophie Creed."

"Before what?"

"I think you know what I'm going to ask you."

"I have no idea what you're going to ask me." But he did.

"Ever since I met you, there's been one thing I couldn't figure out. You never told me the *details* of Amy's mother dying. You never wanted to talk about it. I've found that when a person's lived through something like that, he needs the important people in his life to know what happened. But you don't talk about it."

"You're right." And the game was up. Crystal was intelligent. To lie to her at this point, to continue the lie, would be both wrong and insulting. "Sophie is Amy's mother. When she was eighteen, she left Amy to pursue a career in music."

"How old were you? Nineteen, you must've been. Good grief. You must've been angry. No wonder you told Amy her mother was dead."

"I didn't tell her that because I was angry. I told her because it was simpler." Their sneakers crunched on the rock and gravel and dirt. A spring trickled down the rock wall to their right as they hiked uphill. The elevation was nine thousand feet, but they were both used to it. "It's still simpler."

Crystal stopped. In the starlight, he felt her looking at him. "Oh, please. William, she *knows*."

"What do you mean? Who knows what?"

"Amy. She doesn't know *what* she knows, but part of her realizes that you've lied to her. She's a very sharp girl. And doesn't Sophie want her to learn the truth?"

"I honestly don't know—and I don't particularly care. *I* don't want her to learn the truth."

"Then why on earth do you let her mother come around here?"

Good question.

He'd felt pushed into helping her with Loki. By coincidence. By circumstance. But then he'd invited her to play music. Later he'd decided that Sophie had ensnared him, had coaxed that invitation from him with the bait of his own musical ego.

Why had he let it happen?

Because she has more right to know Amy than I do.

But that was neither honest nor true.

Crystal exclaimed, "When were you planning to tell me, William? Or were you?"

"I knew I had to tell you. But I wasn't sure how. I was afraid you'd want Amy to find out the truth. It's better to leave things as they are, Crystal. You have to believe that. You don't know everything."

"Does Sophie?"

"She's the only one who does. Do you understand, Crystal? It's imperative that you drop this."

"Don't tell me to drop this. I'm going to be your wife. I have a right to know."

Silence cloaked the night. Sigurd sniffed the road.

The black was darker than knowledge.

Crystal said, "Maybe… I think with Amy's mother on the scene—they get along so well—"

He saw it coming and didn't stop it, knew he

shouldn't, knew he should feel gratitude for her good sense and good manners.

"—it's not the time for her to get a new stepmother. Her birth mother lives here now. It's obvious you enjoy each other's company."

"We don't."

"Whatever. I'm not comfortable with it."

And she took the ring that had cost him too much off her finger and returned it to him, and he imagined what the woman at the gallery where they'd bought it would say and wondered how much of a refund he could get.

"I love you, William. But I'm not doing you any favors letting you live this lie."

"You don't know what the lie is." He wished it unsaid.

She gazed at him through the nothing of night. "Actually, I'm beginning to form a good guess."

HE DIDN'T ASK for her guess and she didn't give it.

When they returned to the house, Crystal said she'd rather not go inside but that she hoped the two of them and Amy would remain friends.

He said he intended nothing else, and he held the door for her while she climbed into the Lexus.

He came inside to find Amy and Sophie standing side by side, practicing dance movements.

"I'm learning *adavus,"* Amy told him. "That's the unit of dance. But Sophie says there are a hundred and twenty."

"Ah." *She knows,* Crystal had insisted. What did Amy know or suspect? Not that the woman beside her was her natural mother.

Remembering Sophie's indignant reaction to his lie, he thought of the lie she'd left *him* to tell, the agreed-upon lie, all the distorted stories that had worked until now and must continue to work and yet would never allow him to be free, nor free her either.

Sophie made herself stand, forced herself to leave them. "We didn't get much music played, but I really should get home." Because Crystal had gone.

Because of things that had happened long ago.

And the feelings within her when she'd danced that night.

"I'll walk you out."

Her dogs were waiting in the Tundra, because that had been the most convenient place for them. Another time, she'd said, she would try bringing them into William's house where Sigurd, Tala and Thunder lived and slept.

She put her violin in the front seat.

"I think we should tell her."

Sophie spun. He wanted to tell Amy! It was that easy. "Oh, William, I'm so—"

"I think we should tell her everything."

She stilled, sensing a steel in him that made her picture him easily in the uniform of a law enforcement officer. "I don't think so. I don't think it would be good for her."

"Sometimes things are neither good for us nor bad for us but just part of us. It's part of her, and she knows. On some level, she knows."

Sophie shook her head. The knowledge would be horrifying for Amy, affecting her sense of self. "Please, no. Please, no."

William knew he was hearing what she'd said to Amy's father fifteen years before.

He heard and knew he couldn't tell his daughter that she'd been conceived during her mother's rape.

He couldn't tell Amy that she wasn't his daughter at all.

CHAPTER SIX

IT WAS THE SOLEMN SECRET the two of them shared. Alone. Well—not completely alone, because Sophie had spoken to many therapists over the years. There had been things to get over. The therapists had heard the whole story. They all respected her opinion that it would be harmful for Amy to know that she'd been conceived when her mother was raped.

They all understood why Sophie had walked away from her daughter.

It had been an acquaintance rape. Two days after her graduation from the performing arts high school in Chicago that her parents had let her attend, apart from them, her music theory teacher had taken her to the opera. For Sophie, it had been a dream come true. Patrick Wray was brilliant, handsome, charming, inspiring. She'd had a crush on him forever and couldn't believe he'd invited her to go to the opera with him. He must be attracted to her. All those times he'd talked to her about places he'd visited in Colorado as a child, his family making an annual pilgrimage to one mountain community or another… Even if all he wanted was to develop their friendship, that was flattering.

He drove a vintage Porsche, a Carrera. After *Don Giovanni* he'd driven out to Navy Pier. Then, in the car, in the darkness, he'd asked if he could kiss her.

It had been strange and wonderful. He was thirty-five. But she was ready for this, for an exciting romance with this man.

At some point, however, she knew.

He was too eager, too fast, and the way he said certain things, told her to take off her top *now*, not as a lover but as someone enjoying a show.

She'd said, *Let's not do this.*

He'd repeated what he wanted her to do.

She'd said, *I really don't want to.* And then she was afraid.

He'd kept saying what he wanted her to do. She'd done it. To the next command, she'd said, *Please, no.* And on it went.

When it was over, he asked if she'd liked it.

Two months later, when she'd realized she was pregnant and told her best friend in the Ouray summer orchestra program, William Ludlow, what had happened, he'd said, *He raped you.*

And that was when she understood what had happened.

But still she doubted. She thought she'd always doubt, always wonder, *Did* I ask for it?

Therapist after therapist, she had asked, *Was it rape?*

Therapist after therapist had said, *Yes!* Or *No means no,* which troubled Sophie because she wasn't sure that, for men, no always meant no.

Only time and knowing many men, had helped her see that plenty of them understood *No.* And *Please, no.* And *Please don't.* Other men did not behave as Patrick Wray had.

She'd planned to have an abortion. But it didn't feel like the right solution. Her hero-worship for Patrick had been based on some real qualities. As a teacher, he'd made his subject come alive. He was a mathematician as well as a musician.

Yet she feared and hated him and did not want to bear his child.

She hadn't known what to do.

The last thing she had expected was William's help.

William had not raped her. William had not kissed her. After she'd told him everything, he'd hugged her.

He had been her friend and taken her for ice cream.

He'd finally told her she could tell people the baby was his, could put his name on the birth certificate if she liked.

One day, he was sitting on the grass in the Ouray town park waiting for her to come out from the hot springs pool after swimming. When she did and saw him sitting on the lawn, talking to a mother and her two children, laughing with one of them, he glanced in her direction and smiled the smile that was like the sun beaming on everything around him, and she fell in love.

Abrupt, hard and final.

They'd moved to Carbondale together and, in Glenwood Springs, he'd sold Toyotas.

He had never pressured her for sex. He was careful of her, appreciative of small things—the insides of her wrists, her smell when she woke up in the morning, the skin below her jaw. But mostly she knew that she—she, Sophie, the Sophie inside the skin—was loved.

It was only as the birth approached that she'd known she was doing the wrong thing. She didn't want to be married at eighteen, and she didn't want to raise Patrick Wray's child. If she did, someday her rage would boil over and she would tell the child the truth. She wasn't ready to give up her life for this.

William had said, fine, he would do it. He would raise the child.

Driving home from Mount Sneffels K-9, from his house, she wished she could believe that the resurgence of attraction she'd felt for him that night was real, had any lasting basis.

He hadn't meant what he'd suggested, that they should tell Amy everything. When she'd objected, he'd finally said he supposed she was right.

And he'd told her that Crystal had broken their engagement. No—that Crystal had guessed the truth *and* broken the engagement.

Then Amy will guess, too, Sophie had said.

As she lay in her bed that night, her instinct was to put the dogs in her truck, hitch on her gypsy wagon and go.

She'd never even told her parents the truth about Amy's biological father. Biology included or aside, William *was* Amy's father now. Legally, morally and in every way that mattered. Everything had worked out for Amy, worked out as well as Sophie could possibly have imagined—better, perhaps.

Though William was in favor of telling Amy that Sophie was her mother, Sophie was no longer sure. *If it ain't broke, don't fix it.* Amy really didn't need to know the truth. The only compelling reason for telling her was so that she wouldn't guess.

Amy had an amended birth certificate. That was how Sophie had wanted it. William was named as the father, the mother left blank. That would require some explaining on his part someday.

What a mess we've made.

What a mess I've made.

Should she leave Ouray? Would that solve the problem? It seemed to her now that she'd left Amy for selfish reasons and that to reenter her life would be equally selfish.

Of course Crystal had broken the engagement. William had lied to her. The woman would've had to be crazy or stupid to marry him after that, and Sophie didn't think Crystal was either. In fact, she'd begun to rather like her.

Unable to sleep, she got up and, checking that her parents' door down the hall was closed—and James was, therefore, inside with them—she let Cinders and Loki out and led the way downstairs to the kitchen.

Playing music or singing would disturb her parents—but the gypsy wagon provided a bit of sound insulation. She could go out there.

She took her violin, though she wasn't sure she'd play it; she might just sing or write a song.

The rape had never been a memory of terror. It wasn't like that. It was simply awful, something she preferred not to think about. What remained on a day-to-day basis, what could not be avoided, was what it had done to her.

Before, the world had seemed one way.

Afterward, it was different.

And yes, she still felt anger toward Patrick Wray. Yes, that anger sometimes directed itself at whatever man happened to be in front of her, doing some small thing that even vaguely reminded her of what she hadn't been able to stop.

She wanted to be the way she'd been, believing in love between men and women, *trusting* people, trusting half the species. William had done so much for her, had helped her. He was good. He'd delighted in her.

What had happened to her back then had not been the only shaping event in her life or even the most important. Hers was a meaningful life. She'd succeeded in a difficult career.

Until your band quit, Creed.

She *enjoyed* life.

Or had, unreservedly, until that virus had damaged her hearing.

She'd gone on. Gone on from being raped, gone on from the biologically wrenching separation from her child.

I have to go on from here, too.

A musician with inadequate hearing, struggling even to communicate with the people around her. Once she'd lost her hearing, there'd been so many misunderstandings at gigs.

She was blessed in William, she reminded herself, blessed that he had agreed to father her daughter. Even when she'd left, part of her had loved Amy, had felt compelled to love her, and William had arisen like an angel to care for Amy, to stand by her, to be her father. He was a good father, and the affection between him and Amy was plain.

She'd only asked him once why and how he could give up years of his life, how he could limit his own freedom, by caring for a daughter not really his.

He'd gazed at her middle, grown big with the child, and said, "I think it's what I have to do. That's all."

Ambiguous, yet strongly felt.

She had never mistrusted him. And she understood why it must have been easier to tell Amy that her mother was dead.

But what now?

What now?

SHE KEPT HOPING Fiona would call in the morning, say the band had changed their minds.

She didn't. They hadn't.

Sophie broke down and called Gavin, her best friend in the band. She couldn't bear to call Lalasa, to face so baldly what felt like betrayal.

"Hi, Sophie. How's your ear?"

"No better." What would be the point in lying? Nothing. "So," she said. "You quit."

"Well, I prefer to think of it as changing trajectories."

Sophie wondered how he could possibly think she'd find that distinction anything but completely meaningless.

"It's because I'm not that good, isn't it?" she said.

"You're good." He spoke as though the point was completely irrelevant.

"Not good enough."

"You could be more—sensitive. Toward the people around you. But that isn't why I chose a new trajectory."

If he used that word again…

"I'm producing a CD. For The Heathen."

Grunge-punk. Not particularly good grunge-punk, either. "That'll go platinum," she responded before she could stop herself.

Silence.

Gavin often spoke with his silence. This time he said, *What did I mention about insensitivity.*

"So," he asked, "want to do some background vocals on it?"

She hung up on him.

"SOPHIE, the phone's for you," her mother called upstairs just before noon.

This would be Lalasa, trying to make peace.

She lifted the nearest receiver.

"Sophie?"

"Hi, William."

"I wanted to see how you're doing."

Oh, just great. I have no career. I have no life. What I have is two great German shepherd dogs. "Fine. Why wouldn't I be?"

"You were upset last night."

She said nothing.

"Amy wanted me to ask you over for dinner and to see if you'd bring some Indian dance music. She said you told her you had some."

"Oh. Do you think that's a good idea?"

"I told you last night what I think."

"So, if I come over, we tell her—about me. Not the rest."

"Ultimately, that part is up to you. But I think we should tell her everything. She's not your average person. She believes she's—and she is—almost mystical. I don't think the truth would affect her the way you think it would. And she'll be angry with me, as it is, for lying to her. I'd rather not carry on with additional lies."

"Well, I would. I'm convinced this is better for her." The only good answer was to let Amy continue to believe that William was her father, her only father. "You've come around in a hurry."

"Come around to what?"

"Letting me be near her. Why the change?"

Silence. Then, "Guilt."

"Over? Telling her I was dead?"

"Lying to her. Yes."

Ah. "What time is dinner?"

"Why don't you come over at six? And bring your fiddle again."

It was on the tip of her tongue to tell him that her band had quit, but she'd told no one, not even her parents. She couldn't stand to say it out loud.

"YOU'RE SAYING *Crystal* broke it off?" Amy clarified as they waited for Sophie to arrive.

"I've said it three times now."

"But why? She's crazy about you. Was it because of me? Did she say I was mean to her?"

"She didn't. Were you?"

"A bit. Yes. I'm sorry. I didn't mean for this to happen. She was growing on me." Amy stared out the kitchen window. "It was Sophie, wasn't it? Something to do with Sophie. She thought you two had always known each other."

He said, "Tell me again what we decided. About pizza toppings."

"One with spinach, mushrooms and feta cheese. One plain cheese."

"I wasn't sure. I thought we needed to chop up some other ingredient."

"Salad. And I'm doing it, remember, because I make better salads than you do."

"That's true." He was glad Sophie had vetoed telling Amy that he wasn't her natural father. What if that changed his relationship with her? He didn't really think the other lie he'd told her would make a difference in the long run. Crystal might well be right; Amy might already suspect something like the truth.

But he was certain it had never entered her head that he wasn't her natural father.

Once even his mother had said that Amy had inherited his chin.

People saw what you told them was there.

The phone rang.

"Grandma," said Amy. "Have you told her about Crystal?"

"No." And telling his mother his fiancée had jilted him was not the kind of conversation he wanted to have in front of his fourteen-year-old daughter. But it wouldn't be any more pleasant without Amy listening.

"Hi, Mom."

She started in about her flowers, saying he and Amy needed to come and see them. Also, his brother, Jonathan, and Jonathan's wife, Angie, were visiting for two weeks later that month. They couldn't wait to meet Crystal.

"Well..." He dragged out the word. "Crystal—ah—broke our engagement last night."

"What?"

"Yes."

"Why? It didn't have anything to do with that woman, did it?"

"Put Grandma on the speaker phone. I want to hear what she's saying," hissed Amy. "Is she ballistic?"

William shushed her with a wave of his hand, adding, for his mother's benefit, "Amy, turn on the oven."

"I see. You can't talk."

That required no answer.

"Well, I'm not surprised," his mother said. "I told you that you were playing with fire, that she wouldn't like having another woman around, didn't I?"

"You did." Distantly, he noticed his mother returning to a well-established line, treading into the land of His Life with the aim, perhaps, of running the show. Counseling sessions a decade earlier had helped him address the situation but ultimately hadn't changed her. She cloaked her domination in a mother's protectiveness.

Amy called, "Sophie's here!"

"She's not there *again?*"

"Actually, yes."

"Watch it, William. Just wait. I don't want to be proved right again," her mother said. "I'd better let you go and deal with your...guest. This will not end well. She might be able to take Amy away from you, you know. Children that age have a say now."

"Thanks, Mom. I'll talk to you later."

"All right. I love you, sweetheart."

Amy showed Sophie inside, saying, "We put Loki

and Cinders in the yard with Sigurd. Everyone's playing nice, if you can believe it."

"Good."

Sophie set her violin case beside his and Amy's instruments on the high shelf where they kept them.

William glanced at her and saw she looked pale and anxious. Undoubtedly not knowing whether to tell Amy that she was her birth mother.

"Did you bring a CD for Bharata Natya?" asked Amy.

"I brought three. I thought I'd let you keep them here for a while."

"Really?" Amy sounded both ecstatic and disbelieving.

"Really."

"Want to see my room? It's clean. It's always clean, actually. I'm very neat. My dad's more of a slob."

Nervous, Sophie followed her upstairs. What if she and William told Amy the truth and Amy blamed her, thought Sophie had deserted her?

Amy's was not a typical teenager's room. In place of the posters that Sophie thought of as usual hung framed images. There were four. Two William Blake prints. A hanging tapestry showing the goddess Sarasvati. And a small oil painting of a romantic-looking woman with curly dark hair and brown eyes.

Sophie paused to study the painting.

"I bought it at a yard sale," Amy said. "I don't have any pictures of my mother. This fitted my dad's general description. He says it doesn't really look like she did. Anyhow, the woman in the portrait is sort of a symbol of my mother. I talk to my mother, you know."

I'm going to be sick. I have to tell her. Do I dare say it now without consulting William?

Amy was on the floor on a well-worn yoga mat. "Do you ever do yoga?"

"Of course. It helps with Bharata Natya."

"I wish there was somewhere around here I could take classes in Bharata Natya."

She didn't have to tell her any part of the truth. She could just let it go.

But her mouth moved. "Amy, your dad and I talked last night—" The words seemed to have nothing to do with her, as though someone else had scripted them and she was reading them for the first time. "We decided it was best to tell you."

Amy lifted her head, staring, innocent, with no inkling of the magnitude of what was coming.

"Your dad didn't know how to deal with the situation," Sophie explained inadequately. More of those scripted lines, a horrible script.

Amy's beautiful complexion, flawless white, pink-cheeked, seemed frozen, unreal.

"Amy, I'm your birth mother."

Amy blinked once, shaking her head, looking less than pleased, mostly stunned.

"I realized," Sophie continued, "when you began talking to me downtown, when you told me your father's name—and yours. I didn't come back to Ouray intending to meet you or intrude on your life. It just...happened...that you and I met—and then saw each other again. But I don't feel it's right to deceive you any longer."

Amy seemed dumbfounded. She still didn't speak.

"Your dad and I were best friends all through high school, during the summers. We both came here each year with our parents. We played music together."

"I can't believe this," Amy said. "You knew each other. Crystal was right. Crystal guessed. She guessed all along. She knew my dad had lied to me."

And to her. Sophie didn't add it.

"Does my dad know you're telling me this?" Amy demanded.

"We've talked about it."

Sophie had imagined many reactions in Amy, reactions to this news. She had not imagined rage.

The rage was a contained adolescent rage, righteous and real.

"I'm sorry," Sophie said. "I thought—I thought you'd want to know."

Amy stared up at the portrait on her wall, then at Sophie. "I knew my mother wasn't dead. I'm really not surprised it's you."

Her voice had become matter-of-fact.

"Should we—go be with your dad?" Sophie asked. "Do you want to talk with him about this?"

"Oh, yeah," said Amy. "Oh, yeah. I want to see what hypocrisy he has to say now."

"Hypocrisy?"

"'Tell the truth, Amy. Always tell the truth. You did the right thing.' But you don't know what I'm talking about."

Sophie knew exactly what she was talking about. "Do you want to tell me?"

"Sure." Amy shrugged. "Why not? When I was little in Denver, I went to a barbecue with my dad and I walked in on his boss being the back-door man to this fifteen-year-old girl. It was pretty disgusting. He said I was lying, and he got me alone and said that if I didn't say it was a lie he'd kill my dad." Her voice was shaking. "I've never told anyone that."

Sophie's own secret burned within her. It was not a secret for Amy to hear. "You must have been terrified."

"I'm *still* terrified. I probably always will be. But the point is, my dad definitely believed me, and he kept telling me to always tell the truth, which I couldn't. I was too afraid. 'Always tell the truth.' What a load of crap. People can't stand the truth." She shot a look at Sophie. "So what are you doing here, anyhow? Obviously, you didn't want me before."

That was true.

It was not a truth Sophie would ever utter aloud.

She had not wanted this reminder of her life's most degrading, most powerless moment. Childbirth had helped restore her, somehow, but it hadn't made her believe that she could raise that baby without screaming her rage and resentment and hatred of Patrick Wray.

But now, with Amy, with Amy whom she knew, knew and somehow *loved,* the rage and resentment and hatred were as nothing. Or rather, they had nothing to do with the young woman before her.

"Maybe I'm here," she said, "to be a friend to you. Whatever helps make your life better."

"You didn't want me because you wanted to be a musician, to be a star," Amy declared.

"I believed music was my destiny and that it was the best thing for me to do with my life."

"Didn't you love my dad at all?"

The unasked question flew at Sophie.

Didn't you love me?

"I loved your dad, and I loved you. I did the only thing I believed I could do. I didn't think I could be a good mother. I still don't think so."

Amy stared at her and abruptly stood up. "I agree." She walked out of her room.

Sophie followed her downstairs, meeting William's eyes.

He knew, then, that she'd told Amy.

Amy grabbed a pair of running shoes from beside the kitchen counter. Pulling them on, she snapped at William, "Thank you for lying to me. It's the best idea you ever had, and I mean that quite sincerely. I liked your fiction better than these facts."

She walked out of the house and slammed the door.

Sophie knew not to follow her.

William reached for a bottle of wine on the counter and jabbed a corkscrew into it.

Sophie said, "I shouldn't have told her."

"I wanted you to."

"I wish she *could* know everything, but my reasons are selfish. I want her to forgive me." Sophie took down her violin and opened the case.

William watched her tune, watched her profile with its strong, straight nose. He checked the pizzas in the oven, then put on a pair of boots and stepped outside, shutting the door behind him.

Amy was with the dogs. She'd gone inside Thunder's kennel with him and was petting him and receiving a kiss on the face in return. When he saw William, the Cane Corso came toward him, wagging his tail, ears back.

William stood watching her until she said, "I knew I was being lied to. But I thought it was for a better reason than this. Why didn't you just say, 'She was young and had other things she'd rather do'?"

"I didn't want you to feel abandoned."

She cracked an unamused smile. "You know, she's a pretty good musician, but she's not *that* good. It's not like her music has made this major impact on the world. She's not Mozart. For that matter, she's not even Joni Mitchell."

William was glad Sophie couldn't hear her.

And that surprised him. The last thing he'd ever expected to feel toward Sophie Creed was compassion.

Yet wasn't compassion for her what had taken him into law enforcement, as though by becoming a cop he could prevent even one acquaintance rape, one rape of any kind? Perhaps he'd turned to the K-9 unit because he'd found he could do so little.

And found that at some fundamental level he was in the wrong line of work.

Dogs were the right line.

"If she was really good, really talented, I would admit that her decision made sense."

"No matter how good she is," William said, "it doesn't make sense for anyone to walk away from you, Amy." Except, perhaps, for the reason Sophie had. The *real* reason. That reason he'd always been able to understand—when he'd remembered it above his own pain.

What had hurt was that she hadn't wanted to stay with him.

Amy gave a bitter laugh. "You know, you really don't get it. *'Always tell the truth, Amy,'*" she mimicked.

He said nothing. He deserved her scorn.

"You two aren't, like, involved *now,* are you?"

"No. We barely know each other—as the people we are now. We lived together when she was pregnant with you."

"Then she dumped both of us," Amy said with bright sarcasm and anger like a honed knife.

Unable to explain why it was more complicated than that, he again said nothing.

"Of course, my knowing the truth doesn't change anything, does it? Aside from the fact that she now lives here. Maybe she's decided she'd rather have me than her career."

Was that hope in her voice? Cautious, William kept his reaction to the possibility that Sophie might prefer motherhood to career—not likely—to himself. "I think I'll go back inside. The pizza's probably got another twenty minutes. Then it has to cool."

He heard Sophie's violin as he neared the house, pausing in the yard to invite Loki to come inside with him.

When he went in, he took his own violin from the shelf. Loki greeted Sophie and lay at her feet, angelic.

They were playing Mozart when Amy entered, bringing Thunder.

Loki stood up and growled.

Thunder growled back.

Sophie stopped playing. "Wrrrong," she corrected Loki, as Amy grabbed Thunder's collar and corrected him. Sophie set her violin in its case on the counter before taking Loki by the collar.

"Put him on a lead," William told her.

"Your dog's aggressive," Amy muttered.

"That's why she came to Mount Sneffels K-9," her father said.

"Thunder shouldn't have to leave his own house," Amy responded. "This is his territory."

"Excuse me," William said, "this is my territory." He downed Thunder with a hand signal.

"I'll take Loki out," Sophie offered.

"Let's give them a minute. Put him in a down."

Sophie felt Amy watching her with hostile eyes. *Well, you didn't expect her to love you, did you?*

No, but she'd expected—foolishly—that Amy would like her as much as she had at their last meeting.

It was painful to remain under the circumstances. Sophie was used to being liked—well, yes, there'd been problems with her band, personality conflicts, but *usually* people liked her.

Suddenly, her daughter did not.

What would it be like if *she* suddenly met her birth mother? Sophie wasn't sure she'd appreciate it. Her parents were her family.

As she held Loki's collar, she remembered the emergency room in Carbondale. Amy had been born so fast.

When William released him from a down, Thunder

came over to sniff Loki, and Loki remained in his down. Surprisingly, he allowed Thunder to sniff him.

Finally Thunder's tail wagged.

"Friends," William said. "Release him."

She did, and the two dogs showed signs of wanting to play.

"Not in the house," said William, which seemed to be a command Thunder knew.

"Do you want to hear your birth story?" Sophie asked Amy.

"You obviously weren't happy about it."

"That's not accurate."

"Did you shed even one tear?"

"Yes, I did." *More than you know, for reasons you'll never know.*

Amy jerked her chin up, and her pointed chin was Sophie's. She stood ten feet away, and the Cane Corso lay down at her feet with a small sigh, Loki stooping in puppy stance nearby.

Sophie noticed how Amy's figure was like hers, although she was taller than Sophie. And she had Sophie's nose, too.

"Thunder," William warned. "Not in the house."

The Cane Corso gave him a look of deep disappointment. Loki lay down with his front paws beside the other dog's.

Sophie could barely remember Patrick Wray's face as she searched for him in Amy's. She remembered his enthusiasm in the classroom and his insistence in his car. She remembered that it hurt and when it was over she had felt awful, awful.

Then he'd asked her if she'd liked it.

But Amy growing inside her had not been a hated burden. A problem, yes. But William had taken care of her, doing small things. She'd liked milk when she had morning sickness. He'd gone to the store. For a time, she had planned to raise the baby with him.

When she'd made love with him the first time she'd cried.

He was never urgent about sex. He took it slowly and stopped if she was upset. He'd been very good to her.

There was no *healing* from the wound. There was getting past it, going on, accepting that it was one of the things that had happened to her.

And William had been her *friend.* Such a friend.

During the worries, the fears, she had asked him, *What if something's wrong with the baby? What if it only has one arm?*

He had said, *It'll just be more special.*

Yes, her mate selection had been excellent. She had chosen the perfect father for the child she hadn't chosen to conceive.

That truth, in some very difficult way, *was* beautiful, but they had decided not to tell Amy. It was impossible to know what was right.

Amy sank down on the Adirondack-style couch with its thick cushions and arms of bent and twisted wood.

Sophie took the risk. She came and sat beside her. "Amy, I'm sorry. I didn't know whether to tell you or not. I was so happy you wanted to handle Cinders in class—and learn Bharata Natya. It's one of my favorite things. I was just happy to know you a little bit. Then, I began to think you should be told the truth, that it was right to tell you."

Amy blinked as she sat stiffly, her back slightly arched. The quiet dignity of her face was that of a Cassandra, of one who knows more than she is told, who speaks the truth and is not believed and who is used to the pain of that phenomenon. "I forgive you," she said. "I suppose I can imagine somebody wanting to do other things than raise a baby. I'm not going to be nasty, if that's what you're both worried about."

"It's not," they said at the same instant.

She stared, a frown knitting her brow. "Then what?"

"Amy, I—we love you." William shook his head at her. "We want you to be happy. We're worried you're unhappy, in pain." But the "we" sounded awkward, unnatural. There was no "we." He and Sophie were separate individuals, not partners.

"It's really just as though I was given up and adopted," Amy said. "Or something like that. Except then I'd have an adoptive mother, at least."

Sophie had felt guilty at various times for not raising the child she'd conceived when Patrick Wray had raped her. But it had always been only a passing sense of culpability, overshadowed by the knowledge that she could not have borne it. She would have become resentful and angry. She had done plenty in bringing the baby into the world and relinquishing her to be raised by someone else.

Her guilt about deserting William was keener. But raising Amy had been his choice. She had begged him not to do it, to let the baby be put up for adoption.

But he'd fallen in love with Amy at her birth—perhaps before that. He was, he said, her father already; he couldn't help it.

Amy shrugged. "It's not the worst thing that could happen. And I knew. I knew all along that she wasn't dead." She didn't add, *That you weren't.* Almost as though Sophie didn't exist. "I just had no idea what the real story was. I thought she *couldn't* raise me."

Barbs, barbs, cutting, cutting.

Sophie put away her violin and William his.

"You know," said Amy, "my dad could've been a professional musician, too. Still could. Everyone says so."

William reflected in wonder, amazed that the girl who could be so mature, so adult, one moment, could be so childish the next. So spiteful.

"I respect Crystal," she continued, addressing William this time, "for breaking your engagement.

So did he, but he didn't say so. She was being rude, and his tolerance waned.

It was a tense meal, and afterward both Amy and Sophie felt too stuffed to practice Bharata Natya. But Sophie brought in the CDs, which she'd said she would leave.

She said they—she and Loki and Cinders—had better go.

William offered to walk her out, and Amy threw them a look of disgust.

It's not like that, Sophie thought, wanting to laugh at Amy's apparent fear. She wasn't going to fall in love with William, nor he with her. They were different people than they'd been at eighteen. They'd been friends, and she knew they still could be, could pick up as friends where they'd left off.

Of course, she never fell in love easily. Patrick Wray had seen to that. In every relationship she'd had since, she'd held the cards and she'd kept them. Sometimes she wished she *could* fall in love, could feel with the depth she'd once known.

But she didn't believe that "falling in love" was about love. It was, in Sophie's view, a psychological phenomenon. People fell in love with others who had some quality the lover wished to acquire for herself. Or maybe there was someone in her life whose approval she'd desperately wanted yet had never received, and the falling in love experience was a repetition of that.

Her parents loved each other. Sophie believed in their kind of love, which had its basis in shared interests, a shared life. Her parents seemed to take care of each other, which was unique in her experience. Granted, she'd known men who wanted her to take care of them—but not the reverse.

In any case, marriage was what her parents had. Commitment was what they had. But it didn't show her how she, with her experiences, could marry anyone.

Or how to love.

Out at her truck, William said, "She'll be fine. It was the right thing to do."

"I'm not sure. In an adoption—well, there's no way my birth mother would be able to spring herself on me." She took a breath. "Since this is the night for telling the truth, I may as well tell you that the Wayfairers have split up. My hearing loss was, I guess…well, one problem too many. I'm not easy to work with," she added.

"You'll do fine as an acoustic soloist if you want."

She didn't answer.

"Or you can learn to train dogs, and I'll put you on as an assistant."

She smiled halfheartedly.

"That's why you're now living here?" he asked. "The band breaking up?"

"That and my hearing loss. Yes."

"So—we'll see you in class."

Good grief. Talk about an anticlimax. *What did you expect him to say, Sophie?* "I guess so."

"Try to be more committed," he told her, starting to walk away. "To your dogs."

CHAPTER SEVEN

SOPHIE AND HER MOTHER started seeds in plastic greenhouse trays in the sunroom on Thursday just after noon. Cinders lay at Sophie's feet, and James raced back and forth beside the windows, barking at Loki in the yard. Each bark stabbed in Sophie's left ear, until she held her hand over her ear to stop the pain.

"Sophie, I'm sorry, is his barking hurting your ear?"

"I think you should let him out with Loki and let them work it out," Sophie said. She was beginning to feel that James's aggression toward Loki was yet another of his ploys to get her mother's attention.

"I'm afraid Loki will rip one of his ears off."

"I have the same concern on Loki's behalf. But I think if we let them out there together, they'll have to make their peace." Sophie had the feeling she should clear the plan with William, but she couldn't bear the Schipperke's barking any more—not on top of other tension.

She hadn't heard from Amy or William, and she'd told her parents neither that Amy now knew that Sophie was her birth mother nor that her band had quit. It all felt like failure. Fourteen years ago, she'd been sure she couldn't be a good mother to Amy—and she wouldn't be able to take care of her. She'd told William, *I can't. She'll always remind me.*

But now Patrick Wray's part in it seemed irrelevant.

She loved Amy for herself and because she, Sophie, had given birth to her.

Her mother let James out.

Sophie watched through the window as James tore toward her dog, snarling.

Loki outran him, turned around and chased him, a dog-smile on his face the whole time.

"They'll be fine," said Sophie. And the sunroom was quiet.

Her mother kept her head bent over the seeds. "Um, someone asked me, Sophie—I didn't know what to say. But they asked if you'd sing for their wedding."

Sophie forced herself to relax, not to take the request as a statement on her future prospects as a musician. "Who?"

"I don't think you've met them. They're this very nice couple who go to our church here."

Sing at a wedding? *Maybe that's all I'll be able to do now. Weddings, funerals and birthday parties.*

And she could fail at that, too. What if she was terrible? What if she was flat?

"I don't know if you can do solo performances," her mother said.

"Why not?" snapped Sophie, Sophie of the perfect pitch, Sophie who had sung solo, *a capella*, in Carnegie Hall.

"Well—because of your contracts. Legally. You're one of the Wayfairers."

"Mom." She planted another seed, looking forward to seeing it come up, anticipating the growth of small things. "My band quit. The Wayfairers have broken up."

Her mother stared. "Why? You're so successful."

"They say I'm difficult. I mean, that's not the only thing. Don't tell Dad. Don't tell him they say I'm hard to get along with. He'll lecture me about it. I have to work this out on my own."

"I don't keep things from him, Sophie. You know that."

"Whatever," Sophie answered. "I don't know about the wedding. I guess I could do it. If I can hear well enough." She took a breath. "I'd like to stay here. If that's all right. Perhaps beyond the summer. I just don't know what I'm going to do. I think I might get another kind of job. You know. Take a break."

"Don't give up, Sophie," her mother replied. "You're always welcome here. And you can certainly stay after we leave. But you're talented. I believe in you, and I always will."

"Thanks, Mom." Now came the hard part. *"And..."* She drew it out. "We—I—told Amy that I'm her natural mother."

"You did." Her mother repeated it numbly, shocked, no longer looking at the seeds, her blue eyes fastened on Sophie's face.

"Yes. She wasn't thrilled."

"She will be, though," Amanda predicted. "And Sophie, I so want to know her and for her to know me as her grandmother and your dad as her grandfather."

"I want that too. But neither of them have called since I told her. I'm going tonight, of course, to class." She glanced toward the yard, where Loki was still chasing and teasing James, who continued to snarl at the big shepherd. "If you brought James— Amy's handling Cinders in that class, you know."

"We can't come tonight. I've promised to help get ready for the Elks rummage sale. I don't suppose he'd let me start next week."

"I'll ask, if you like."

"Thank you. I'd like that," Amanda concluded. "Yes, I'll try it."

SHE ARRIVED EARLY for class and caught him alone. She put Loki in a down-stay which he seemed for once willing to hold. Thunder lay in a down-stay near William's feet. Cinders was waiting in the car; Amy had not yet appeared.

"William, I guess that was a joke—your saying I could help you train dogs." She spoke uncertainly.

William, his black hair tousled, wore a Mount Sneffels K-9 T-shirt and blue jeans.

Sophie reflected how strange it was that just proximity, just seeing a lot of someone, could start attraction.

Attraction was what she felt. Her eyes strayed more and more often to his dark eyes under those thick black eyebrows. He had a bit of beard, a bit of mustache. He looked rumpled and wild, a gypsy prince, Heathcliff with glasses for interest. And he could play the violin better than she did.

"It wasn't a joke," he told her. "Do you want to learn to train dogs?"

"You can't afford to pay me."

"I pay other people. I pay agitators to come and entice protection dogs to bite. When I'm boarding and training dogs but have to go away for some reason, I pay someone to take care of the place—and the dogs."

"But if I was—well, if I was an apprentice dog trainer, you wouldn't pay me. I mean, I'd think the arrangement would be for me to pay you—for learning."

He shrugged. "Think you'd like to learn to be a dog trainer?"

"It might be...good experience—for getting along with people."

"I'll say," William agreed. "An instructor has to do a lot of—well—biting his tongue."

"But how can people learn if you don't say what's on your mind?"

"You don't have to say *everything* that's on your mind."

Wasn't that what her band manager, Fiona, had implied? "Are you suggesting you might tell them one thing they're doing wrong but not something else?"

"I might."

"What if I offend one of your clients?"

"Sometimes I do myself. Say you take a couple who's gone all day at work, five days a week, and they go and get a German shepherd puppy. They've picked, first of all, a puppy—and it's never great for a puppy to be alone all day. On top of that, they've chosen a large breed that needs a lot of training. They're asking for trouble. Usually when I see this kind of situation, it's after aggression problems have started."

"So, is it usual for you to have private sessions with clients who have aggressive dogs?"

"I've attained a bit of a reputation for being good at that." As he spoke, he wondered why he was unveiling his world to her, why he'd let her through the parting of that veil. Yet Crystal had never been terribly interested in his business. "I try to keep things versatile. Breeding and training protection dogs can be lucrative, while obedience training usually isn't. But it's good to let the public know that you're a real dog trainer as well, one who can teach dogs Come, Sit, Down, Stay and Heel." He gestured with his left hand. "And I publish. Animal behavior. In any case," William said, "between Amy and me, we could teach you to teach obedience classes."

"But I can't hear."

She could tell he'd forgotten this.

He took a moment to consider. "How would you feel about training hearing dogs?"

"Why would you want to do that?"

"Because there's an inadequate supply of dogs for the demand—and because you're hearing impaired. You'd have to set up a separate business—non-profit, which Mount Sneffels K-9 definitely is not. At least that's the idea. Making a profit."

Sophie cracked another smile. "I don't know anything about training hearing dogs."

"It's much less complicated than guide dog training. Dogs can be sound-trained very easily—and often shelter dogs make the best candidates. But to start with, why not train Loki for sound work?"

"Do you think I could? Could he learn that?"

"Oh, you'll have no trouble teaching him the sound work. He's food-oriented, which will make him very trainable. But service dogs also have to be perfectly behaved. That'll be the challenge."

Sophie noticed something, something she'd observed several times since coming to Ouray. When she was focused on dog training, there was no opportunity to worry about her career, no time to envision herself as not good enough. She, Sophie Creed, ceased to be so important, ceased to be an issue. "I'll try," she said. "It's—kind of you."

"Do you *need* a job?" he asked.

She reflected on the wedding her mother had mentioned. She had a job—as a wedding singer. The thought made her half sick. "Not really."

"Amy is my main part-time employee. But I can give you a few hours here and there. At less than minimum wage since you'll be learning."

"Fine. Thanks."

"What sounds would you like Loki to tell you about?"

"Traffic. I mean, it's scary walking downtown if I

have to cross the street. I don't hear cars on my left at all. He and Cinders have started kind of naturally protecting me."

"What other sounds?"

"I can't hear the stove timer. I can't hear the phone ring, but I'm not sure I want to. I can't hear the tea kettle."

"You lost a lot of hearing, didn't you?"

"Yes. The other ear's fine, though."

"That'll make it easier for you to train Loki." Briefly, he told her how, with food, she could begin encouraging Loki to tell her about sounds. "He'll probably think it's a lot of fun. Dogs like a job to do."

"Then Cinders won't have a job, though."

"We'll figure out something else for her. We can see if she's suited for protection work, if you like. She seems to have a strong play drive."

Sophie frowned slightly. "She's not very aggressive."

"Right."

"You mean, that's good?"

"Aggression is undesirable. Period."

"Hello."

Sophie jumped. She hadn't noticed Amy entering the training barn, hadn't heard or seen her.

She joined them in the ring. "I think I'm ready to learn a new *adavu.*"

She's not completely furious, Sophie thought. *She's still interested in Bharata Natya.* "Okay."

"Sophie's going to apprentice with me," William told Amy.

"I'm sure," Amy replied with more than a trace of cynicism. "Where's Cinders? Shall I get her?"

After class, when Amy had gone to put Cinders back in Sophie's truck, William suggested, "Why don't we put Loki in one of the kennels—or you can put him in your truck with Cinders—and you can be an agitator for me? I got a bullmastiff at the animal shelter in Durango yesterday, and I'm going to see if he wants to work. I'll show you how I start protection dogs. Come on. Let's put some protective gear on you."

Sophie met her daughter out at the Toyota, where Amy was offering Cinders water. Putting Loki in the truck with the other shepherd, Sophie said, "I'm going to help your dad. Then we can dance a bit."

"Maybe." Amy shrugged indifferently.

She followed Sophie inside and over to a small room on one side of the barn, where William sorted out protective clothing for Sophie, to put on over her camisole "Now, because you're being an agitator," he explained, "you should anticipate never having a relationship with this dog. We never use owners for agitators, never use any kids at all, never use friends of the owner who will be seeing the dog in the future. But the bullmastiff is a prospect for a guy on Martha's Vineyard who loves the breed and wants a protection dog."

"You're going to take him to the vet, aren't you," Sophie asked, "and make sure his hips are sound?"

"I'm going to make sure *everything* is sound."

"What if he's not healthy?"

He smiled. "Then I have another dog. And we try to make him forget that you were an agitator."

"How old is he?"

"A year."

"What was he doing at the pound?"

"His owners got him, and then they had to move, and they couldn't take him," explained Amy. "That place, the La Plata County Humane Society—they have the best dogs. Sometimes they call my dad when they have especially good ones. We've gotten two Catahoula Leopard Dogs from them."

"What do you do with them?"

"Train them as hunting dogs. Sell them," Amy answered. She watched her father hold a bite suit up against Sophie's body, smaller than Amy's own.

Amy said, "So, do you have parents?"

"Yes. I was adopted. My adoptive parents are my parents. They want to know you."

Amy seemed to consider this. "Do they get along with each other?" she asked.

Did William's parents so obviously *not* get along? "Yes. Quite well."

William abruptly turned from Sophie and his daughter, then swung back and handed the bite suit to Sophie.

In his eyes, she saw something intense and unfathomable, something she didn't understand at all.

She'd felt it before—the dark and hidden. Having to do with the places he'd lived and the way he'd lived as a child. Of course, it could be her imagination. She could be projecting secrecy onto him. But life had taught her that one's secrets were sometimes connected with a private shame that when voiced, could shrink in magnitude. If William had a secret, it was likely to be something like that.

What she was seeing was probably—*must be*—his part in their secret: that he was not Amy's biological father. And probably would like to be.

She wished she could open his head and go inside with him, and visit his childhood and know what he'd learned in that landscape.

Amy said, "Being an agitator is only scary at first. I mean, this dog is big enough to knock you over."

"We're just training a bit today," said William. "The dog won't even know what to do yet."

Amy looked amused.

"So what do I do?" Sophie asked.

William sighed. "Nothing for which you'll need the bite suit." He put it away and grabbed a pole with a burlap sack tied to the end. "Let's go try to interest him in this."

AFTER SHE'D SPENT ten minutes trying to entice the bull-mastiff to bite at the burlap sack and after she'd played tug-of-war with him, she and William put the dog—they were calling him Sport—away and walked toward the house, or the cabin as Sophie found herself calling it.

She liked William's house, liked how small it was, liked the simple log-and-fieldstone design, the freedom of the loft, the cherry stain of the counters and cabinets in the kitchen, and the master bedroom tucked under the gable roof on the second floor. The walls were recycled pine planks. It was no bigger than it needed to be.

On the way to the house, she couldn't help repeating, "This is *not* what I expected to find you doing."

"What did you expect?" Mild curiosity.

"Something academic, I suppose. I mean, I don't associate your childhood with dogs. Did you ever have one?"

"Never. We traveled too much."

It wasn't as though he'd never said anything about his childhood. He'd said he'd lived with a people whose culture was too different for Americans to understand. Cannibalism, he'd said, had been prohibited before he was born, but his nurse had practiced ritual cannibalism of deceased relatives, a rite of mourning, years before he knew her. She contracted the virus *kuru* from unsanitary preparation of the body. He had watched her begin to slur her words, walk drunkenly, fall down, laugh for no reason and finally die because of what she'd done a dozen years earlier, before cannibalism was outlawed.

Sophie remembered him saying, *You really can't imagine. You can't imagine living with people who are that different from you. Nobody can. I couldn't if I hadn't lived with them. It changes everything.*

No, she couldn't. Yet she could imagine the horror of a six-year-old child, watching his trusted nurse become sick, infirm and insane before his eyes. Not to mention learning that it was because the woman had eaten part of another person.

She glanced up just outside the front door, surprised to see William studying her before reaching for the doorknob.

"What?"

"You're very pretty. I guess you know that."

She knew that when she'd performed at the Telluride Bluegrass Festival, she was the musician most men had rushed to photograph. But she realized it wasn't just the way she looked. They appreciated that she could play the fiddle—and the harmonica, the latter better than most musicians of either sex.

"Thank you," she said. She appreciated being told she was pretty by William, William who had once harbored bitter feelings toward her and said bitter things.

From around the side of the wraparound porch, they heard Amy calling, "Dad! Dad, did you come inside? Where are you?"

They followed the sound of her voice, and she thrust the portable phone at William.

"It's Grandma," she said.

Sophie asked Amy, "Want to show me how you're doing with what we already learned?"

Dance. "Okay."

They went and William stayed outside. "Hello?"

"Hi. Have you heard from Crystal?"

"No." The morning after she'd broken their engagement, she'd called and set a time to come and get some clothes of hers that she'd left at his house. When she came to get them, she'd said she would be in Ouray all summer, perhaps looking for property.

William hadn't asked why she was buying property when she didn't intend to stay, when she wanted to move back to the city, to any real city, which meant a city larger than cities in any part of Colorado.

"Amy said Sophie's there."

He'd told his mother that Sophie had told Amy the truth—well, the same truth his parents knew. His mother had said, *I warned you she'd do that. Next thing she'll be moving back to Ouray to stay.*

He had told her that was happening, too.

Now, she said, "Crystal told me she had good seats to the Chamber Music Festival this summer. She was planning to ask you and Amy, and I wondered if she'd called."

"She hasn't."

"You know what Sophie Creed's going to try next, William. You know, don't you? You can guess, can't you?"

"No."

"She's going to try to get her claws into you."

Claws. Well, his mother had never exactly adored Sophie. But her new campaign against Amy's mother was unwelcome. Now he had to do something he disliked having to do. "I'd rather not discuss it," he said, aware that he might have to restate this more strongly and employ other tactics he disliked. Completely ignoring her personal comments and changing the subject so abruptly that she would get the picture. Not taking her calls but letting the answering machine pick up.

A therapist had put forth the proposition that his mother always wanted to be first in his life. Since his mother knew that Amy already was, that made little sense to William. But learning to establish boundaries with her had been necessary.

"Just don't say I didn't warn you. I wouldn't be surprised," said his mother, "if she tries to get pregnant again. After all, her career is on the rocks, you said."

He didn't remember saying that. He remembered saying that Sophie had lost some hearing because of a virus and was taking a break from performing. He was tempted to say he couldn't imagine Sophie doing such a thing. Instead, he said, "I need to get off the phone."

"All right. I understand. But don't be naive. She may want to make you marry her. You own some valuable property in Ouray County. You have a successful business."

"Bye, Mom." He hung up without waiting for a reply. That she didn't like Sophie bothered him a little. That she warned him about Sophie angered him.

As for his "successful" business, his mother's description of his net worth varied considerably. She had complained that it would never be enough to satisfy Crystal in the long run. She'd said that for his own good and Amy's, he should try to find a more lucrative profession. But now, with the arrival of Sophie Creed, his mother had decided that he was wealthy enough for her to marry him for his money.

The phone rang again, and he checked the caller ID as he walked inside. His mother. He let the machine get it, and his mother's voice came into the living room for Sophie and Amy to hear as well.

"I just wanted to tell you that Dad's leaving for New Guinea again as soon as he can," the message began.

William schooled his features. He'd learned early in

life that if he showed any distress over his father's departures—his father's flights from his mother—his own reaction instantly became a weapon in his mother's arsenal against her husband. *Think of William! Think of Jonathan! You're their father! They need you.*

This was a war from which William had long been AWOL. He refused to side with either parent. He knew too much—and too little.

"....he wants me to come," the message continued cheerfully, "but he knows I can't, not this time of year, not with everything I have to do at the botanical gardens. Anyhow, I'm apologizing on his behalf. I know you could use your father's support right now, too. You've just ended an engagement, and your daughter's mother has shown up. Before you ask her to move in, think through what she'll be able to demand in the way of visitation rights."

William switched off the volume on the answering machine, looked directly at Sophie. "I'm sorry."

"Hasn't changed much, has she?" murmured Sophie.

Amy glanced between them, no doubt interested by this view of her birth mother's relationship with her grandmother.

"No," William conceded, unwilling to say more about it. He knew why his mother behaved the way she did toward Sophie, why she seemed to want to control his as well as his brother's life. But he never spoke of it. What would be the point?

"Does she still call you every night at dinnertime?" Sophie sounded amused. His mother's phone calls had been a problem for both of them when they'd lived together.

And he remembered Crystal saying, *Your mother calls you on the phone every single night and talks for a half hour?*

William nodded.

"Sometimes," Amy said, "he puts her on the speaker phone, and it's like talk radio spouting life advice. Doctor Moira."

William smiled. "You two look a lot alike when you smirk."

They laughed, looking even more alike.

"Grandma says I look like *you,*" Amy told him.

"How are your parents?" he asked Sophie.

"Well, they're all right." She remembered then to ask if it was too late for James to join the class.

"Normally, yes. In this case, we'll make a useful exception. You can teach her what we covered in the first two classes."

"I'm not sure she'll listen to me," Sophie said doubtfully.

"That surprises me."

Sophie turned to him.

"Everyone else listens to you," he said. "You'll do fine. Dominant women make excellent dog trainers."

Was he baiting her? She wasn't sure she liked being called a dominant woman by William Ludlow. Her response came out automatically, as though some part of her remembered a skill she'd been sure she'd lost. "The way I assert myself impresses people. A crowd gathered yesterday to watch me work up the nerve to buy a postage stamp." As soon as she'd said it, she decided she hadn't been very funny, but William seemed to fight a smile.

Amy, however, had stopped smiling entirely. Sophie couldn't understand why. She'd shown Sophie how she practiced the first *adavu* they'd learned. Sophie had been preparing to show her another when the answering machine went on, with William's mother broadcasting her thoughts. Was *that* the problem?

She looked questioningly at her daughter.

Amy lifted an eyebrow. "You're really going to help train dogs?"

"Shouldn't I?"

"Well, you can't train dogs if you can't hear," said Amy.

Listening, William was strongly reminded of his mother. "Not true," he said. "And yes, Sophie's going to join us as a part-time employee."

"She's too small to be a good agitator. She's smaller than me."

Why was Amy doing this? he wondered. In the past few days, ever since she'd learned that Sophie was her natural mother, she had gone from child to woman and back again on an average of every six seconds.

"She'll clean kennels and learn to teach classes."

Amy continued talking almost as though Sophie wasn't there. "I mean, she had a career that was so important to her she didn't want to raise me, and now she's, what, starting a whole *new* career?"

"Part-time employee usually doesn't equal whole new career," he answered. "And you're being rude."

"I'm being truthful, but I forgot—that's a punishable offense."

Sophie thought of interjecting that she didn't have to take William up on his offer, that she didn't have to do it.

But her relationship with Amy wasn't her only—or even her most pressing—problem.

The problem was that she was a musician who'd lost her hearing. It was worse, or seemed worse to her, than if she'd gone completely deaf. The way she was now, she could hear some notes and not hear others.

She might *need* a new career.

It wasn't something she wanted to think about, but

some feeling she couldn't name, some intuition, told her not to back out of her agreement with William. "I want to learn to train dogs."

"Well," Amy said, "then I guess you'll do it."

She turned and went upstairs without another word.

CHAPTER EIGHT

"SUMMER," William told Sophie the following week, "is the best time to have dog-training classes. I can use the city park for some of them."

"Why aren't you doing them all here?" Sophie asked. She and William and Amy sat at the kitchen counter where Amy was shelling peas she and William had grown in the small greenhouse attached to the south side of the cabin

"In Beginner Two class, I like the dogs to work in a place with distractions. Also, some of these people want to show in obedience trials, and often those are held on lawns. We'll have Beginner One and Puppy Kindergarten here."

"And you want me to be there for all the classes?"

"Don't you want to be?" His look said, *Don't you want to learn to train dogs? Isn't that what you told me?*

"I don't know. There's a wedding."

"I didn't realize you knew anyone here." William frowned, seeming preoccupied. "Anyhow, there are no classes on the weekends."

"I'll have to practice."

"You're going to *perform* at a wedding?"

He needn't sound so incredulous. "Yes," she managed with dignity and didn't add, *I couldn't say no*. Because she could have refused. But her father had pointed out that the groom was the son of an old friend of *his*, that the bride had been through some "really difficult times," that they'd *begged* her parents just to *ask*. It was certainly nice to have anyone at all begging her to perform. Quickly Sophie explained, "It's not like that's my job or anything. Come to think of it..." Voice trailing off, she glanced between him and Amy. "Would you two like to do this with me? This wedding gig?"

Amy said, "Count me out."

"You're a good musician!" Sophie told her.

"No, I plan on running away to catch sexually transmitted diseases and get pregnant," Amy replied blandly, with that half-ancient dignity that seemed so alien in a fourteen-year-old wearing braces. "I absolutely cannot stand up in a church and sing 'The Wedding Song' and 'Sunrise, Sunset.'" She squinted at Sophie. "Or even 'Now, I Believe.' I'm surprised *you're* doing that. But I guess maybe your options are shrinking."

Sophie was getting used to Amy's smart mouth, but this was close to the bone. She tried to ignore it. "Weddings are romantic," she told Amy, disliking the hypocrisy of the statement.

She hated weddings.

She did not believe in love or happily ever after or any of that, and she felt stupid trying to convince Amy that she did.

"*You* think they're romantic?" asked Amy, with an incredulity Sophie could only respect.

They all heard tires on gravel outside. William stood up.

Amy peered out the window and smiled like the Cheshire cat.

A moment later, William opened the screen door to his mother.

"Oh," she said. "Hello, Sophie."

"Hello, Moira," Sophie responded.

"You've been spending a lot of time over here," William's mother observed. "Honey," she addressed her son, "I brought you and Amy some organic fruit from Ridgway. Oh, the peas look wonderful, sweetie," she told Amy.

Sophie observed the bags under William's nonetheless beautiful mother's eyes and figured they were from too many with-and-after-dinner glasses of wine.

"When are you taking off on the road again?" Moira asked her. "I imagine you have a busy traveling schedule. Are you on a concert tour now?"

"No." Sophie knew perfectly well that William had told his mother all about her hearing loss and that Moira was simply finding a new and different way to ask how soon she would be leaving. She thought of asking if Bill—William's father—had left for New Guinea yet but decided to spare Moira the question, as she wished William's mother had spared her.

She knew there was no simple truth. Too easy to say that Bill Ludlow always left, traveling alone, to get away from his wife. Also, for years they *had* traveled together.

But William had made remarks once or twice suggesting that his father liked going alone so he could fool around with other women. *Not that he's monogamous when my mom's around. But if she's not there, he doesn't have to listen to her complain about it.*

Complain?

If her spouse behaved that way, Sophie knew she'd do more than complain.

She said, "I'm just trying to persuade William and Amy to perform with me at a wedding on the Fourth of July weekend."

"Well, neither of them have ever wanted to be professional musicians. Either of them *could* be, you understand," Moira continued.

"But I'm a dog trainer," William supplied, as though the explanation was necessary. "I'll be happy to play with you, though, Sophie."

"Thank you," she exclaimed.

Moira said, "I've always felt you should do more with your music, William."

"I am not getting on a music stage with braces on my teeth," Amy announced. She gathered up the peas.

"What brings you by, Mom?" William asked.

"The organic produce, and actually I picked up some things for Amy, if she's interested. There's a new boutique in Ridgway, and I thought these were cute."

Amy turned, interested to see what her grandmother had purchased. "Oh, nice. I like the leggings. Mmm—that's a bit girly for me, don't you think?"

"You look nice in pink. It's cute. What do you think, Sophie?"

A raspberry-colored camisole with cotton lace trim.

"I like it," Sophie said truthfully. "And I've seen you wear that color, Amy."

"Crystal helped me pick it out," Moira replied. "She has such good taste."

"She gave up on William though," Sophie said before she thought better of it. "I didn't mean that how it sounded."

"It wasn't *William* she had trouble with, dear," Moira said. "The time before a wedding is always stressful, especially for the bride, and I think you were a bit of a surprise."

"I was surprised, too," Amy put in, "that Dad lied to me. And also to Crystal, of course."

Sophie wished she could go to Papua New Guinea with William's father; she wished she were already there. Amy was a smart-mouth. It was summer. She wasn't in school. There were no bad grades to complain about, no objectionable friends, no boys. She was just a girl who almost seemed to be from a different world.

But she's not. The nature part came from me—and... And the nurture came from these people.

"*Your* parents must be glad to see you," said Moira. "Amy, what do you think of this? I thought it was cute. You don't wear dresses much, but Crystal and I just kind of went crazy."

"I never wear blue."

"But it would be nice with your skin. Look."

"It doesn't suit me."

"All right, I'll take it back. Crystal was afraid it might be too young for you."

"Why are you shopping with Dad's ex-fiancée?" asked Amy, making a show of bewilderment.

"Oh, things can change. And she'll *always* be a friend of the family. She and your father have so much in common, both having traveled."

"You ever been anywhere?" William asked Sophie.

For the first time since Moira had arrived—in fact, since she herself had shown up at Mount Sneffels K-9 that day, Sophie felt like laughing. True, she hadn't traveled as much as William had, but her parents had moved a bit when she was growing up, as her father accepted different parishes, and after she'd become a professional musician she'd visited Europe, Africa, India and South America.

Sophie made a point of shrugging. "Some."

"What do *your* parents do?" Amy suddenly demanded.

"My father is a pastor. When I was little, very little, he was an itinerant preacher, but he's since moved into having his own congregations."

Moira said nothing for a moment. "Grandpa and I have always felt that organized religion causes wars."

"Is that what caused the ones in our family?" William murmured.

"Don't get smart," replied his mother. "We just wanted you and Jonathan to see the world with a vision undistorted by prejudice. And look at the kinds of things done in the name of religion, even in New Guinea."

"Like what?" Amy tried on the raspberry camisole over the lavender one she wore. It looked good on her.

"Well, for instance, the Fore's religious beliefs led them to consume the bodies of dead relatives, and people used to get *kuru* and die, like your dad's nurse."

"Now, *that's* one of the major world religions," said William.

"And most religions oppress women one way or another," Moira continued.

"Many things," Sophie said, "contribute to the oppression of women."

"I doubt *you've* had much experience with that," Moira retorted. "You've certainly always done exactly what you wanted. No one's oppressing you. I don't expect you'd like the compromises family life requires. I suppose it's nice that you have parents with spirituality, but I don't see that their views have informed *your* life."

William leaned back against the refrigerator and gazed at an eight-by-ten of Sigurd that adorned it. "Well, I know I'm a lot happier," he said, "since I came to believe in Dog."

Everyone smiled, and the tension dissipated.

When Moira left, she took Amy with her, promising her a trip to the bookstore downtown to see what new hardcover novels were in, although Amy said she was actually burning to read Nietzsche.

"He died alone and insane," her grandmother told her briskly, "but we'll see if we can find you something of his."

Sophie and William stayed in the cabin. The dogs were all outside, Sophie's kenneled with his.

Watching Moira's Saturn drive away with Amy in the passenger seat, Sophie said, "I should go."

As though he hadn't heard, William said, "I think she's afraid of being supplanted."

"Your mother?"

"Yes."

"You'd marry a woman," Sophie said incredulously, "who wants to be your mother?"

"Never. I meant that she's important in Amy's life."

Sophie tried to revise her opinion of William's situation with his mother. As she'd always seen it, Moira Ludlow would never let go of him. No woman would ever be good enough for her oldest son. Let him get engaged to Crystal again, and Moira would target her, the restored fiancée. Whoever married William would also be marrying his mother and his relationship with his mother.

But maybe not. Moira clearly *tried* to run his life. To what extent did she succeed?

Not that it matters to me, Sophie assured herself. *William can marry or not marry whomever he wants.*

She would never marry. Once she'd actually said to one of the Wayfairers after a *very* rare wedding gig, for an industry friend, *I can't imagine doing this. Being the bride, with my family and friends around me happy that I've decided to spend the rest of my life with one person. It makes no sense to me.*

Did she still feel that way?

Yes.

But there was something different in how she regarded William, had always regarded him. As someone who would always be present in her life, even if she never saw him. As someone who in some way would always belong particularly to her.

Which wasn't logical at all.

"Sophie."

She looked at him.

"I have to go to Durango. I was going to go tomorrow, but I could drive over the mountains today. There's supposed to be a Tibetan mastiff at the humane society. They're unusual and can be good protection dogs. Want to go look? We can sound-test some dogs as hearing dogs."

"Today? What about Amy?"

"I'll call my mom's cell. Amy already said she doesn't want to go to Durango."

Twenty minutes later, they'd climbed into William's Forester, leaving Loki and Cinders together in one of the runs. If they picked up a new dog at the animal shelter, it would be better to accustom him to the other dogs slowly, rather than by forced confinement in a car.

Sophie wore a tank top a slightly duskier shade of pink than the camisole Amy had just been given and, over it, a faded blue hooded zip-up sweatshirt. Her pants were low-cut eggshell, flared, and she wore an old pair of running shoes. Her hair was loose, her bangs blowing lightly around her eyes. Glancing in the side mirror, she was surprised to feel that she looked pretty.

It's because I'm with him. He makes me feel pretty.

It was true and subtle. William had a way of dropping nice things other people said about her—her singing, her appearance.

Looking over at him, she saw the familiar cleft chin, the hollows in his cheeks. But it had been a boy's face long ago. Now, it was a man's, and he was attractive as a man.

As he drove up the first hairpins of the Million Dollar Highway, with its great drops, its views of finger-thin waterfalls cutting vertical volcanic rock, he sang the first lines of "Dark as a Dungeon," a coal-mining song by Merle Travis.

They used to sing it together, used to sing so many songs together.

Sophie picked up the harmony, and for the briefest moment, only the safest glimpse, he caught her eye.

She felt a charge she remembered from long ago.

She had been raped. She had decided she *never* wanted a lover.

And then she had wanted William, who only hugged her occasionally, who once kissed her hand.

He had shown her what it was to be lovers.

He had not been a virgin, and he'd never said where he learned it.

What was never in question for her, back then, was his essential goodness.

Was he still good? How many women had there been before Crystal?

He did not touch her.

Twenty-five winding miles separated Ouray from Silverton, which sat at 9,318 feet. Then, another fifty miles to Durango. Three mountain passes between Ouray and Durango.

In Silverton, William said, "Want to stop for coffee or anything?"

"Only if you do."

"Let's."

They went to the Animas Coffeehouse, decorated with mining relics, Tibetan prayer flags and modern art framed in toilet seats. They shared a small wooden table outside.

Admiring William's profile—his jaw in particular—Sophie said abruptly, "*You* should reproduce."

He eyed her, smiled a bit, then eyed a Victorian across the street. "Thank you."

No other comment, and she felt she'd said something awkward, that perhaps it was wrong to remind him that Amy did not carry his genes. But William had never shown resentment of that—just an unusual gratitude for her as a child.

"But I guess it's never happened," she said, knowing she was digging.

"No." He sighed. "Sophie, I wanted that with *you.* Sometimes I'm still angry when I meet couples who've been together since they were sixteen. No, angry isn't the right word for it. But I believed it *could* have worked. Now—" he shook his head "—I hope I have a better comprehension of what you went through. So you and I did our growing up separately."

Sophie sat breathing in the high mountain sunshine, missing Loki and Cinders, who hadn't been this far from her in months. "I'm impressed that you've managed to draw some boundaries with your mother. That can't have been easy."

"It's still not easy. She wants me to side with her against—" He stopped, shrugged.

His father? Yes. And she was possessive. Intrusive. Overbearing. For survival, William had become aloof, reserved.

Secretive.

"Does Crystal want kids?" she asked.

"She wanted the one I have."

Sophie said, with less truth than she would've liked, "I'm sorry my appearance interfered with everything. I'm sorry your engagement's broken."

"Are you?"

His tone made her look up.

She found him staring across the street.

"That's a new Victorian," he said. "I like how they've painted the outside—those designs."

"Yes. It's nice. Are *you* sorry?"

"Sure." He drained the mug that had held his cappuccino. "Ready to go save a dog or two from death row?"

"Yes."

"I HAVE TWO DOGS," she said. "I need to train one of them—Loki, we decided—as a hearing dog."

"But if you train another hearing dog—for something to do, for money, for experience, for any reason—we'll have no trouble finding a partner for that dog."

"Well, let's have fun sound-testing them anyhow," Sophie said as they went inside. "But I can't stand this. There are so many good dogs in these places."

William didn't answer. He greeted a middle-aged woman with very short black hair who stood behind the counter.

"Hi, Will," she said. "Come to see our Tibetan mastiff?"

"Your *alleged* Tibetan mastiff. And maybe to sound-test some dogs. We're going to try training a hearing dog."

"Now *that's* a good idea. I know some people who do that down in Bayfield if you want to talk with them."

"Thanks. I would."

He let Sophie precede him down the hallway, following painted paw prints the size of dinner plates toward the kennels, which lined both sides of four aisles. More dogs were outside. They found the alleged Tibetan mastiff against the back wall.

William took one look and shook his head.

"What?" asked Sophie.

"I bet you can figure it out."

"Too small? Not a Tibetan mastiff?"

"The latter. I don't like his conformation either." He nodded and walked on, pausing beside a golden-colored dog with a creamy chest.

"He looks kind of like a Shiba Inu," said Sophie. Its card identified the dog as a "Carolina Dog."

"He's not," said William. "And he's not a Carolina Dog." He crouched beside the door, and the dog came forward, tongue hanging out. "I know what you are, mate."

"What is he?"

"This is a New Guinea Singing Dog."

"They're really from New Guinea?"

"Yes."

"Do they *sing?*"

"They do. It's kind of like wolves howling. There's nothing like hearing a bunch of them together."

Sophie felt tears sting behind her eyes. Her damn hearing. Coyotes had lived near her when she was in Nevada and when she was in California. There was nothing she'd preferred to listening to their song. But even that was different now. After she'd lost her hearing, she'd known they were yipping and singing only when Loki and Cinders had told her. Then she'd put both dogs on lead and gone outside to try to listen.

Everything sounded so different now.

And look how different your life is, *Sophie.*

Living in Ouray, visiting an animal shelter with William Ludlow, preparing to sing at a wedding.

I feel like such a failure.

Why had this happened? Why had it happened now, when she was so near the culmination of her dreams?

"How did the dog get here," she managed to ask, "if it's from New Guinea?"

"Imported or maybe bred here. I saw one once on the street in Denver with someone. They were wild in the Highlands of New Guinea. But people have domesticated them here."

"Are you going to adopt this dog?" she asked.

He scrutinized the dog as it stood and jumped against the chain link. "Yes. I think I am."

"He's too small for protection work. And you'll only have one. You won't have a chorus."

"One will be fine. Maybe I'll find him a malamute friend. Let's go look for a hearing dog, too."

"Won't this dog work?"

"Probably not. Different agenda. A good sound dog needs an agenda that involves telling you about sound. Come take a look at this one. Do you have our noise makers?"

Sophie removed the day pack she'd been carrying as she followed William to a kennel in the next aisle. The dog springing against the chain link and barking, hurting Sophie's bad ear, was a Sheltie cross.

"I can't, William." She covered her ear. "That dog would drive me nuts. I can't do this."

"What do you...that ear?"

She moved away from the hysterical dog so she could hear him.

"What do you hear from that ear?"

"Distortion," she replied. "Donald Duck sounds. Barking like that hurts. If that's the kind of dogs deaf people need, I can't train them, because I can't stand that."

He studied her thoughtfully. "Come on, let's try another dog. I know the one."

Sophie stood outside the kennel of a quiet but wriggly hound-terrier cross while William walked further down the aisle, out of sight, and set off the alarm clock with its electronic beep. Sophie couldn't hear the clock, not with the racket the dogs were making, but the little mixed breed in front of her cocked her head to one side, then jumped against the chain link. She shook her head several times as though trying to explain the source of the sound.

When the woman from the front desk came to let the dog out, Sophie and William tested her on retrieving—she brought a ball back to William promptly—and assessed her dominance level, which was low.

"This is a good dog," said William.

Sophie thought about that. He seemed to love large protective breeds, as she did. This dog could fit in a five-gallon paint bucket, but William seemed both satisfied and impressed with her.

They adopted the New Guinea Singing Dog and the terrier cross, naming the latter Spinner, because she became ecstatic and seemed to spin in place on her back legs, and took them from the shelter to the walk-in veterinary clinic where William had taken many of his dogs from time to time.

The vet brought both dogs up to date on shots and wormed them. Finishing with Spinner, she gave her a kiss. "This one's a sweetie," she said.

William told the vet their plan for training Spinner as a hearing dog, and the vet predicted, "You won't want to part with her."

Abruptly, Sophie's heart seemed to hurt.

She held the dog's lead on the way to the Forester but no longer spoke to her.

William noticed her silence. "You okay?"

"This isn't the right job for me," Sophie said.

"Why not?"

"Whatever you and Amy think, it wasn't easy for me to give up a child for adoption. I don't think I can do it with dogs, either, especially with one dog after another."

In the car, he stared at the steering wheel for several seconds before turning the key.

"I do it," he said, "with protection dogs, and it is hard. But it's satisfying, too. I think you'll find it quite different from parting with Amy."

HE TOOK HER to an Indian restaurant on the way out of town. The food was excellent. They had left Spinner and Tenor—the singing dog—in crates in the car. During the meal, they talked about what kind of food Amy preferred, about what his life had been like when Amy was a toddler, how he'd dealt, later, with dilemmas like sex education.

"I let my mother tell her."

"How did it go?"

"My mother told me that after she'd explained the facts to Amy, who was eight at the time, Amy said, 'It's sort of gross, Grandma. My head is swimming.'"

Sophie laughed. "Have you had other girlfriends before Crystal?"

"Yes."

"What made you think you wanted to marry her?" Sophie asked.

He shrugged. "It was more the timing than her. I realized I'd never married anyone because I was looking for a soul mate. And there are lots of soul mates out there for each of us. It's just—who we choose to be with."

Sophie nodded.

William studied the bow of her full lips, the tilt of her dark eyes.

Sophie turned back to her food, trembling slightly and not knowing why.

"What about you?" he asked.

"I've been solo for a few years. I've dated guys but not—well, for three years or so, as I said."

"Too busy?"

"It's not just that. I realized that a love relationship wasn't even in my top five priorities. Relationships really require a lot. I wanted to write music, write more songs I felt proud of. I want to perform. I love being in front of an audience. There's a pulse—it's almost like your own pulse, you know."

She expected an expression of cynicism or bitterness from him. It wasn't there.

"Sophie," he said unexpectedly. "Losing your hearing isn't going to make a bit of difference to what you do musically. You're stronger than that kind of obstacle. Your fire burns hotter."

It was the last thing she'd expected to hear, and he was the last man she'd expected to say it.

"Thanks. Thanks," she repeated.

He insisted on paying for the meal. "I can't let you pay any of it," he said, shaking his head at her money.

"Why not?"

"You're the mother of my child. You're a woman. Old-fashioned reasons."

"I won't fight you." Smiling, she put her money away.

They took Spinner and Tenor for a brief walk. Spinner didn't know the first or second thing about walking on a leash. She barked at a fire hydrant. That was when Tenor sat down and began to sing. Just for a moment. A dog a half block away or so howled back.

Sophie could hear both the singer and the howler—not completely, but she *could* hear them.

When they returned to the Forester, Sophie put Spinner back in the crate they'd picked up. "I can't take her to my mom's house."

William unlocked her door. "Amy says you have a fifth wheel or something."

"A gypsy wagon," Sophie corrected.

"If your parents…well, start getting on your nerves—or even if they don't—you and Loki and Cinders could park up at my place. There's room. Fenced space for the dogs to run."

"Your mother would love that."

"Well, she doesn't pick who lives with us."

Lives with us.

That was an invitation. But what kind? What did it mean?

He walked around the car and climbed in the driver's seat.

"Thanks for dinner," she said again.

"I think you're my oldest friend," he said.

"I suppose you're mine."

He turned to look over his shoulder, to back the truck out.

He hadn't been going to kiss her, after all. As they headed north again, Sophie realized that was what she'd been expecting—and that she'd wanted it to happen.

CHAPTER NINE

IT ALL GOT TO HER that night, as she lay down to sleep in her bedroom at her parents' house. She'd left Spinner with William. Loki and Cinders lay in their crates with the doors open. During the night they would get up, move around the room, return to their beds, get drinks of water from the toilet in the bathroom.

When she'd come home, she'd gone out to the gypsy wagon to write music. What she'd done had been less than brilliant, but not every song she wrote *would* be great. That was the nature of creativity.

What bothered her was that she'd lost the fire William had insisted she still possessed. She'd lost the ability to believe. The bride and groom of the July wedding wanted to get together with her to discuss musical selections. They'd hoped for a band to play at the reception but had been thrilled at the prospect of Sophie singing during the ceremony.

They would want "Now, I Believe."

But I don't believe.

And anyone who heard her and saw her face would know.

She had written that song so long ago, too.

She had written it for William, before Amy was born.

She had sung it for him only once or twice. Then she'd understood that her singing made him uneasy, that he knew she was going to leave, that he knew she would choose music over him.

That had been the song of a woman who'd believed, then been raped, then learned that love wasn't dead, after all.

But William had accused her of abandoning her child—her rapist's child.

Was that when she'd stopped believing?

No. There were other men, other disappointments. She'd given up her daughter only to discover that virtually every man she became romantically involved with seemed to want *something* she couldn't give, seemed to want her to be something she couldn't, seemed to care most about how she could change to be his idea of what a partner should be. She'd been with clingers, with liars, with controllers.

They all seem so screwed up.

William didn't, but she didn't trust that appearance, and it never took her long to remember that his mother had always seemed to exert an unwholesome influence on his life. *She'll always criticize whatever woman he marries.* There could be no marriage—no marriage of growth, of growing *together*—when one of the partners had never really left home.

But she sensed that William actually *had,* that he was not living a life his mother had planned for him.

I don't believe. In love. That's the problem.

She cried.

Not hard, not sobbing.

Hers was a quiet despair that in the morning would give way to the satisfaction of seeing the faces of her dogs, of training them, of making them happy.

What if William had kissed her tonight?

It would've been the beginning of something guaranteed to further shatter her faith in love. Much better to be "just friends" with him, because she did believe in friendship. It was the gold standard of relationships.

But that didn't explain why she felt so empty now.

When she was a little girl, a little girl who'd been adopted, whose origins were known only in an unformed, mobile way, origins that still seemed to her somehow romantic and special, she had thought there was a soul mate for her. She had sometimes felt his presence in the earliest morning when she'd just awakened, the sense that he'd been with her in sleep, but couldn't meet her in present time or waking hours.

Once, one morning, a frosty Colorado morning, she had awakened with William beside her, a younger William, beautiful as very young men can be. His eyes had looked into hers, and she'd experienced the same floating feelings as when she woke from unremembered dreams and knew her soul mate had been with her.

She'd been certain her soul mate was William, and she'd written "Now, I Believe," which, fifteen years later, was still her most popular and best-loved song.

That, she thought, was something to cry about.

All she'd ever been was the writer of a popular wedding song, and now she had become a wedding singer.

Which was all the Wayfairers—the ex-Wayfairers—thought she was good for, anyhow.

WILLIAM WAS CLEANING the kennels in the morning when he heard tires in the driveway. He expected to see Sophie. Expected? Hoped? He wasn't sure.

What he was sure of was that Sophie Creed was promised beyond simple relationships between men and women. She was promised to her heart. She'd been lucky enough to recognize that commitment earlier in life. But now she was doubting it, thinking of becoming a dog trainer with him.

And he'd observed that she was happiest when training her dogs. Many people were. The concentration was on something outside of oneself, and that made for happiness.

The car didn't belong to Sophie.

Nor was it Crystal's Lexus.

It was an old Toyota Land Cruiser.

His father's car.

William continued cleaning the kennels, power washing them because it was summer. Sophie had done it the last time she'd been at the house, but William liked to do a thorough job more than once a week. He waved to his father as Bill Ludlow climbed from the green vehicle with its white roof.

His father was built like William—not quite six feet—and wiry. William knew his father was attractive to women. Crystal had said he was "charismatic, really," after Bill turned on the charm, enthusiastic about William's choice of fiancée. Now he wore his iron-flecked hair short. It still retained the untidiness that characterized William's, too, sticking up at odd and rakish angles on top, unwilling to lie flat.

"Hi, Dad."

His father stood silently outside the chain link, watching William. "That actually looks like good meditation," he said.

"It is."

"Well, I came to say goodbye."

"You're taking off so soon?"

"Yes. I was lucky in my timing. I was able to book a flight immediately."

Once again, his father couldn't wait to get away from his mother, couldn't wait to pursue his infidelities. William wished he felt nothing about this, but he was sullied by it as his brother was. It wasn't the relationship he wanted with his wife. Not only because of the pain created by infidelity—substantial—but because he would no longer like himself.

"Let me finish here," he said, "and we can go inside. Want some coffee?"

"I'd enjoy that. Thank you."

As they walked to the house a few minutes later, Bill said, "So Sophie's back."

"Yes."

"I always liked her."

William considered a fact about his father. He could keep a secret. Many times, he'd been tempted to confide to Bill that Sophie had been raped. But it wasn't his secret to tell.

It was Sophie's.

"How's Amy taking it?"

"Moody. But she's a teenage girl. We can't lay all her moodiness at her birth mother's feet."

"Sophie doesn't want to take a more active role with her?"

"I think she does." Inside, William poured some coffee beans into the grinder.

"And Crystal's out of the picture?"

"Yes."

His father nodded slowly.

Amy came down from the loft. "Hi, Grandpa."

"Hi, beautiful." When she approached the trestle bench where he sat, he reached up and gave her a quick hug. "Want to come to New Guinea?"

"Absolutely not."

Bill's grin showed that he'd expected that response. William prayed his father wouldn't ask, even in jest, how she could pass it up. Amy would answer, would accuse his father of fleeing his marriage, would accuse William of driving Sophie off, then of driving Crystal off, of keeping secrets, of lying lying lying.

Or so he imagined.

Amy had a CD in her hand and took it over to the stereo. William wondered if she'd put it on. Was she going to share Indian dance music—his father would like it—and show him the *adavus* that her mother had taught her?

But what she put on was the first Wayfairers CD. The title song was "Now, I Believe."

"Waking one morning when I was small/ I discovered you'd been there, too/ not beside me/ my other part...."

William hadn't listened to the words in years, hadn't listened to the enviable violin solo, nor to the surprisingly *happy* harmonica.

"This song was written the year I was born," said Amy. "She must've written it for you, Dad. Or, I suppose, for someone afterward."

"She wrote it for me. She wrote it before you were born. In fact, she may have written it for you."

Though he knew she hadn't. It wasn't until he'd seen the change wrought in Sophie by her teacher's rape that he'd begun to understand rape. It was, he thought, deadening, enraging, so many conflicting things.

Mostly, he remembered that she used to cry after making love with him, not a happy romantic sort of crying, just a miserable sort.

He had touched wounds, raw wounds.

It had been hard, hard to think he, too, was doing something that made her cry.

It wasn't that simple, though. He always said, *We don't have to do this.*

What would she be like now as a lover?

She would have moved on, to some degree, anyhow.

Rape changed her. She's never been the same; she never will be. With a sense of failure he remembered his idealistic intentions as he went into the police academy. Rape prevention programs. Helping victims. Instead it had been traffic tickets and drug busts. Narcotic searches had led him to dogs. He had prevented no rapes.

After the one song, Amy switched CDs. "Grandpa, I'm learning Bharata Natya, classical Indian dance. Sophie is teaching me—well, teaching me some. She says she doesn't know all that much herself."

Before Bill Ludlow left, he asked Amy, "What would you like me to bring you from PNG?"

"A weapon." She smiled. She had been giving the same answer since she was seven, and now she had quite a collection of spears and knives and fighting sticks.

"A weapon, for a change," Bill answered. That was part of the ritual, too.

"Just this once," Amy begged.

William laughed, still thinking of Sophie's song.

She might believe now—though he doubted it.

He certainly did not.

Not in the kind of soul mate the song suggested. But he did believe in lasting partnerships between men and women. His parents were no example of marital felicity, and yet… They loved each other. To an almost appalling extreme.

But if he'd ever had a soulmate, a woman who was twin to him as man, it would have been—and still must be—Sophie Creed.

IN THE MORNING, Sophie and her parents sat down to breakfast together—a rare event even now, when she was living with them in Ouray.

"I'm helping William with dog training," Sophie said. "I just want to try something different because of what's happened with my hearing."

Both parents stared. Neither said a word.

Until James jumped up on Amanda again, and Amanda exclaimed, "Down, James, down," in a voice no different from the one she used to tell him she loved his great big ears.

"Tell him, 'Off,' Mom, because 'Down' means you want him to lie down." The night before, she'd begun showing her mother the dog-training basics William had taught in the first two classes. The instruction had gone well, and her mother had thanked her. "Anyhow, he offered—he invited me to leave the gypsy wagon at his place. You know, to stay up there and train dogs."

Again, they said nothing.

Dan's lips had formed a thin line.

"What?" Sophie demanded.

"You really think your musical career is over?" asked Dan doubtfully.

"No," she snapped. "I mean, I don't know. But I don't want to spend my life doing weddings."

"By the way, don't forget that the bride and groom are coming today at eleven."

"I haven't forgotten."

"Of course, you're free to move up there," he said. "We'll miss you, but we understand."

"Well, I have to train another dog. I mean—I'm going to train another dog. William thought I might like to train hearing dogs."

"I'd think he, of all people, would know better," said her mother. "He knows how much you love music."

"Please let's not talk about music," she said.

"And when are we going to get to see Amy?"

"Mom will meet her at class."

"We should ask her over for dinner," Dan suggested.

"You know, I think we should," Amanda put in. "Her and William, of course."

"Fine," Sophie said brightly. "Well, I'm going to go walk Cinders and Loki before the bride and groom get here."

THEIR NAMES WERE Jodie and Micah, and they wanted "Now, I Believe" and "My Island Just Got Bigger" and "Utility Bills" for the wedding and asked if Sophie knew "Ave Maria." Sophie broached the idea of having two other musicians—playing the violin and clarinet.

"Oh, great!" exclaimed Jodie. "And we were going to ask. I mean, your mother said we wouldn't be able to get your band, too. And we probably can't afford you for our reception."

This was the part of being a wedding singer that she particularly disliked. Monetary discussions. And she wasn't going to hire Fiona, the Wayfairers' manager, to book her for weddings. Setting aside the reception question, she named her fee for the ceremony.

Bride and groom looked at each other.

Micah said, "It's worth it."

Sophie thought of her hearing and prayed it *would* be worth it to them. Forget training dogs. She was going to have to practice playing and singing. She'd need another musician to tell her if she was flat, to tell her what she was missing, to tell her in a shared language.

William, of course.

She mentioned that the same two people who played at the wedding itself might be able to play the reception with her.

Jodie told her how much they'd budgeted for a band.

"If my friends will perform with me, I'll do it for that."

Jodie's smile almost made it worth it to Sophie.

She'd never been an innocent coed planning her wedding, glowing with excitement at the big day. Definitely, absolutely, she had never wanted to be.

But for a moment, in the glow of Jodie's shining eyes, she could believe that marrying someone, promising to be with that person forever, was to embark on a noble—and interesting—journey.

"Thanks," Sophie said.

"For what?"

"You have a wonderful smile. I'm looking forward to the wedding. I hope all your dreams come true."

SHE DIDN'T CALL before she went to William's. She put Loki and Cinders in the car, hitched up the gypsy wagon and headed for the Camp Bird Road.

The first person she saw was Amy, walking alone up the road with Tala off-lead. Sophie slowed beside her. "Want a ride?"

"Okay."

Amy climbed in, and when Tala jumped inside, both Cinders and Loki barked, then sniffed Tala and settled down. "You've got your gypsy wagon," Amy said.

"Want to help me paint over Wayfairers?"

"What are you going to put on instead?" Amy asked.

"Wedding Singer?" Sophie made a face, saying that she wasn't serious—and that she did not like singing at weddings. "Please do this wedding with me," said Sophie. "They want us at their reception, too."

"How can you make reception music with only three people?" Amy demanded.

"We'll give them variety. And we'll practice. They said they want a little dancing and lots of background music."

"What kind of wedding has no dancing?" Amy asked.

"They do want *some*. You know—bride and groom. Groom and bride's mother, bride and groom's father, et cetera—"

"—Et cetera, et cetera," Amy finished. "Are you going somewhere? Are you leaving?"

"No. Why?"

"You have your rig."

"Oh. Your dad said I could move it up to your place."

Amy lifted her eyebrows.

Sophie said, "Please do the wedding with me."

"Who are the people? Do I know them?"

"Jodie and Micah?" Sophie turned down the Mount Sneffels K-9 driveway.

"No. But I'm sure people I know will be there." She looked worried about this.

"So what? You're a good musician. You know what, Amy? A lot of life—the good parts—you can't worry what people think. Life is too brilliant. Just go forth and be yourself."

Amy glanced over at her. "That's what you did."

"I guess so. I'm not always proud of it. I'm not proud that I didn't stay and raise you."

"And you're not really here now. Are you?" Amy asked, her voice holding a cynical edge Sophie had heard in it often since Amy had learned she was her birth mother.

Yet the cynical edge explained something to her. Plainly. *She thinks I'm going to walk out of her life again.*

Am I?

If she still did have a career, if her hearing spontaneously improved—which no one had suggested it would, not enough to make a huge difference—would she just leave Ouray again? Or if she truly learned to compensate and decided to pick up where she'd left off or move forth alone, stronger, to even more challenging horizons, would she just leave Amy and William?

It wasn't as though either of them needed her.

But that distrustful note in Amy's voice said something different.

She opened her mouth to say, *I'm really here now,* because she knew that was what her daughter needed to hear.

But the words didn't come out. Who would believe them? Could she make promises?

If this girl needs me, can I sacrifice my own dreams for her?

Strange, Amy was no longer the daughter of Patrick Wray. The resemblance must be there, but Sophie didn't see it, didn't remember Patrick Wray's face well enough to make the connection. Amy was, however, *her* flesh and blood—and William's daughter, clearly the most important person in William's life.

Even Crystal had been willing to become a stepmother to Amy.

If her daughter loved and needed her, wouldn't that be more than enough?

"I'm in your life," Sophie said abruptly, "to stay. If I return to the stage, if I work professionally again, I will remain in your life. I'll take you with me on tour if your father lets you come and if you want to go. Truthfully, I haven't been sure you want me around. And I definitely don't feel I have any right to inflict myself on you."

"Then why are you spending so much time with my dad?"

In the hope you'll want me near. Was it fair to Amy to say this?

"Friendship?" she answered. "This hearing loss has been pretty awful. My band quit. Training dogs keeps my mind off the stuff that isn't so good right now." She smiled. "Also, your dad plays the violin better than I do. Believe it or not, when we play together, I learn quite a bit from the experience. Are you disappointed he's not marrying Crystal?" Sophie parked behind William's Forester. She would ask him the best place to put the gypsy wagon.

"No," Amy answered. "I knew he wouldn't marry her."

Sophie switched the key to the off position.

"I know things sometimes," Amy continued.

"Has he been engaged before?"

"Just to you, I think. I always thought the two of you were married."

"No."

"He wanted to be married. Right?"

Sophie considered this. "I was pregnant with you, and we were both focused on you. We loved each other. A lot," she said, more to herself than to Amy. Most of what she remembered was laughter. They had stayed up late playing Scrabble—open dictionary. He had teased her with horrible scenarios he would inflict upon her when she was his spouse. Papua New Guinea had been one of them, although she'd thought he'd spoken of it a bit wistfully.

She opened her door and Amy opened hers.

"Dad!" Amy yelled. "We're going to be the wedding band!"

SOPHIE WORKED with Cinders and Loki. William said one of the men he hired as agitators would be up later in the day. They could do some protection work with Cinders then.

In the meantime, he gave Sophie some ideas about starting to train Spinner for sound work.

Using food, Sophie soon accustomed Spinner to the timer on William's microwave. Every time it went off, Spinner jumped up, barking at Sophie.

"Next," William told her, "you'll want her to come and get you and tell you when she hears the sound. She will. She's eager to work."

He introduced Sophie to the idea of targets, areas in the house where the dog would go on command, to signal or for other reasons.

Sophie noticed that Tenor, the New Guinea Singing Dog, followed William everywhere. William had leads with hooks on them secured to various points in the house and training ring and outside, as well. When he was doing something he thought Tenor would interrupt, he simply hooked one of the leads to the dog's collar.

"Dad loves that dog," Amy told Sophie as they—and William—took out their instruments in the living room to practice.

Sophie had scrawled down the songs they would be performing at the ceremony and at the reception.

"Did you write 'Now, I Believe' for my dad?" Amy asked bluntly.

"Yes."

Amy frowned.

"What?"

"I think that's more disillusioning than if you hadn't."

"Why?" asked William.

"Well, you're not together. Not that I want you to be. It just confirms my belief that love doesn't really last."

"Your grandparents have been married more than thirty years," William objected.

"And I know why. For you and Uncle Jonathan.

Grandma says so all the time. It makes me glad you two didn't stay together for me."

Both Sophie and William stared at her.

Ignoring their looks, Amy said, "Don't you have to tune?"

They disregarded the suggestion. William said, "Shall we do 'Now, I Believe' as a duet?"

"Yes," Sophie answered emphatically, knowing William had suggested it to put paid to Amy's adolescent angst.

"You don't have to listen," he told Amy. "We know the possibility of enduring love is anathema to you."

"Ha ha." She set the sheet music that Sophie had provided on her music stand and started practicing with her clarinet.

She seemed not to hear as Sophie began to sing "Now, I Believe." William tuned his violin, disregarding the other two, but picked up the second verse.

"Climbing trees, skinned knees, half-pipe dreams… I never had to see your face…no mine or yours, no us, I've known your soul before, and we go on forever…."

"You have a nice voice, Dad," said Amy.

Sophie nodded. "Very nice."

"I feel like the Von Trapp Family," said Amy, but this time she was smiling.

William grinned and reached up a hand, a hand that touched a thick waving lock of Sophie's thick, dark hair with its shimmers of auburn. "Your mom's inspiring. That's all."

Sophie's throat dried up, and her heart pounded solidly.

Now, she thought. *Now I could almost believe again.*

CHAPTER TEN

"AMY, TELL ME what you like to do when you're not in school," said Amanda, setting a loaf of garlic bread on the table. It was the kind that was frozen, then heated up in the oven.

Amy said, "Is that Pepperidge Farm garlic bread? It's my favorite!" she said as her grandmother nodded.

Sophie was tremendously proud of her daughter, proud of the job William had done in helping her become the kind of person who was enthusiastic about the food when she was a guest. She seemed uncommonly self-possessed for someone her age.

"Actually, I like social studies and history," Amy said. "I'm not much of a language person, which is weird, considering how my dad and my grandfather are. I must not have inherited the gene."

Sophie tried to breathe normally. She went through all the motions perfectly, didn't even look at William to watch him do the same.

Nobody knows the truth but William and me. We can keep the secret. There's no need for Amy ever to know about this.

"What class are you in?" Dan asked.

"I'll be a sophomore next year."

"So the girl involved in that unpleasantness we read about in the paper isn't in your class."

"No, she graduated this year."

"What unpleasantness?" asked Sophie.

William shook his head, as though to dismiss the topic.

"She was raped by a guy at a party," Amy told her. "It shouldn't even have been in the paper. Her name wasn't, but this is Ouray, so everyone knows who it was."

"Unpleasantness?" Sophie repeated incredulously, suddenly shaking. Acquaintance rape as "unpleasantness"? She realized too late that she was trapped, that the ingredients were there; rage was inevitable, but this rage would confine itself to trembling, to fighting to control herself, to fear, to horror.

"Well, he's saying it didn't happen," her father explained, "and there's no evidence. He's an adult, and he's got quite a bright future, admitted to an accelerated medical program. I don't know the people. There've been some letters about it in the paper."

Her chest had tightened. "If she said it happened," Sophie nearly hissed, "I'm sure it probably did."

"Well, innocent until proven guilty."

He doesn't know. He doesn't know. She reminded herself of that, and at the same time a hatred fifteen years suppressed, fifteen years forgotten and now remembered, forgotten and remembered like this, resurfaced again, rushing through her.

Amy shrugged. "Maybe true, maybe not."

"It's not a very nice topic for dinner, dear." Amanda laid a hand on her husband's forearm.

Sophie tried to focus on the quiche that she herself had made. She'd made three of them: asparagus, mushroom, spinach and feta. Besides the quiche, there was a creamy cucumber soup and Greek salad.

I can't eat.

She could only try to breathe.

Twice. Twice in five minutes Patrick Wray had come up.

Of course, the first was just Amy's innocent reference to her genes, genes that could never have been hers. The second—the "unpleasantness."

Sophie wished she knew who the girl was, wished she could help her.

She had volunteered on a rape crisis line in the past. It had helped, helped her feel solidarity with other women. It had *not* helped her love men again.

William scratched the back of his neck, then made a performance of pausing. "Hey, Sophie. Sophie, is this a tick?"

But he stood up before she could check, and she knew what he was doing.

She knew there was no tick.

"Let's go outside where there's better light," she said.

"The light in the bathroom's good," her mother offered.

The dogs were outside, and that was the direction Sophie chose, outside and away from the windows.

Five dogs—Loki, Cinders, James, Spinner and Tenor—charged up to them. Sophie and William ignored their pleas for attention, and the dogs ran off, chasing each other around the yard.

William said, "Want to take the dogs for a walk?"

"We can't. I just have to relax. I'm fine. I'm really fine. It's not like it happened last week. He just made me mad. He doesn't *know*."

"You never told them."

"Of course I never told them. I promised you."

"Not everything. I just thought you might've told them you were raped."

"It would've turned complicated in a hurry."

"How about a glass of that wine your father offered?"

"They buy horrible wine."

William laughed. "Shall we say there was a tick or wasn't?"

"Wasn't. But let's try to spend a lot of time talking about ticks. Rocky Mountain Spotted Fever. That should keep the conversation in safe waters."

He put his arm around her shoulders as he steered her toward the solarium and into the house.

Sophie shuddered beneath his touch, feeling an old terrifying, disconcerting mixture of comfort and distrust, of wanting to be embraced and wanting to be safe and untouched. But with William, there was no anger at presumption, none of the annoyance and suspicion she would have felt toward another man. He was her friend, he knew her, and his embrace was as safe and straightforward as embraces came.

No ulterior motive.

They paused in the solarium as he shut the door, and he gazed at her for a moment. She'd braided her hair in one thick braid, but she'd also braided a series of small four-stranded French braids near the front, to keep the wisps back. Seeing his expression, she said, "What?"

"I've always loved your neck."

She saw then in her mind's eye, felt in its memory, times she'd lain on her back with her head in his lap and he had stroked her throat.

She had never feared his fingers on her throat.

What would have been terrifying from someone else, from him was safe, cherishing.

She smiled.

"If I kissed you sometime, would you hit me?" he asked with the sensitive and delightful smile of a man who was very sure she wouldn't hit him.

"Yes," she said and walked ahead of him into the house.

"Good," he said behind her. "I love it when you hit."

At the table, Amanda said, "Was it a tick?"

"No," Sophie said.

"Yes," William answered in the same moment.

"It hadn't attached itself," Sophie embroidered.

"That's what I meant," William told them.

Amy turned away from the others to roll her eyes, and Amanda said, "I don't know if there's Lyme disease here, but you don't want to get it."

THEY HAD COME to her parents' house together in William's Forester, and they returned to William's the same way, taking the dogs they'd brought.

In the back seat, Amy said, "James…the worst-behaved dogs I've ever seen. I tried to…Amanda that she's…his bad habits, but she wasn't having any of it. Would you say a…Owner type, Dad?"

"Yes."

"What?" Sophie turned around to see her daughter, wishing she'd heard what Amy had said about her mother and the Schipperke.

"Dad has this book…William Campbell…animal behaviorist. It's…list of owner archetypes. I said Amanda's a Seductive Owner. Like…begs…to behave decently…."

Sophie shot a look at William. "What kind of owner am I?"

"Anthropomorphic."

"I am not!"

"You asked." He turned up the gravel Camp Bird Road. The evening was warm and the air thick with dust from the preceding vehicle.

"Explain."

"You think Loki misbehaves in public to embarrass you. That's ridiculous."

"Well, why does he do it then?"

"Possibly because you anticipate it happening, you get stressed out, maybe he senses weakness and an opportunity to do what he wants instead of what you want."

Sophie had not yet spent the night in the gypsy wagon at William's. Each night, she took Loki and Cinders and drove home. She told her parents she was using the gypsy wagon, her portable home, as a studio, a place to write music and be alone. And basically that was true.

During dinner she'd caught her father looking between her and William with interest. Her father believed, perhaps more strongly than anyone, that she should have married William and stayed with him. Sophie's mother wasn't critical of her decision. Well, her father wasn't, either, not really, but Sophie knew how he felt because he'd told her.

Once.

Her parents tended to give their opinion once. It had been very effective as a means of influencing her when she was growing up.

But about her and William's relationship now, they seemed to have no opinion. She knew they felt that people who were lovers should also be married, but she and William weren't lovers.

They'd been thrilled to meet Amy, of course.

Sophie said, "Amy, want to practice Bharata Natya before I put the dogs in my car to head down the hill?"

"Yes."

They all went inside, and Amy put on her favorite Indian dance CD.

While Amy practiced the two *adavus* she'd learned, Sophie watched critically from the kitchen area. She and William leaned side by side against the glossy, cherry-stained kitchen counters, as beautiful and truly rustic as the rest of the little cabin.

When his hand covered hers, just for a moment, she first thought she was imagining it.

Her legs seemed to melt.

Now I believe in desire, she thought.

She didn't want to fall in love or be in love, but she realized that both were beginning to happen, and she was terrified.

If she allowed herself to love William and he broke her heart, she would be unable to leave, to run away from the pain. She would not desert Amy. This time, she'd promised.

Being close to William had never looked more complicated.

Before she could begin to define how she felt, he moved his hand.

"Well—" he yawned. "I have some dogs to work with."

She knew there were four protection dogs on the premises that he was training for other people. This service was his most lucrative. But protection training wasn't just a matter of bite work. All dogs needed obedience training, and complete reliability was required in a protection dog. He threw her a glance. "When Amy wears out, you can come help me, if you want."

You can come kiss me, you can come have the kiss I promised, Sophie translated.

She did not reply.

THE DOG BELONGING to the man whom Amy called simply "the Hummer" was nearly ready to go. The client had asked him to be trained as a family protector. He wanted a European shepherd to wait in the Humvee, to be prepared to spring from an open window if he saw a family member threatened or attacked.

The dog, Friedrich, was impressive. Training dogs was never something to be done by formula—and yet it was. Certain techniques worked with certain dogs.

William checked Friedrich's stand-stays, recall, basic obedience. He was putting the dog back in his kennel when the door to the training barn opened.

Sophie came in.

"Hi. What's Amy doing?"

"She's online on your computer, making a wish list of saris, et cetera, for Bharata Natya. I really ought to introduce her to Lalasa, but I haven't spoken to Lalasa since the band broke up. I guess I'm angry."

William asked, "Can I see the inside of that gypsy wagon of yours?"

He turned off the lights in the barn, and they walked out to the wagon together.

"I have a little solar generator, but it's not set up right now. I just have flashlights."

They entered through the back door of the wagon, and Sophie grabbed a flashlight and turned it on. There was a rag rug and the bed, covered with a patchwork quilt, a wedding ring pattern.

Ducking beneath the roof, William shut the door.

"Cozy," he said and kissed her.

They moved to the bed, and she killed the flashlight.

"I wish I could see you," he said.

She pushed open the curtains at the foot of the bed to let in the starlight.

"Better."

The anguish pounded within her. She couldn't identify it, didn't want to. But she said, "I *don't* believe, William. It's a problem I have now."

In the darkness, she saw a trace of his smile, a smile from a craggy face, the face of Tolkien's true Aragorn, she thought, or it would be when William aged.

"Which don't you believe?" he asked. "That you have a soul mate in the world? Or ordinary old happily ever after?"

"The latter."

"You think you have a soul mate?"

"Part of me will probably always think it's you. Part of me will always think we lived a twin existence, you in Papua New Guinea, me in the United States. When we were children. You know. Like our souls used to leave our bodies and be together."

"When we make music," he said, "I'm certain you're my soul mate. What about happily-ever-after don't you believe?"

"I don't believe it's to be my fate. That's all."

His eyebrows drew together. "You might want to let go of that vision."

She laughed.

"Do *you* believe?" she asked.

"I believe," he said. "Actually, with you, I believe I have a better chance of happiness than I would have with Crystal. You and I have common interests. Consider people who are married for a long time. It's shared history, in part, that holds them together. It makes a difference to me that I've known you so long, although we've been separated. We remember things. The other day you mentioned that girl who used to play flute—"

"Patty. Why can't you remember her name?"

"See? I even like the way you snipe at me over trivialities. I must secretly want that, Sophie, that level of familiarity." He frowned again. "That *was* part of the problem with Crystal."

"What?"

"She couldn't dish out a really serious hard time the way you can."

"I never give you a hard time!"

He grinned in the dark. "Only when my mother calls."

"I think it's nice that your mother calls you. You have a mother and don't expect me to be your mother. Also, I won't have to train you to let someone else run your life, because your mother's been telling you what to do since you were a kid."

"Like I said, I'm so glad you never give me a hard time, Sophie."

"I'm thinking of going professional with it," she said. Her head rested against his arm. He smelled like wood smoke and vaguely of good dog smells, the smells of clean dogs who got lots of exercise and occasionally swam in cold mountain rivers and streams. "Anthropomorphic dog owner," she muttered.

"You're completely anthropomorphic."

"What other categories are there?"

"Placating-Submissive."

"You're sure that's not my mother?"

"No. Amy had her pegged. Seductive. She's constantly bribing that dog."

They lay together, looking at each other.

"I dated one man," she said, "who used to call me on the phone just to talk, and he'd sit there and tell me what supplements he was taking. Like 'Right now, I'm having my L-glutamine,' as if I didn't have anything better to do than listen to the sound of his voice."

"Probably lonely," said William.

"I attribute it to a weak mind. Mine, for sleeping with him. I used to spend a whole lot of time not regretting, William, but when I get involved with men I seem to end up with nothing but regrets. I was doing a tour once, and a guy I dated calls me up at 6:00 a.m. and leaves this loud, horrible message saying that I'm Miss Destructo and he really thinks I need help, and it's too bad because he really loves me and thinks we should have a life together. I'd broken up with him! Did he think this would endear him to me?"

William's lips twitched again. "We're none of us perfect, Sophie."

"I don't mind imperfection. I mind moments of extreme human weakness. I mind that I *pity* my former lovers, not because they suffer over not being with me anymore, but because they're so *clueless* about what women want and need."

"What *do* women want and need?" William actually sat up as he said this.

"I want a *man.* I mean, if I'm in a relationship. Like an equal. I don't want an eternal adolescent. Like Gavin, my bass player, my *former* bass player. He thought nothing of calling at dinnertime, finding out what I was making, and asking if he could come over and have some. What I hate most about it is that I have *contempt* for these people. I dated this guy from Texas. It was a nightmare. He'd sit down with really interesting people, and all he'd ask was how many miles they had on their vehicles and what they thought about the Broncos' chances. The way I felt in situations like that makes me not like who I am. Why do I hate men?"

William squinted. "Say again what it is that women want?"

She sat up, raising two fingers in turn. "One. Freedom. No bullies, no people building fences around me. Two. An adult! I mean, if it's a partnership, it should be a partnership. I am so tired of men who are children. They—and the bullies, the future domestic terrorists—*always* want to get married. The ones who are least suited to marriage."

"You're a bit intimidating in this mood, Sophie."

She relaxed against his arm again. "Being raped might have ruined me. That, or giving up Amy. Or something. I can't allow myself to be vulnerable. I become like some creature who spits poison. Or a Gorgon. Then—" her laugh was a half sob "—I agree to sing at a wedding."

"Want to hear a good joke? This guy finds a bottle in this old house, and he rubs it," William said, "and a genie comes out. And the genie says he'll give him one wish. The guy says, 'Just one?' But then he says, 'Well, I've always wanted to go to Hawaii, but I'm afraid to fly, and I get seasick. I'd really like for someone to build a bridge from California to Hawaii so I could drive there.' And the genie says, 'Oh, come on. Think of the engineering difficulties. Think of the legal problems—where we'd have to get permission to build a bridge across a huge stretch of the Pacific Ocean. What state, what country, would own the bridge? It's impossible.' The guy is disappointed, but he sighs and says, 'Well, if I can't have a bridge to Hawaii, I guess what I'd like most is to understand women.' The genie says, 'You want two lanes or four?'"

Sophie laughed.

"Sophie, if you make love with me tonight, I promise to behave like an adult for one out of every twenty-four hours, and I promise to check up on you and watch your every movement only during the minutes I'm not training dogs. I'll have a detective service do the rest. And on our anniversary every year you'll get the night off and won't have to make dinner or clean house. And you can have all the friends you want, as long as I approve of them. And you can talk to your family whenever I say so."

She laughed again, less heartily. She understood that his joking was an acknowledgement of what led up and added up to marital abuse, and she believed she wouldn't see those things from him. But her fears seemed physical, cellular, something she couldn't overcome.

And the picture his joking painted was too vivid.

"Don't joke about it," she murmured.

"Sorry. I was trying to say that I know what you're talking about, and it's not who I am or plan to be."

"I really don't know what you want." It came out more quietly than she'd tried to say it.

"A drummer," he said. "For your wedding gig."

"*Our* wedding gig. And you're right."

"Too bad my father took off."

"That's right," Sophie recalled. "He drums well. I'm sure he doesn't have the right equipment, though. When did he leave?"

"The other day."

Silence.

There was pain in that silence, the pain of his father's infidelity, still ongoing. His father would pursue women, outside of his marriage, until he could no longer walk and speak.

"Would Lalasa do it?" William asked.

"I hate Lalasa." Which wasn't true.

"Because she quit?"

"No, because I can't stand her. She's a scene-stealer. The bride will hate her."

"I never met her," said William. "You've told me she was a good percussionist."

Better than good, more than a percussionist.

A friend.

Who seemed to have ceased being a friend.

Who hadn't called Sophie since the band's breakup.

She didn't know where the tears were coming from. "William, I can't be with you. Because—don't you see?—I can't get along with people. I'm so full of *hate* that I sabotage all my relationships. Even my manager said so."

His hand linked with hers. "Sophie."

"What?"

"Just be at peace. Just relax. You can take your dogs for a walk if you want."

"What's wrong with me, William?"

"You were raped, and I'm not sure people really heal from that. I know they're never the same again. You told me that a long time ago, and I believed you. You said, 'The world used to be one way, and now it's another.' You're not a bad person, Sophie, and you're not hateful. You're just…"

"Just what?"

"You're not going to let it happen again. And I think it's hard to go through life always ready for combat."

The tears that had started earlier dampened the sleeve of his T-shirt, dampened the cotton over his chest, over his heart.

When he held her, the quiet vibration between them was electric. It was not sexual—not just or first—but spiritual. The attraction was of mind and heart, and she felt more intimate with him in this embrace, in which he held his sexuality apart from her, than she had in couplings with men she'd believed she loved.

But she had known—*known*—that none was her soul mate, that there was a man she'd loved more and better.

No wonder I destroyed those relationships. I loved someone else.

He said, "It's never exactly about making love with you. I think I've known you since before there were stars."

More tears, tears for the time she had spent trying to love other men.

"Are you all right?"

"Yes," she said.

He gazed down at her face, heart-shaped, white in the moonlight, brown eyes showing beneath long, thick lashes. "I could look at you forever," he whispered.

"William," she said, feeling the desperation in herself, the exhaustion, "this has to last. It has to."

He saw the fight within her. He knew what she fought. She fought ownership. Like Tolkien's Eowyn, she feared a cage.

She always would, and he wasn't sure she could ever let go enough to live a commitment. He suspected that was what Patrick Wray had done to her, and it leaped into his mind that Amy was Patrick Wray's natural daughter.

Sophie had no trust now.

Except maybe, he realized, in him.

He kissed her, felt her lips part against his mouth. She rolled toward him on the bed, which creaked beneath them, and lay over him, her lips on his throat.

During the vast quiet waves washing through her, he held her with arms that he hoped would never be a cage.

CHAPTER ELEVEN

SHE CHOSE TO GO HOME that night. She took Spinner, as well as Loki and Cinders. Her parents were asleep when she got in.

Creeping up to bed, she felt torn between the love she felt for William and the security of solitude, of sleeping alone. She rarely put on music to sleep. Now she wished she had William singing to her, his voice solid and resonant, authentic as something ancient, as the voice of a bard, telling truths.

She remembered what he'd said to her earlier that night. *I am for him what he is for me,* she told herself.

That wasn't the trouble. The trouble was her. The trouble was her inability to let go, to give herself totally to any relationship, be it with her daughter or with a man.

It occurred to her that she hadn't thought about her hearing loss for hours.

She realized she *was* adjusting to the different way things now sounded. When was the last time she'd jumped at a loud noise? Well, other than James's bark.

Also, it was hours since she'd wondered whether she had any future in music.

She *could* sing.

She had asked William if she was on key. Her hearing sometimes cut out so badly.

But he said that her perfect pitch had been preserved.

Why had she returned to her parents' house?

Well, she and William had agreed it would have been too much for Amy to find Sophie wandering out of her father's bedroom in the morning.

Sometime, William had said. Sometime she would stay.

So many sometimes.

But there was a sometime that must never happen. Her daughter must never learn what had been done to her, Sophie. That time must not come to pass.

In the morning, at breakfast, her mother said, "You were out late. Practicing for the wedding?" She didn't wait for Sophie to answer, having had years to know a Sophie before coffee. "I like Amy. William's done a very good job with her—or I should say William and Moira. I know his mother's always given him lots of help. But I do think Amy's glad to have you, Sophie. At this age—hers—it's important not to underestimate your importance to her. She may not seem like it, but she needs you."

Her mother was right. Amy *did* seem as though she didn't need Sophie. Sophie managed a precaffeinated nod, then wandered into the living room and lifted the lid on the baby grand piano. Her parents had it tuned every summer, and it was time again, but it wasn't unbearable as it was. Loki, Cinders, James and Spinner arranged themselves on the carpet nearby. James growled at Spinner and ran up to her, snapping.

She played some Mozart and Liszt, and her mother came in, drying her hands on a dish towel. "That sounds so nice, Sophie."

"The dogs?" asked Sophie, who could hear nothing else.

"No, the..."

She nodded absently, knowing her mother would understand that she couldn't hear.

She returned to the kitchen and drank coffee, gnawed on a piece of toast and began thinking of music. Laughing with William.

When the talking's more important than touch...

She wanted to be alone to write music, and she hurried back up to her room and grabbed a notebook to scrawl down lyrics.

She hadn't seen Amy last night, after she'd gone out to the gypsy wagon with William. How would Amy react to learning that her mother and father were intimate?

It sounded like a silly question, but Sophie remembered growing up and feeling absolute horror at the disgusting thought that her parents could engage in that act *with each other.*

Better for Amy not to know now. After all, William had been engaged to someone else about a week earlier. This might not last, either, might not last another day.

HE CALLED at nine-thirty that morning.

She answered, and he said, "Hi. It's me."

Her heart thudded, and she was sure he was about to tell her that it had all been a mistake. "Oh, hi," she said. "What is it?"

He laughed. How she liked his laugh, how she wanted to hear its sound, how it relieved her now. It was sexy and sweet and rueful, maybe rueful for his own feelings. That was how she wanted to read it, that he was laughing at himself for thinking she might be glad to hear from him the morning after they'd made love.

He said, "You're busy?"

"No. I mean, I just got up. I always get up earlier and let the dogs out, then I sleep some more. I haven't had enough coffee." He must remember how difficult she was, how she sometimes *had* to get those extra few hours of sleep, how she could barely speak before coffee—which she hadn't touched during her pregnancy. She'd been so different back then, and so had he. This—what lay between them now—was something entirely new and unique.

"So, before you have more coffee, can you say if you—if I've crossed your mind since you left last night?"

"Not once."

He laughed again, now a laugh of confidence that she was teasing him with a lie. "When can you come over?"

"I need to go check out the church where the wedding's going to be and also the place where the reception's being held, and then my mother and I are going to Grand Junction. I don't know when we'll be back."

"Tonight?"

"Let's say tomorrow sometime." Minutes later, when she'd hung up, she wasn't sure if she was trying to create distance between them to protect herself from a broken heart—or just from commitment.

TOMMY TRAVIS WAS STAYING with his grandparents a quarter mile down the Camp Bird Road from Mount Sneffels K-9. He was sixteen and would be a junior the following year.

He had never spoken to Amy, nor she to him, and Amy liked it that way. It wasn't that she didn't like boys. It was just that she'd never met one she thought was worth making herself ridiculous over.

Her father had shaken his head after learning, from another neighbor, that Tommy had been in trouble with the law—possibly gang-related trouble—in California. Her father never seemed to have much faith in kids starting out as bad boys and then straightening out.

Tommy Travis was riding a mountain bike up the

Camp Bird Road when Amy reached the top of the driveway with Sigurd, whom she was taking for some tracking practice.

"Cool dog."

"He's my dad's. You should wear a helmet," she told him.

He shrugged. "I'm not going far."

Amy made a face that she hoped expressed what she thought of his logic. The road was steep. It was rocky. If you fell on your head, you spent the rest of your life as a vegetable.

"Maybe you already *did* fall on your head," she said.

"What do you mean?"

No, he'd just been that way from birth. "Never mind."

"What's your name?" he asked.

"Amy."

"I've never seen a dog like that before."

She didn't apologize for his disadvantaged upbringing.

"I'm Tommy Travis."

"I know. Sigurd, heel."

"That's his name?"

The guy was attractive, if a teenager with a less-than-average IQ could be, and that was how Amy perceived him. She knew, however, that he had his own car, a Jeep.

"It's from Norse legend," Amy said.

"What kind of dog is that?"

"He's a German shepherd." *Hello?*

"I've never seen a black one."

She said nothing.

"So. What do people do around here?"

Amy never knew what to say when anyone asked her that. She didn't think she'd ever been bored in her life.

What did a person do anywhere? And Ouray was the most beautiful place in Colorado.

But she had plenty of classmates who maintained that what set Ouray apart *was* that there was nothing to do.

"Hike?"

"Want to go hiking sometime?"

Okay, she was flattered. She was popular, and she'd been asked to dance at dances, but it was unusual for a boy who was older and as nice-looking as Tommy Travis to ask her if she wanted to—well, hiking wasn't really a date.

"I go all the time," she said indifferently, because she knew, instinctively, that boys liked indifference and didn't like little girls with crushes. "We can go together sometime, if you want, I guess."

"Cool. Is this where you live?"

"Yeah."

"Your dad's the dog trainer?"

Amy figured this was obvious. "Right again."

"What does your mom do?"

Amy was used to saying that her mother was dead. She didn't now.

Nor did she say that her mother was Sophie Creed. Most kids her age liked the Wayfairers, who were cool. But what if Tommy decided he liked her *because* her mother was Sophie Creed? People did that. "She's a singer."

"A singer?"

"A wedding singer," said Amy with a kind of vengeful satisfaction. "She sings at people's weddings and stuff. And plays the violin."

"Interesting," he answered and sounded as though he really thought it was. "Well, do you, like, have a phone?"

"HE WANTS TO take you to a movie," William said the following afternoon, his voice all on one note. If he'd been asked to pick out a first date for his daughter, it would *not* have been Tommy Travis, about whom his feelings were ambivalent even before the kid had showed interest in Amy.

"Just in Ouray. Good grief, Dad, the theater's even at this end of Main Street."

"In his car." William had picked up the phone in the training barn, surprised to hear a male whose voice had changed asking for his daughter. But he'd gone to find Amy.

Ten minutes later, Amy had come out and said nonchalantly that she was going to the movies that night with Tommy Travis from down the road, okay?

He has a deep voice, William had wanted to say. None of the stupid responses that came to him seemed at all adequate.

He asked, "How old is he?"

"I think he's sixteen?"

He hated when she answered his questions with statements that were questions.

He hated how mature she sounded when he knew that his most basic concerns hadn't even occurred to her.

You are not driving down the Camp Bird Road with anyone who's had his license for less than a decade!

He'd never considered himself hard-wired for law enforcement, but his immediate instinct was to call in every favor he could to find out exactly what Tommy had done. He knew also that he would do it. Later. "No."

"No?"

As though he amused her. *No, as in you're trying to tell me what to do, as in you're forbidding me to go on a date?*

"You can go to the movies but not in his car."

"What?"

"You have a long life ahead of you. I don't want it ruined by a yahoo driving you off the Camp Bird Road."

"Oh, for crying out loud," she exclaimed. "That's ridiculous! How are we supposed to get there?"

"Walk. It's good for your heart."

"It's, like, more than a mile!"

William grinned in spite of himself. Tommy Travis was not local, probably wasn't truly acclimated. It would be a good way to wear him out. "Ah, after the years I spent in Papua New Guinea, walking four miles a day just for—"

Amy's look scorned his immaturity. "Is it just too much to ask that we not go through this undignified nonsense? I'm fourteen. He has his own vehicle. He'll come to the door. He'll meet you. And he'll drive us to the theater."

"If you think I'm being unfair, you can ask your mother's opinion."

"I think I'll ask Grandma's."

William tensed. His mother was a little too willing to keep Amy in her court by spoiling her.

"Actually," he said, "I don't know what your grandmother will say. But I can take a good guess what your mother will say. And no matter what either of them says, you are not getting in his car."

"You know, of course, that you can't really stop me."

What had happened to her? This was an entirely new approach to getting along with each other. Two weeks earlier, he'd have said he had the most levelheaded teenager in Ouray County.

You can't stop me.

He had seen this behavior in dogs.

"That's true," he told her, "but I can make you understand that my way is the one that will make you happiest."

"But it's not."

He was sure it was, but didn't yet know how he'd convince his daughter of that.

Bribery? He never used it with dogs, but she was more complicated than any dog.

Offer her another alternative?

Like what? She was hardly going to agree to his driving them to the movie. What was Tommy Travis doing pursuing Amy, anyhow? William had heard that Tommy was in Ouray because he'd been in trouble in Newport Beach, California, where his mother lived. The fact that he was from a beach community and liked Amy, who still wore braces, made William extremely suspicious. He doubted they'd talked long enough for Tommy to discover Amy's intelligence and sense of humor.

He had a new idea. He could go talk to Tommy Travis and make Tommy see that he'd be happier not aspiring to date Amy Ludlow.

"Suppose," Amy said. "Suppose Sophie said I could go, would you let me?"

His answer was dependent on whether or not he believed Sophie would let her go. But if he gambled and let Sophie decide, he'd have to live with her decision.

Sophie, who was raped in her teacher's car at the age of seventeen?

"If she says no," he said, "will you abide by that decision?"

Amy considered this. "Yes." She snatched the portable from the desk where William had set it.

He watched her, absolutely certain how it would go.

But Amy surprised him. "Do you think you could come over? My dad and I have appointed you arbiter in a dispute."

William wished he could hear Sophie's reply.

"The loser," Amy promised, "will not hold it against you."

"NO," SAID SOPHIE, with exactly the expression on her face William had expected to see. "Your dad's right. Tommy hasn't been driving long. It's a difficult road, and a car can get out of control very fast. Also, you barely know him. You don't want to get in a car with a guy you barely know."

"Like he's going to do something to me?"

"*I* have no idea," Sophie said. "You never know what people are going to do. But it helps if you know somebody for a long time and well."

"How am I supposed to get to know him when my dad won't let me go out with him?"

"Did he say you couldn't go out with him? I thought this was about the guy's Jeep."

"Tommy won't want me to go out with him if I can't go anywhere in his car."

"Nice guy," Sophie murmured.

William was pretty sure that only he and possibly Sophie herself, not Amy, heard the slight tremor in Sophie's voice.

Amy frowned at Sophie. "Are you all right?"

Sophie nodded. "Fine."

"Well," Amy raised one shoulder in a shrug, "I can see your point about that. And I can see the point about the road. The guy hasn't lived here even a month, after all."

William stared.

"Also, I don't really want to go. I'd rather stay home and be with my dog. Tala's my best friend."

Manipulation.

Sophie didn't seem to recognize it. She also seemed

immune to any pathos in Amy's words. "I'd feel the same way," she said. "Hey, if I go to Denver sometime to a dance workshop, do you want to come? If there's a weekend seminar, I'd like to go."

"We can look on the Internet!" Amy suggested.

"Do you have to call that guy and give him some kind of an answer?"

"Yes." She rolled her eyes. Then she laughed. "I'll say, yeah, my parents want to see it, too. Let's all walk down together. We'll come by at six-thirty."

"*What* movie do I want to see?" Sophie asked.

"Actually, it's Horror Night. *Arachnophobia.*"

"Did I ever mention that this is a problem of mine?" Sophie asked. "Oh, well, no sacrifice is too great for testing the intentions of your prospective boyfriend."

Amy had that look of sharp interest and intelligence, of general thoughtfulness she assumed when she suddenly became older than her years. "Really? You think we should all go?"

"Yes, I do." *I won't leave you,* Sophie promised again. *This time, I won't leave.*

William slipped out of the room and the cabin, heading for the barn to make a few phone calls.

THEY PRACTICED music that afternoon, preparing for the wedding, which was only a few weeks off. Then, Sophie and Amy trained, fed and watered dogs and cleaned kennels.

Afterward, Amy ran upstairs to change before the movie.

They left behind all the dogs but Spinner. William had gotten her an orange cape, and Sophie had stenciled on it HEARING DOG IN TRAINING. As an assistance dog in training, Spinner was allowed in the movie theater. Sophie brought along a squirt gun to spray at Spinner if she made any noise.

Tommy Travis—William had learned he'd been in trouble not for gang activity or drugs but in connection with a fight—sat on a stone wall outside his grandparents' tall, gray-sided modern house with its immense south-facing windows. "Bye, Grandma," he called and stood up when he saw Sophie, William and Amy. His grandmother came to the screen door and waved at them, and William, Sophie and Amy walked up to the house to say hello.

Amy made the introductions. Mrs. Grant, Travis's grandmother, seemed surprised to hear Sophie introduced as "my mother," and Sophie saw Amy flush.

How could you do that to her, William? Were you so sure she'd never meet me, never learn I existed?

Amy and Tommy walked yards ahead of them down the road, talking and only occasionally glancing back.

"I don't like him," said William decisively. Not the fight, not trouble with the law—no, he didn't like what he suspected Tommy wanted from Amy.

Sophie glanced at him and gave Spinner a leash correction. The little dog was adapting to a lead very well, and William had said that the walk to the theater would probably be the longest she'd ever experienced.

"That guy's too old for her." William said this and looked at Sophie, as though the statement was one with which she would certainly agree.

"He seems okay to me."

"I knew you'd never let her get in a car with him."

"You were right about that," Sophie said. "It terrifies me that what happened to me could happen to her. I almost want to tell her—not everything, but just that it happened to me—to impress upon her that it can really happen and it's really awful. I don't know about her, but I didn't quite get the picture until—"

"I was surprised," William said, walking on the side of her good ear, "that you didn't call the police. Back then, I was surprised." His experience in Denver had helped him understand the reluctance of rape victims to come forward. Being disbelieved…

"I didn't understand that it was rape. Not till—well—till you said it. You know that."

"I know."

"Let's not talk about it," she said. "I worry about Amy. It's not fair to assume that our friend up there has that in mind. But I want to protect Amy. Not just from him. From the whole world. I couldn't stand it if that happened to her. I've wondered sometimes if I was an easy victim because I was adopted and thought I was unlovable or something, but I've come to believe it could happen to anyone."

"True."

"And any high school senior would be thrilled to have a date with the teacher on whom she'd had a big crush. I didn't grasp how inappropriate it was."

"All true," William agreed. "Don't let Spinner do that. Tell her 'No sniff,' so she keeps her head up and pays attention to you."

"No sniff," said Sophie with a swift leash correction.

The kids rounded a bend in the road ahead of them and were briefly out of sight.

William said, "Can you stay tonight?"

"I don't think Amy's ready for that."

"I can't stop thinking about you."

"Really?"

"Yes."

"Don't tell your mother. She'll have a lot to say about how miserable I'm going to make you in the short *and* long run."

"Sophie."

"What?" She glanced at him.

He shook his head.

She understood what he meant. "I know. I'm being off-putting. Gavin, my bass player, used to tell me that my *wit* did not become me."

"Your wit isn't a problem."

"I'm jaded, and it shows. That's what was behind my comment. It's awful. I know it's awful. I don't like it, and sometimes I think if I could just *love* again, really love, with innocence, instead of from this stance of absolute cynicism, I'd have part of my soul back again, the part I lost."

"When did you lose it?"

The day you accused me of abandoning Amy.

That wasn't precisely true, nor was it true that she'd simply left and he'd been heartbroken. When he'd known she was leaving, it had become clear to her that he didn't love her. Things had been said which should not have been said.

But it wasn't just William.

Since living with William during her pregnancy, since leaving him and Amy, she had believed and hoped more than once.

But love was not what it seemed to be. Every man she'd met seemed to need such major change to become a reasonable life partner that partnership seemed more like a project than a relationship. A man like that needed a woman willing to make him the center of her world.

Granted, some men, like Gavin, seemed to want to make the relationship the center of the world, but that annoyed her, too. The world was bigger than that. She had her music, she had her dogs, and she wanted to contribute to the world around her, to help people who needed help.

One of her boyfriends had insisted, *Well, you can do that.*

When? In between giving him so much attention that she fell into bed at 9:00 p.m. every night, too tired to play a song, let alone write one?

Did all relationships take that much energy?

William wanted to know when she'd lost the part of her soul she'd said she'd lost.

"It seemed to happen over time. Once I realized it was gone—well, I don't have much hope of being that person again or even the kind of person who can love as a woman should be able to love. I can relate to monks and nuns and all those people, who simply want to love the Divine best, who want to live in that kind of rapture."

He smiled a little.

"What?"

"I'm just thinking of what your parents would tell you."

"What?"

"I think the biggest challenge in their faith is to love *people.*"

The tears she'd shed the other night, in his arms, echoed behind her eyes. "I know. It's not hard to love you—or Amy. I just—"

He looked at her.

She didn't answer and knew she didn't have to.

BECAUSE IT WAS Horror Night at the theater, actually a benefit for the local search and rescue, there was wine and cheese available in the lobby—though only to adults. Sophie and William both passed on it on the way in. Nobody stopped Spinner in her orange cape, and the dog was quiet during the movie, settling down to sleep at Sophie's feet. Tommy and Amy slipped over to the side of the theater, in search of seats apart from Sophie and William.

Before the lights went down, Crystal entered the theater with a tall and very handsome man Sophie had never seen before.

"There's Crystal," she whispered to William.

"I see her."

"Who's her friend?"

"He's a teacher, I think. From Crested Butte or Aspen. He's in Ouray for a two-week family reunion. She said he was her oldest brother's buddy in high school. In Chicago. They ran into each other at the hot springs pool. She mentioned it the last time I saw her." When she'd come to get her belongings from his house. "They're just friends, I think."

"If they weren't would it bother you?"

"Not remotely. I'm glad."

"Why?"

"She wants to be part of a couple."

"Any couple?"

"Sometimes it felt that way."

The lights went down, and William put his mouth near her ear. "What if I chew on you a bit, during the movie?"

"Bad example for Spinner," Sophie answered. But she leaned against his shoulder, and his scent and his flesh, muscle and bone, were as comfortable to her as her violin and favorite bow.

SOPHIE ENJOYED the movie, which was full of the kind of spidery surprises that made her feel completely justified in clinging to William.

Afterward, she and William remained in their seats and looked for Amy and Tommy.

Crystal and her date came up the aisle.

William and Sophie each gave a small wave.

Crystal detoured the man into the row in front of

William and Sophie. Her eyes, instead of sweeping over Sophie as though she wasn't there, which Sophie had half anticipated, fell directly upon her.

"Sophie. Do you recognize this man? He remembers you."

Sophie did not recognize him.

But she knew.

"I was telling Crystal that long before you were rich and famous, you used to have quite the crush on me," he said. "It's a flattering recollection. I'd love to play music with you sometime."

CHAPTER TWELVE

THE THING SHE MOST WANTED in that moment was to tell Crystal that her date, her oldest brother's high school buddy Patrick Wray, had raped Sophie Creed. No, the thing she most wanted was to say it to him, to say, *You raped me when I was seventeen, and that's what I remember.*

The rage inside her was so intense she almost thought the words would pour out of her. But it was the kind of shaking rage that held a fear her body would never forget. Uncontrollable trembling shot through her, and she stood, glad to be on the aisle with Spinner, wishing Spinner was Cinders or Loki. William stood, too, and she couldn't look at him.

She stared at Patrick Wray, who wore his graying hair in a sleek ponytail, and said, "Never speak to me again for any reason."

She strode out of the theater and into the lobby without waiting for William or for Amy and Tommy.

PATRICK WRAY STARED after her in bewilderment. "I can't explain that," he said. "Shouldn't I have teased her?"

William said, "Good night, Crystal," and stepped out into the aisle.

Amy's father.

Sophie's rapist.

Sophie was all right, wherever she was, probably downstairs on the street by now.

He had to get Amy out of the building without meeting this man.

Don't be stupid. Crystal will introduce him, but no one has any reason to think more of it.

If only Sophie had done less, done nothing Crystal might mention again, talking freely at some point about Amy's mother's inexplicable behavior.

Yet William couldn't think of any better thing for Sophie to have done.

She was not on the street below.

He found her waiting directly beside the ladies' room door, drinking red wine from a plastic cup beside a board advertising hats and shirts bearing the logo of the local search and rescue group.

Sophie pushed away from the wall, joined William and handed him Spinner's lead. But she looked at someone behind him.

"Patrick," she said, the tremor in her voice audible, William thought, to no one but him, "I must have mistaken you for someone else. Some wine, you two?"

"None for me," Crystal said.

"Thank you," said Patrick.

Sophie handed him an empty glass, and picked up a bottle from the nearby display. She met his eyes and said, "Tell me when to stop."

William knew what was about to happen. *Amy,* he thought. He wanted to warn Sophie that her daughter—*Patrick Wray's daughter*—was about to witness this, but he couldn't make a sound.

Amy and Tommy stepped from the theater and into the lobby and stopped beside them. Tommy was giving a long lazy stretch and appreciating Amy's backside. William noted this. *It's not her best feature, buddy.*

The red wine splashed into the glass, filled it.

"Stop," Wray said.

The wine continued to pour, the bottle shaking, dark red splattering Wray's Birkenstocks, his socks and his cream-colored linen pants.

"Stop. Hey, stop! What are you doing?" He stepped back, trying to get out of the way. Red wine had stained his hand, pooled on his pants, colored his shoes and socks. "Are you crazy?"

Sophie set the wine bottle back on the table, drained her own glass and looked at his overflowing one, then said, "Did you like it?"

"That is not what happened."

Sophie felt the quaking in her chest. It was perfect pitch, a difficult note faultlessly reached. No. It was a thundering she'd never known before.

It was satisfaction.

Because, by his very protest, Patrick Wray had just confessed to raping her fifteen years earlier.

ON THE STREET, Sophie shivered, zipping up her sweat-shirt.

"Sophie, what was that about?" Amy asked, ignoring Tommy.

William shook his head at his daughter and put an arm around Sophie's shoulders. "Home?" he asked her.

"Sure." Her voice shook. She shook. How could she have done that in front of Amy? How could she explain?

Though she liked her own actions given the circumstance, it didn't help. Nothing she'd done had helped, and nothing could. Seeing him was a nightmare, and she felt like throwing up. There really was no getting over it. Just going on.

"Had you seen that movie before?" she made herself ask Tommy and Amy.

"Did you know Crystal's date?" Amy asked, ignoring her father.

"Yes."

Don't tell her, William thought. *Don't tell her.*

"I hope I didn't embarrass anyone. Besides myself." Now there was shame in her loss of temper, shame in her inability to observe simple courtesy.

William wasn't sure what to say or do to make her feel better. He said, "You know, with dogs, you can't teach them by *telling* them. You have to *show* them." He hugged her.

"Thanks," she muttered.

Amy gazed at them both keenly.

William said, "Amy, would you please take this dog's lead?"

Amy took it. "Let's go, Spinner, silly dog." She strode ahead with Tommy and glanced back once.

William wrapped both arms around Sophie and felt the helplessness of a man who could not fix the situation, who knew of no way to make things right.

"SOPHIE'S SLEEPING OVER," William told Amy.

Amy blinked, a dramatic blink. "Have you changed the sheets since Crystal was here?"

Crystal hadn't slept over for months.

Too many girlfriends, too much rotation, too much serial monogamy.

He said, "Good night," and went into his room with Sophie and shut the door.

A few minutes later, he heard Amy's door softly close.

"That's one milestone out of the way," he said to Sophie, who stood staring at his queen-size bed in its frame of twisted and bent logs and twigs. It was tucked under the gabled ceiling and covered with a patchwork quilt. "You all right?"

"Sure." She shrugged, still visibly quaking.

"Oh, Sophie." He sank down on the edge of the bed and rubbed his face. "I'm sorry. She called him by some nickname that had something to do with her brother, something I can't even remember. I had no idea."

"Neither did I. I can't believe he admitted to her—or to anyone—that he knew me."

"Oh, come on. He was your music teacher, wasn't he, and you're a success story."

"Music theory. Just—it's like he thinks he's untouchable. And he *is*. He did that, and he's completely untouchable."

"People's habits have a way of catching up with them. If his haven't yet, they will."

"Did you hear what he said? 'That is not what happened.' He *knew*."

"I caught that."

"You believe it's what happened, don't you? That I said, 'No.'"

"I've always believed you, Sophie." He stripped off his shirt, then his jeans.

"I can't make love," she whispered. "I can't."

"That's fine. You don't have to. You just have to listen to my jokes."

She groaned and switched off the light.

As she pulled her camisole over her head he said, "This man comes home from work one day, and there's a snail, on his doorstep. So he picks it up and tosses it out in the yard."

She kicked off her jeans.

"Two years pass. Two years. And the man's at home one night—*two years later*—and there's a knock at the door. He goes and opens the door, and it's that same snail. And the snail says, 'What was that about?'"

Sophie climbed into bed with him. Laughing.

Shaking.

I'll never be all right. I'll never be normal *again.*

AMY LAY AWAKE. She thought for a short time about Sophie acting so—well, almost insane. Obviously, she and Crystal's new man had history.

The sense of knowing, the knowingness that was with her so much, the curse of Cassandra, blanketed her. She *knew,* though she couldn't name what she knew.

They're still keeping secrets. That had to do with my dad, too.

Her ruminations gave way to infinitely more interesting speculation about Tommy Travis. During the movie he'd taken her hand once. He seemed much older than her and as though he felt his greater experience. What did he want with her? While they'd walked ahead of her dad and Sophie, he had told Amy that he'd been in jail in California. Just overnight. It was very stupid, he said. He got in a fight, and his friend was hurt, and he knocked somebody out with his skateboard. Jail was bad. *Never go to jail, Amy,* he'd said.

But he seemed nice, not like a thug at all. He was a skater and a surfer, and he wanted to live in Colorado in the winter so he could snowboard, too. He'd asked if she knew how—she didn't, just skijoring with Tala and Sigurd. When they said goodbye at his driveway, he had said, "Well, I'll see you sometime."

That was all.

He didn't want to see her again—that couldn't be plainer.

Sophie didn't want me, either.

The thought crept in.

Her birth mother would take off again. Amy expected it.

She tried to ignore the fact that Sophie was across the way in the big bedroom under the gables.

That was probably the only reason she'd stuck around this long. To sleep with Amy's dad.

Tommy, in any case, had never heard of Sophie Creed and seemed not to recognize her. He'd definitely heard the Wayfairers; everyone had. But he didn't know who Sophie was. It wasn't as though she'd ever been on the cover of *Rolling Stone.*

The scene upstairs at the Ouray theater, the wine bottle shaking in Sophie's hand as she poured and poured and poured… *Did you like it?* She had seemed almost crazy.

But Crystal's date had understood whatever Sophie was saying.

That is not what happened.

Very strange.

But really, there was nothing to give her that sense of dread—and of knowing, and not knowing what she knew.

SOPHIE FELT HIS SKIN. Warm skin against her cheek. It was the middle of the night, and the man was William, and she was safe.

She could make love with him.

Yes, after fifteen years, even though she'd seen Patrick Wray only hours earlier.

She could do the sexual part and have an orgasm.

What she couldn't bring to that bed was her heart.

"Sophie." He hugged her.

They kissed, and she wanted to believe that this man was different, that he would be different for her in the long run.

I can't love. What is wrong with me?

Patrick Wray had not made her this jaded. Time had. Witnessing the world. She'd come to believe that sex was for physical pleasure but love—love was different.

Not necessarily related. She loved her parents, certain friends, her dogs, and now Amy—finally, surprisingly. She supposed she loved William in friendship. But she could no longer connect friendship, anything so non-threatening, to sexual desire, to consummation.

"William?"

"Yes."

"Do you believe in happily ever after?"

"I do."

"You know Gavin?"

"I don't, but yes, I know who he is."

Sophie found her cheek against a heartbeat, against breath. "He is obsessed with talking about the relationship. Even if you're just friends. It's exhausting."

"'Love does not consist in gazing at each other but in looking outward together in the same direction.'"

Sophie stilled. "*Yes.* That's what I mean." *And William knows, too.*

"Antoine de Saint-Exupéry."

William thinks love is looking outward together in the same direction.

His body felt different to her at once. His touch felt different. She questioned: Had he just *said* an impressive thing, the way Gavin always did? Her bass player was so full of clichés and soundbites she sometimes wanted to throw up listening to him.

But William was different.

William rarely talked about himself.

He wasn't boring.

He wasn't boring because he *did* look outward, instead of perceiving the world and everything in it as an audience riveted on the spellbinding drama of him.

Something like trust settled within her.

She parted to him, feeling like a young flower waking up.

But he only touched her, stroking her throat, kissing her lips.

"I can do this," she said.

"What?"

"If you—if I think of love that way, as looking outward together in the same direction—I can do it."

William rolled onto his back beside her and took her right hand in his left.

She stared up at the ceiling, just shadows in the dark.

But William saw the dark, too.

They saw it together.

CHAPTER THIRTEEN

"SOPHIE, it's for you. Can you talk on the phone yet?"

William, up, dressed, had probably already worked with several dogs. Sophie didn't know the time but it felt like 10:00 a.m. or so.

"You let me sleep," she observed gratefully.

He pressed the mute button and said, "It's Crystal, for you. I have no idea what she wants. I can tell her you're asleep or in the shower."

Wary, Sophie sat up and reached for the phone. William stood in the doorway for just a moment, then turned and descended the steps, giving her privacy.

"Hello?"

"Sophie, it's Crystal. I didn't know what to do."

This did not sound like a woman calling to lecture her ex-fiancée's lover on proper wine-serving.

"What?"

"I saw everything last night."

Sophie's breath caught. Of course, Crystal didn't mean *everything* as Sophie understood the concept.

"I saw what you did, and I understood why you must have done it, and then he pretended ignorance. Sophie, I believe you, and I told him so."

Sophie did not ask what Crystal believed. She said, "Thank you. How do you—"

"I was raped by two guys my freshman year of college. I quit school. It changed my whole life. But it's probably why I went to work for The Company."

"I didn't know. William never said anything."

"Well—he wouldn't, would he? He's a pretty decent guy if you can accept that his daughter will always be the most important female in his life, closely followed by his mother."

Sophie made a sound that was an attempt to laugh. His love for Amy didn't bother her at all. "Thanks for saying what you did, Crystal. To me. Thank you for calling."

"It sucks when men do stuff like—well, whatever he did—and then lie about it. It's like you kind of expect they'll see, the irrefutable evidence and own up to what they did, but they never do. Not rapists. And I hope I wasn't speaking out of turn to assume. If I assumed wrong—"

"I can't—" *Say. I can't say out loud to you,* He raped me.

"It's all right. Well, look, I'll see you around, okay? I've got a job offer in Washington day after tomorrow, so I'm scooting out of here. Something tells me I'll wind up back with The Company."

"Good luck, Crystal."

"Good luck to *you.* From this point on, I wouldn't trade places with you, Sophie."

"Why not?" The question sounded stupid but no stranger than Crystal's statement.

"I guess—because I see now that it would never have worked for me. But you're different. You fit in with them. So good luck," she repeated.

SOPHIE DIDN'T SEE Patrick Wray again and wondered if he'd left Ouray after Crystal stood up to him. In the next weeks, she and William and Amy practiced daily for the wedding. They found a drummer in one of the men who worked for William as an agitator. He played percussion for a local band but was willing to do the wedding with them.

Sophie began acting as William's assistant at a Beginning Obedience class. Usually with Loki or Cinders or Spinner, she demonstrated the techniques William wanted the class to learn and helped other students with their dogs while whichever dog she'd brought that night maintained a long down.

Amy had withdrawn, losing interest in classical Indian dance.

It was the week before the wedding, which would be on Saturday, July second, that Sophie figured out why Amy was depressed. Amy was trying to pick out an outfit to wear when the phone rang.

William was downstairs, finishing up a training contract with a client, but he answered the phone and called up the stairs to Amy.

The look on Amy's face told Sophie everything.

She's hoping for someone to call.

Tommy Travis?

It wasn't Tommy Travis but one of Amy's girlfriends. She returned upstairs, clearly upset.

"Is everything all right?" Sophie asked.

"Nothing. That cretin Tommy is going out with Jackie Martin."

"Who's she?"

"A girl in my class. She's probably allowed to ride in his car."

Bad things can happen in cars. Sophie didn't say it. She said, "Are you upset?"

"Well, yeah. I mean, a bit. I must have been a not very good date. He never called me again."

That admission was almost choked out.

Sophie didn't know what to say. "Amy. High school's usually not the best time of anyone's life. It gets better."

"Doesn't look like it from where I'm standing. You guys have used up my generation's resources, stolen the financial security of our country, destroyed the environment. The world is filled with guns and nuclear weapons and war, war, war."

Sophie knew even less to say to this accusation. She said, "Have hope, Amy. Have hope."

"For what? I don't even know what to hope for. A quick end?"

Did she talk this way to William? Did it worry him as much as it was worrying Sophie?

"To your life?"

"No. I'm not suicidal. I just mean—everything. Can you imagine the environmental situation getting *better?* I can't. Anyhow, I'm not interested in dating some surfer just to have high school experiences. It's just not important."

It was important, Sophie thought, but she was glad Amy had some perspective. "I love you, Amy." She had never said this before to her daughter. "I'm grateful that you're part of my life. I feel like you're the biggest blessing I've got."

"I'm not," Amy answered. "Music is. I know that about you. I just know things like that."

Sophie compressed her lips upward in something like a smile. "In a very short time, you've changed my life—changed it again and changed it more. I'm very proud of the person you are. I had nothing to do with it, but I am grateful."

Amy seemed not to hear her. "What about this?"

It was a sleeveless dress, black, countryish.

"It's okay," Sophie said, "but I think it looks young for you. You want to go shopping?"

"Like to Durango?"

"Okay." Sophie shrugged.

"Yes." And Amy said, somewhat ruefully, "Crystal was going to take me shopping a while back. I was really rude to her."

"I like her," Sophie said, remembering Crystal's phone call of support. She thought of that phone call often and things she wished she'd asked. But the questions might have directed Crystal's attention toward a truth she didn't know and mustn't learn—that William wasn't Amy's natural father.

What frightened Sophie most, she supposed, was Patrick Wray's ever finding that out.

But she doubted her former music theory instructor had ever or would ever think as far as pregnancy. That was a scenario Sophie was nearly certain he'd never even considered.

Amy gave her a strange look. "You're not jealous?"

Sophie shook her head. True, William hadn't asked her to marry him, but she hoped he wouldn't. Things were fine as they were. She didn't need a wedding ring. She didn't need a promise.

And if he asked, she wasn't sure what she would say.

She couldn't imagine herself as a bride, couldn't imagine getting married.

It was something she didn't know how to do.

THE MORNING of the second dawned clear. The wedding was at one o'clock and indoors. Her parents would be there. They knew the bride and groom and the couple's family.

William's mother called while Sophie was cooking omelets for herself and William and Amy. Sophie could hear Moira's voice through the receiver from across the room. "Well, I wish I could get to see you play together. It's too bad I won't get to, but I really have to be at the gardens. There are so many tourists this time of year."

"We'll have you over here and give you a concert," William promised.

Amy looked disgusted by this prospect.

"I've barely seen you since Sophie's been around so much."

William saw the expression on Sophie's face, similar to an expression he'd seen more than once on Crystal's. Annoyance, perhaps, that his mother was intruding on family time.

Family time.

This is my family.

His mother was, too. He couldn't have gotten by, raising Amy, without his mother's help, without her emotional support. In many ways, at various times in his life, she'd been his best friend. What his father had put them through, in particular, she and William had shared.

"Well, she's going to be." He almost put his hand to his mouth, as though to catch the word that had escaped.

"Going to be what?"

"Around."

Sophie glanced at him sharply. "Food's ready," she said. "Amy?" She offered their daughter a plate.

"We're going to eat now, Mom," William muttered.

"Of course, you go have a good meal. I'm glad someone's feeding you."

"Thank you. I'll call when we get back and tell you how it went."

"All right. I'll be thrilled to hear."

Sophie handed him a plate with an omelet on it.

After breakfast, Sophie and Amy washed the dishes, then went up to dress for the wedding.

Sophie had bought Amy some flared silk shantung pants and a poet's shirt. They were beautiful on her—elegant, sophisticated, neither too young nor too old. She herself wore a wraparound top and flared wraparound pants. William wore an oxford cloth shirt and khaki chinos, and Brett, the agitator/drummer, wore a white shirt, black pants and paisley summer vest.

They did look like a band.

Brett went ahead to the hotel where the reception would be held to meet with the sound man, whom William knew and said was good. Sophie discovered that she cared far less than she should about the quality of the sound. *I won't be able to tell if it's good or not.*

That was closer to the truth.

She needed someone she could trust—would always need that person—to take care of the sound.

She was proud of what she and Amy and William could do together, and liked Brett's contribution on the drums. She felt more relaxed than she ever had before a gig. She felt a different kind of anticipation than she'd experienced before any of the Wayfairers' shows. Jodie and Micah were so excited to have her sing at their wedding.

It felt good.

What's happening to me?

She was still thinking of that when William parked the Forester behind the church. They had practiced in the church the day before, alone, and had provided a tape for the wedding party to play at the rehearsal.

They carried their instruments into the church. It was an hour before the wedding, but Sophie saw some men in tuxedoes and searched them for the groom.

She saw Patrick.

He was one of the groomsmen. He might be the best man for all she knew.

She took a deep breath and walked back out of the beautiful church, away from the heady scent of flowers.

William had seen, as well. He followed her out. "Are you going to be all right?"

"I cannot *believe* this. I'll have to be. I'll have to be, won't I? I can do it. I can do anything." She heard how hysterical and angry and fierce she sounded. She couldn't stop. "I'll be fine. He is not going to screw this up for these people. I can do it, William. I'm going to do it. I have to do it. I have to be good. I've been looking forward to this."

"Would someone please tell me what's going on and what the problem is with that friend of Crystal's?"

Neither of them had seen Amy come outside.

"It's personal," Sophie snapped. "He did something awful to me. You don't have to know about it. You just have to play the clarinet."

Tears welled in Amy's eyes.

"Oh, shit," said Sophie, dragging a hand through her hair. "I'm sorry. I didn't mean to yell at you. It's not your fault. I'm just upset. I'm really sorry, Amy. Oh, God, please stop crying, Amy. I'm so glad you're here with me. Come on. Let's go back inside."

She ignored Patrick Wray. She could not afford to think of what he'd done so many years before or the fact that he was Amy's biological father, the secret that Amy, who always spoke of "knowing" things, must not learn. Micah, the groom, came over and greeted her and met William and Amy.

"We put 'Sophie Creed and Family' in the program. Does that work?"

"It works great," she said. For some reason, the name made her feel invincible, made her feel that her rapist's presence in the audience—in the wedding party, no less—could make no possible difference to her performance.

When her parents came into the church, she waved to them, thinking just briefly of the secret they didn't know and thinking that sometime soon she might tell them part of it.

The church filled, slowly at first, then quickly.

The minister spoke to Micah at the front of the church. The minutes passed.

Finally, the minister nodded to Sophie.

She and William and Amy drew up their instruments and, in some synchronicity built of love or genes or both, began the wedding march.

The best man and the maid of honor appeared, her in a dark rose color. Then a bridesmaid and Patrick, just another male figure. Then another bridesmaid and another groomsman. And another.

And Jodie.

Her dress was satin, a Grace Kelly in *Rear Window* kind of dress.

Radiant.

One with her violin, Sophie still saw her, saw her slow steps, saw her on her father's arm, saw the tears in her eyes, beneath her minimal veil, and in Micah's eyes, too, as Jodie's father brought her to her future husband.

Sophie's own eyes stung. Half the congregation seemed to have the same reaction: the female half.

How silly. I don't cry at weddings.

Sophie Creed and Family.

I don't sing at weddings if I can help it.

Sophie Creed and Family.

I don't even like to go as a guest.

But her heart spoke to Jodie, said, *You know how to get married, girl.*

The wedding seemed uncommonly beautiful. The bride and groom had such faith in each other. It showed in every moment: gratitude for what they shared and determination to see it through. Sophie found herself badly wanting that for them, happiness and a happily ever after in which, seeing them, she could almost remember how to believe.

After the Gospel reading, Sophie stepped closer to the microphone and began to sing. No accompaniment. She couldn't hear every note she sang, but she knew how they *felt,* because in the past weeks she'd come to trust William's judgment that she was on key, in tune.

"When I was a little girl, dreaming in the night…"

She sensed William beside her.

As he picked up the second verse, she echoed it, harmonizing as they'd practiced.

"I never had to see your face…no mine or yours, no us, I've known your soul before, and we go on forever…."

She was *not* going to cry at this moment. She could cry for the beauty of the wedding, for a wish of joy for the bride and groom, but she could not cry for the truth that sang within her.

And we go on forever….

She felt as though she'd never sung this song before until she heard William beside her, singing, "I never had to see your face; that wasn't how I knew…."

As they finished, they both stepped back, and she didn't look at him.

When the ceremony was over and they'd played the recessional and were putting away their instruments to go to the reception, William seemed strangely subdued.

Sophie was soaring. "That was so beautiful," she said.

"You think?" he murmured.

"Don't you?"

He nodded. "I do."

Amy stared thoughtfully, distractedly, toward the back of the church, where the wedding party had disappeared.

"Are *you* all right?" Sophie asked her.

Amy nodded, casting her eyes down.

As the three of them left the church through the side door, William murmured to Sophie, "Tommy and his grandparents were here. There was a girl with them."

Sophie put her arm around Amy's shoulders.

Amy said, "Can't you just tell me what that guy did?"

Sophie swallowed. There could be no harm in saying this much. "He raped me. On a date. It was a long time ago."

Amy said nothing, looking up with a shocked expression that only the young could produce. The disbelief of the innocent.

"Oh, Mom."

Three heads suddenly lifted, hearing the word.

Sophie laughed. "Maybe it was worth it to hear that." Then she realized what she'd said. She had *meant* that telling Amy was an easy price to pay for hearing her daughter call her "Mom."

But that wasn't what she had *said.*

She fell silent.

Amy said, "Good. Mom." And hugged her.

Sophie released her breath.

Safe again.

She watched William, who was unlocking the Forester, her door first. He met her eyes as though to ask what she was looking at.

"Did you like the wedding?" she asked.

"I'd like to have one," he said, almost through gritted teeth.

He knew.

He knew her.

He knew what she feared, to be caught and held. To be kept from a wide world she loved more than she could love any man.

But somehow not more than she loved her daughter.

Sophie said softly, "Let's enjoy this one."

THE RECEPTION WAS FUN. In some ways, Sophie found it more satisfying than shows with the Wayfairers.

I'm with my family.

Brett was a decent drummer, and Sophie knew the music was good. The guests loved the dancing. She saw Patrick dancing with a couple of the bridesmaids, and it was almost as though he was just another man she didn't know. Almost. Sometimes. In any case, the wine-pouring incident had yielded one desirable effect: he seemed to be keeping his distance from Sophie.

They played for two hours, each had a piece of wedding cake and then they packed up.

William, although he'd played with enthusiasm, remained quiet on the way home.

When they walked inside the cabin, he put away his violin and picked up the phone.

He's not going to let us go on this way, Sophie thought. *He wants a promise. He wants me forever.*

The next thought came to her like a reflex.

He wants to own me and imprison me.

Stupid to think that way, to always feel that way. Why couldn't she trust?

"It was beautiful," he said into the phone. "It was the best musical experience I've ever had and definitely the best wedding I've ever been to."

Sophie tuned out the static-like sound of his mother replying and reflected how loudly Moira spoke; Sophie could hear her from across the room even without the speaker phone on.

As William told his mother the songs they'd played, Sophie put her violin away and headed upstairs.

His mother said, "Well, I hope this is just a one-time thing with her. She'll be going back on the road, won't she?"

"I don't know."

"Be careful, William. I don't like to see you hurt. Especially by her. Again. That woman has caused a lot of people a lot of pain."

"A lot of people?"

"Well, you and Amy is enough."

The two of them had gone up to Amy's room, he supposed. "Amy called her Mom today. That made Sophie really happy."

"I'm glad it's going well. Dad called." An abrupt change in subject. "He got delayed in New Zealand. But he made it. He asked if I'd like to join him, but you know I have the botanical garden to tend. I really can't go this time of year."

"Are you sure?"

"Of course I'm not sure," she said. "I miss him."

What he had seen that day with Jodie and Micah was a beginning. His parents had begun once. And after thirty-plus years, when his father went across the world, his mother missed him. Missed him in a way that transcended knowledge of his infidelity or associated jealousy.

"I'm glad," said William, "that you do."

UPSTAIRS, Sophie and Amy sat on the floor of Amy's room, still in their clothes from the wedding, and stretched. Sophie was able to get her wrists past her heels. Amy could only grab her toes.

"Your legs are longer," Sophie said.

"How old were you?" Amy asked.

How old were you?

A lie foundered on her lips. She couldn't lie about this. But she had to. If she refused to answer, what would Amy say?

How vague could she make it? Should she say, *I'd just graduated from high school.*

No.

"I was a teenager." She couldn't make herself say, *Let me think...* That would be another lie, and Amy's perspective on integrity had undergone too much assault. The situation was impossible.

"My age?"

"Older."

Silence.

Amy sat up, and Sophie imagined for a moment that she could see a third eye blazing on her daughter's forehead.

I know things, Amy always said.

"He's my father, isn't he?" Amy said. "That man."

"William Ludlow is your father."

Amy gazed at her, eyes slightly narrowed. "I get it," she said. "I think I always knew."

Sophie didn't answer. *William, William, where are you at these moments?*

"He doesn't know, does he?" Amy asked.

Sophie was afraid to speak, to shake her head, to affirm Amy's knowledge in any way. Even to say, *Who?* She knew that Amy meant Patrick Wray.

"I don't want him to," Amy said. "Ever."

Sophie said the only thing she could. "Your father is William Ludlow."

Amy drew the soles of her feet together, assuming a yogini pose, stretching. "I knew there was something else you weren't telling me. This explains everything. Everything. You must have hated me."

"No. But I was terrified I would. How wrong I was." Sophie reached across and hugged Amy. She received nothing in response. "Giving birth to you is the best thing, the very best thing, I've ever done."

Amy said, "I don't buy that."

"Maybe some day you'll have a child," Sophie said. "Then you will." She released her.

Amy gazed at her. "I think it's why I'm different."

"I'm glad you're exactly who you are. I wouldn't change anything about you, except to protect you from pain—from life. And that's nobody's right."

"I'm contaminated, though. He's a sick person, and I have his blood in me."

"Rapists aren't born, they're made. At least, that's what I believe."

"I'm never going to have a boyfriend," Amy said. "I'm never getting married. I'm always going to be alone." It didn't sound like a worry but a promise.

"I never wanted to tell you, but I can't lie to you when you ask me outright. You know I can't."

Amy's dark stare was thoughtful. She seemed to be remembering something.

"I'm *glad* you were born," Sophie repeated. "I'm glad I know you, glad you're my daughter and that we're sitting together now." She took a breath, recognizing what she needed to say, even though she hadn't meant it when she'd said it the first time.

Amy, with her strange telepathic sense, seemed to know.

"You're saying it *was* worth it?" Adolescent skepticism.

"Yes." *A few minutes pain and humiliation so I could sit with you now, sure.* But it wasn't that simple. It wasn't a few minutes pain and humiliation. It was a wounding that changed a person forever. And not in a good way. Neutral, at best. Not good.

Had it made her a richer musician, increased her depth of experience, allowed her to see further into the collective mass of humanity?

Maybe.

For that, would she pay the price she'd paid?

She would pay almost anything to be a more effective musician.

Would Amy alone have been worth it? She loved Amy and would, she thought, die for her, but rape was no way to make a child. "Amy—it's as though the two things aren't related. I don't think of what happened like that. It didn't last long and wasn't the worst pain I've ever experienced, but it's horrible. You're miraculous, and precious to me. Whatever the link is, it's not…a price. It's like—it's love, Amy, and that's all I can call it. I love you. Your dad—*your dad, William Ludlow*—loves you. I love you no less because of the way you were conceived. That's all I can say."

And she wouldn't speak aloud what Amy's question had made clear to her. She'd been able to walk away from Amy. She could never have walked away from music. Music kept her alive and always had. It was who she was. The question was, *Could she be musician, mother and partner?*

She watched her daughter's face, hoping she'd said what was right, hoping she'd said enough. "It just doesn't matter," she repeated. "It makes no difference in who you are to me. None."

Amy lifted her eyes, and Sophie saw that she believed.

Believed because her mother hadn't lied to her.

Downstairs, the phone rang, and a moment later William appeared at Amy's door with the cordless.

"Tommy," he said.

CHAPTER FOURTEEN

"SHE ASKED ME. She asked me straight out."

"I know."

"She still—nothing's different, William. You're her father. You always have been. You always will be."

"I'm not bothered about it," he answered. "Really."

Sophie believed him. If William had insecurities—and didn't everyone?—he'd never shared them with her.

Amy, minutes after expressing her intention never to have a boyfriend, had agreed to go for an evening walk with Tommy. She'd taken both Tala and Sigurd with her, telling Sophie, "I think he's just interested now because he's finally realized who you are."

"More likely," Sophie said, "he saw you at the wedding, saw you as the beautiful and talented person you are."

Tommy had come to the cabin to get Amy, and as soon as they were gone, Sophie had told William what happened upstairs.

Now she asked, "So what did your mother have to say? Everything's all right, isn't it?"

"Everything's fine."

"She dislikes me, doesn't she?"

William considered this briefly. True, his mother seemed to strongly dislike Sophie, seeing her as a destructive force in his life and Amy's.

Receiving no answer, Sophie continued. "You know, say you and I were a normal couple who decided to get married," she said, trying to phrase it in a way that would leave no doubt whatsoever that they were *not* that hypothetical couple. "If you and I had marital problems, my parents would blame me, and your mother would also blame me."

William, who had removed vegetables from the refrigerator in preparation for dinner, frowned, then finally smiled, "Sounds good to me."

Sophie shook her head at him in rueful not-quite-amusement. "It's because my parents have always assumed that if I'm involved in any kind of trouble, I caused it. Your mother, in contrast, believes that you and your brother can do no wrong."

"You think differently?"

Sophie elbowed him. Choosing her words carefully, she said, "I think it could cause problems. If people get married, they both really need to leave home, and you never have."

William turned and looked at her as though truly astonished by this perspective. "Amy and I have lived alone since she was two years old."

"Don't be so literal. Your mother's still there for you every moment of every day. Say you marry someone—"

"Someone."

"—and that woman falls short of your expectations. Your mother's always ready to step in and do for you what your spouse can't or won't. She'll always be on hand if your wife doesn't cook the food you like or bring in enough income or stay at home enough or fill in the blank."

Again, an expression of amusement played around his lips.

"It's true!" said Sophie. "You know it is."

He didn't respond, just watched her with a half smile.

"What?" she demanded.

"If you wanted to marry me, I don't think you'd see my mother as an obstacle."

Sophie said, "You don't really care if we get married."

He didn't answer.

"Do you?" she asked. When he still kept silent, she said, "I mean, you were engaged to Crystal, but you haven't asked *me* to marry you."

"Do you want me to?"

"Is that what you asked her?"

"Pretty much." He stretched lazily.

"So you really didn't love her, either."

"There are suddenly a lot of assumptions flying around. Do you want to marry me?"

The thought of marrying anyone terrified her as much as it ever had. But what bothered her more was that William seemed ambivalent. His engagement to Crystal seemed unimportant to him now, and it seemed as though he could take or leave a marriage to Sophie. He was as much an enigma as he'd been fifteen years earlier.

"I assume you're simply seeking information, not proposing marriage." Sophie hurried on before he could deny it. "You said earlier today," she told him patiently, "that you wanted to get married. Or did I mistake you?"

"Not completely. I said something like that. I'll be honest, Sophie. I've never been a huge fan of marriage, even fifteen years ago when I thought the best thing would be to marry you."

"You feel that way because of your parents."

"Let's say their relationship has always made it hard for me to believe that people can live in fidelity and happiness."

Sophie had never known him to say anything like that before. She'd never known he felt that way, and her spirits sagged. Somehow, if at least one of them really believed in marriage, even believed in something *resembling* marriage, there was a chance, a chance for them together.

But William was as much of a cynic as she was. He certainly had more reason than she did to take that position.

"So—you don't want to get married," she said. "I don't especially, either. Days like today make me *want* to believe in marriage. But are you sure you're not just being cynical about marriage," she said, "because you know how I am?"

"No, I'm not at all sure, Sophie." He had begun cutting vegetables, but set down the knife. "Fifteen years ago, I asked you to marry me, and you said yes, and I agreed to raise another man's child as my own. At the eleventh hour—or later—you changed your mind and left. I understand *why* you left, but it hasn't made me a romantic. I'm a father. I like being a father. But I sacrificed a lot. It's been worth it. I wouldn't change my decision. But planning to marry Crystal—who makes choices and knows why she makes them and sticks to them—and marrying you, who always move steadfastly in pursuit of *your* star, are two very different propositions. You couldn't keep a promise to me for more than seven months."

"I was eighteen years old!"

"Point well taken. But tell me how you're different from that eighteen-year-old."

"I've had therapy," Sophie spat. "I recommend it."

He laughed but didn't seem amused.

"Look," she told him, "I haven't involved myself with you again just because of Amy. But if you're saying you're not that interested—"

He put down the knife, spun from the counter and placed his hands on her shoulders. His eyes delved into hers. "I'm interested," he said, "and not just because you're Amy's mother. So we're even."

They gazed at each other for what felt like minutes. Then Sophie looked away. "Okay."

How had they gotten onto this topic? Oh. She'd asked him about his mother. And William's response was perfectly valid. His mother *was* a problem, but she was also an easy, ready-made reason not to marry William Ludlow. Another excuse. *And if I wanted to marry him, I could make his mother like me. I've just never tried very hard.*

Granted, Moira Ludlow would always be a nightmare of a mother-in-law, but she wasn't the reason Sophie didn't want to marry William, the reason that every five minutes or so she felt like fleeing their relationship. What that reason was, she couldn't say.

I wish I could be like Jodie was today, bright-eyed and hopeful, certain of a lasting marriage. She had slept with William every night since she'd seen Patrick Wray at the movies. It was more than comfort from fear or sadness or rage. Much more. But if William asked her to marry him today, what would she say?

"Sophie?"

He was still watching her.

"Yes."

She had the feeling that there was something he wanted to tell her, something he was holding back. But instead of speaking, he kissed her lips, and in the look of his eyes she felt herself wedded beyond one lifetime.

It wasn't just because of what they shared. She had a hard time disbelieving the perfection of chemistry that sang between them. He had kissed her, and her legs seemed to shiver and shake, unsteady. This, too, seemed what lifetimes must be made of.

She said, "Have you had many girlfriends before Crystal?"

"Yes. Well, it depends on what you call many. But I'm not proud of failing to make a relationship work."

"Most people who really want to," Sophie said, "do."

He nodded without argument.

"Why did you tell Amy I was dead?"

"You didn't make it easy, Sophie. I couldn't claim I didn't know who her mother was. It's water under the bridge now, anyway, isn't it?"

"Except that Amy's pretty bitter about the lies both of us have told her. She seems accepting of all of it, but I can't help thinking that the other shoe is waiting to drop."

"Don't worry about it," William said. "Nothing's happened with her yet that I couldn't handle."

The statement shut her out, and she understood something she hadn't before. William was Amy's guardian. And he wasn't necessarily ready to share that responsibility—and privilege—with Sophie.

Sophie said, "I'm back in her life to stay. You realize that, don't you?"

He just looked at her and didn't bother answering at all. Skepticism needed no words.

ON THE MORNING of the Fourth of July, as Sophie was helping her mother cut James's nails, the phone rang.

James gave more dramatic cries of terror over his nails. Ignoring the tantrum, Sophie held his paw firmly and snipped a dewclaw carefully, erring on the side of too long rather than the reverse, which could make him even more resistant to the procedure. She popped a treat in his mouth and said, "Good boy. Look how brave you are." He gave her hysterical kisses until it became clear she was going to cut more nails.

"Sophie, it's for you."

The phone.

Sophie released James, saying, "We're not done, friend."

She took the phone from her mother.

"Sophie, it's Fiona."

"Hi." Why was the manager of the now nonexistent Wayfairers calling her? "What's wrong?"

"Nothing. Nothing. Something's right. Want to tour with your favorite folk legend next year?"

Sophie couldn't believe her ears. "Peter Haight?"

"Right. What do you think? Are you up to it?"

"With no band?"

"He said that you solo, with acoustic, fiddle, guitar or harmonica, are more interesting to him than you with the Wayfairers. He's talking about you two getting together, seeing how it goes. He wants to make a CD with you, then have the two of you tour together."

Amy. Amy was in high school. *I'll be on the road all the time.*

Peter Haight had been her favorite folk musician for ten years. He wrote original songs, upbeat, funny, warm. Musically complete, emotionally sound.

"Does he know about my hearing loss?"

"He said if it's not a problem, it's not a problem."

Sophie knew she could work with her hearing loss. With a sensitive singing partner, it could work.

She remembered moments singing with William, playing with him, at the wedding on Saturday. But she was the only one who'd made music her life. He'd made dogs his.

And Amy. He's made Amy his life.

"I need to sleep on it," Sophie said. She always said that, and Fiona knew it.

"Okay." Fiona laughed. "You sound like your old self when you say that."

"I'll call you sometime tomorrow," said Sophie, "or you can phone me tomorrow night."

"Why don't I let Peter call you? He's actually in Colorado and is hoping to get together and play with you."

Had William been right about her on Saturday? Was he right about her in general? Would it take no more than an offer like this for her to turn her back on him and Amy? "Where is he?"

"In a place called Paonia, north of where you are. He's apparently staying in a yurt and writing songs. Could you go up there?"

Slow down! Please slow down!

Paonia was just hours away. Opportunity was knocking, and she couldn't answer. For the first time in her recollection, she truly couldn't walk through the open doorways in her career. Because she'd given herself to her daughter. She'd made that promise, publicly and privately.

She could already see William's expression, his look as she explained to him and Amy that she was going on tour with Peter Haight. More eloquent and incisive than *I told you so.*

There would be little bitterness in that look, little disappointment. A person had to be hopeful, had to believe in love and fidelity and happily-ever-after, to suffer regret when those things proved false. Neither William nor Amy really believed—because of the choices she, Sophie, had made long ago.

"I— Fiona, I said I'd sleep on it."

If I turn this down because of Amy, let alone because of William, I will regret it—and possibly resent it—for the rest of my life.

"Same old Sophie." Fiona laughed again. "Give her what she's always wanted, and she still says, 'I need to sleep on it.'"

"You probably wished I'd slept on it before being too 'blunt' to band members."

"Touché. No. Sophie, you're a professional, and now is your chance to work with someone as professional as you are, someone talented. I truly feel this is a partnership that can help *both of you* or I wouldn't be in favor of it."

It can't happen.

She might as well say so now.

She had promised Amy. As for having Amy accompany her… Sophie could romanticize the situation all she liked, she could remember that she'd made the suggestion herself, but it would be wrong in too many ways to take Amy with her on tour—provided William even consented.

So she had to choose between her daughter and the kind of chance she'd worked toward her whole career.

"It's so perfect. He wants a fiddler, wants to do a Celtic folk CD. Lots of traditional. You're right up his alley."

Please stop talking. Please stop describing this perfect thing that I feel so unable to turn down and just as unable to accept.

What if she told Amy she'd be back often—once a month or so? What if she told Peter Haight she could do a briefer tour? Three months, say? And really, there'd been no mention of precisely what the tour would entail. United States, Canada, international?

As she hung up the phone, her mother was telling her dog, "James, please hold still. I'm not that strong."

Miraculously, James seemed to calm down.

"That's one I've never seen," Sophie said.

"Well, he understands me." But Sophie was already thinking about something else.

This is why I knew I couldn't marry William. This is

why I didn't stay with him and help him raise Amy. I knew, I knew that when the chance presented itself I wouldn't be able to make the unselfish choice.

I would choose selfishness instead.

Creativity was always a good choice, selfish or not, which was a discussion she didn't need to have with herself. She felt bad enough.

Forty-eight hours before, she'd been sure she could be content to train dogs, play at the occasional wedding or party with William or Amy, maybe work with hearing dogs.

Now, she *knew,* knew again, that wasn't what she'd been made for. She'd been made to care first for her music, and there was no way a fourteen-year-old girl could understand that. No reason she should be expected to.

"Is everything all right?"

Sophie didn't realize how long she'd been silent. She sighed. Why not tell her mother? This woman who had adopted her as an infant had, time and again, proven to be an excellent and nonjudgmental listener. Sitting down at the kitchen table as her mother managed to snip the Schipperke's toenails, Sophie unveiled her problem, the proposition that had been laid before her.

"I'm young. This is when I should be performing."

"Sophie, you'll be performing your whole life. I don't say that to persuade you that you should be here for Amy now. I don't know what you should do about playing with Peter Haight. I just mean that you care about people, you care about audiences. You're a warm person who'll always move people's hearts. Life is long."

"I'm sure you're right."

Amanda lifted her head. "You don't sound sure. I think you need to consider how you'll feel with each outcome. But I do have to say that your daughter will only be fourteen once. The time to be with her is perhaps more of a once-in-a-lifetime chance than the one your career is offering."

Sophie nodded. "I know. There's no outcome to make me feel good. I can't go. I know I can't. But I'm angry that this should happen now. That I should've come back here, made the choices I've made, when I could be singing onstage with Peter Haight." She sagged in her seat. "I don't mean that. I'd rather know Amy than anything." She sighed. "William's expecting me to pick up and walk away as soon as I feel like it."

Her mother looked at her, looked hard. "Is that what's keeping you from accepting?"

"What? William? No." But there was no doubt that his reaction would be difficult to stand.

"Is it that you've promised Amy?" her mother clarified.

"Oh. No. No." *Amy needs me.* That was the truth of it. *And I need her.*

Knowing Amy was helping Sophie heal the wound that had formed when she'd turned away from her newborn daughter.

That knowledge made it a bit easier to contemplate the answer she knew she had to give Fiona the next day.

"Thanks, Mom," she said. "You asked the right question. I want to be with Amy. That's why I'm not accepting."

"Not William?"

Another relevant question.

Could she want to be with William, could she feel that same loyalty to him, feel that he needed her?

He so clearly *didn't* need her or anyone, which was undoubtedly one of the things she found appealing about him.

"William's an adult. He doesn't need me."

"I think you may need him," her mother said. "But maybe I'm wrong. You've always been so self-reliant."

"Well, William is not a good man to need."

Her mother gave her a look of surprise but didn't question the statement.

Still feeling sick inside over the chance that had presented itself now, when it was impossible to accept, Sophie collected Loki, Cinders and Spinner from the yard and headed to the place she was beginning to call home—with some encouragement from both William and Amy.

In fact, Saturday night, possibly to take some of the sting out of what he'd said after the wedding, William had told her, *You pretty much live here. I hope you feel like this is home.*

It hadn't persuaded her to move more of her belongings to his house, however, except a few T-shirts and pairs of shorts.

But she liked the cabin and was touched that William and Amy wanted her there with them. William had designed the house. It was small, just a thousand square feet, yet certainly big enough for the three of them. It was easy to imagine winter evenings around the woodstove, snow falling outside.

And she liked William's world, liked training dogs.

I'm happy here, she thought as she turned down the driveway. *And I'll continue to be happy.*

It needn't feel like a prison, and it needn't feel as if she was making the wrong choice by giving up something that would've been a splendid reward for her hard work.

She wouldn't even tell William. She couldn't bear to say what she was turning down, and if he even looked at her wrong, gave her even the slightest expression of *knowing* that she'd be unable to resist Peter Haight's offer, she would be paralyzed with anger. Because she could turn it down, and that was exactly what she was doing.

She found William in the training barn, and he invited her to work one of the protection-dogs-in-training on obedience.

Sophie agreed. The dog was a handsome European German shepherd named Klaus. He was a powerful dog, and it took her some time to get his attention.

"He's young," William said. He was working with an Akita-mastiff cross, a dog whose aggression was a problem for his owners. "Just use your usual patience."

For Sophie, that involved stopping as soon as Klaus pulled on the leash and waiting for him to look at her and ask what was going on. Then she gave him the heel command in Czechoslavakian, which was the language the dog knew. William had a large painted sign on one wall, listing basic commands in English, German and Czechoslavakian.

Even working with the dog, her whole concentration on what she was doing, she felt an emptiness and wondered if she was turning against her values, turning against what she really wanted, who she hoped to be.

After she'd taken the dog through basic obedience exercises and brought him to William and Brett, who had just arrived to act as agitator, she headed into the cabin. Amy didn't seem to be around, and she hadn't asked William where she was.

Sophie took the guitar she played less frequently than her violin and went up to the open space in the loft. She'd taken a pen and pad of paper with her and started finger picking. The words flowed easily. In song, she could express the pull between her heart, which owed itself to Amy and loved Amy, and her soul, her art, which claimed her.

As she wrote and picked out the melody, she realized again that the richness of experience in being a mother and knowing her daughter inspired her creatively. It was more fertile than her life as a single and unencumbered artist.

I have to make both things work. I will always write songs and sing and play them. But I'm a mother, and I'm bound to my daughter now.

And William?

Sophie didn't know the answer.

Where was Amy, anyway?

When she'd played the new song through once more, she stood and walked to Amy's room, knocking at the door again, peering in.

Amy's bed was unmade, her journal lying on top of the sheets, a pair of clogs strewn across the floor. There was a dog crate at the foot of her bed, a wire Life Stages crate, in which Tala slept at night.

Sophie returned downstairs. She checked the time, knew William and Brett would be done practicing bite work, and went into the training barn. Brett was peeling out of a bite suit. The dog had been put away.

"Where's Amy?"

William smiled at her. "Climbing Mount Sneffels. With Tommy."

Sophie had never climbed the mountain, which was over fourteen thousand feet, during any of her summers in Ouray. She knew that the trailhead was at the very top of the Camp Bird Road. "Did you drive them to the trailhead?"

"Actually, yes."

"How will they get down? They'll be too tired to walk back here after climbing the mountain." She wasn't sure how far it was to the trailhead—several miles, at least.

"That was their decision. They got an early start." He glanced at the clock. "I suppose we could drive up and look for them."

Sophie nodded vigorously.

He drove the old Land Cruiser. They took only Spinner and Tenor, because with any of the bigger dogs along, Amy and Tommy wouldn't fit in the back. It was nearly impossible to converse, would have been impossible even if she'd had two perfect ears instead of one.

Yet Sophie shouted over the engine and the rattling and the sound of tires on gravel, all the static that prevented her from understanding speech. "Isn't it dangerous? Don't people die up there?"

"People…highways, too. Amy knows…look out for."

"How do they die?"

"About one…year…talus…boulder."

It was no kind of answer.

"Are there other people up there if they get into trouble?"

"This…year? On the Fourth of July?…a million."

Sophie had almost forgotten it was the Fourth of July, which, in Ouray, was hard to do. She'd had to drive around the parade that morning. Downtown, the firemen would be trying to knock each other over with jets of water from their hoses. That night, tourists and people from all over the county and from neighboring Montrose County to the north would line the streets for the fireworks, which would be set off from Ouray's Ampitheater Campground.

The road was crowded, the air thick with dust, parking areas at the trailheads packed, campgrounds full.

William squeezed in beside a Toyota truck near the trailhead. No sign of Amy and Tommy. "Want to walk up a ways?"

She'd worn her hiking boots. "Sure."

They climbed out, and William tossed her a plastic water bottle from behind his seat and took another himself. They let the dogs out, snapping leads on them.

The bottom was an easy trail, gentle and pleasant. She and William and the dogs had to move off it several times within the first ten minutes, however, to make way for hikers coming down.

Sophie saw William nod to the hikers, heard some of them speak but not what they said. His face wore a puzzled expression.

"What is it?"

"Amy and Tommy were nearly the first people up here this morning. They were at the trailhead at six-thirty."

And yet she and William had passed people who'd already been to the top.

"If either of them had been hurt," William said, "we would know. Let's go see the register at the trailhead."

He and Sophie retraced their steps and read the ledger. Amy had signed it for both of them. If they'd come down, they hadn't signed out.

William chewed his lip, squinted up the trail through his sunglasses, then eyed the surrounding mountains.

"Is there any chance—" Sophie felt so stupid saying it "—that they never went up?" She didn't know why she suggested it. Was she denying the possibility that her daughter had come to harm on Mount Sneffels?

No. It was what Amy talked about so much, that kind of *knowing*. She *didn't* know. But she wondered.

William studied her thoughtfully.

"Are there rangers?" Sophie wondered. "Anyone we could ask if there's been an accident?"

"If anything like that had happened, I would've heard the rescue vehicles, the helicopter, whatever. I always do."

"Could they just be taking their time? Tommy's from sea level, after all."

"True. But I'm thinking about your question."

The other question. Had they actually climbed the mountain?

"Where else would they have gone, though?" Sophie asked. "They couldn't go anywhere but back down the Camp Bird Road, could they? Or up another hiking trail?"

William's expression grew more thoughtful—with hints of displeasure.

"What is it?" she asked.

He shook his head. "Something that defies belief. I left them at six-thirty. That's pretty early for any of their friends, I imagine."

"So what do you think they did?"

"I think, as you said, they're taking their time climbing Mount Sneffels. Want to resume our walk? Or we could head over to the stream, give the dogs a drink."

"Let's do that. I wish I'd brought binoculars," answered Sophie.

For the next hour, they watched the dogs run back and forth in the trickle of water coming down the bowl of green to the south of Mount Sneffels, above Yankee Boy Basin. Marmots poked their heads out of dens and stood up on their back legs to whistle at one another. Spinner kept charging after them, then coming back and spinning around in front of Sophie, as though the marmots' vocalizations were a sound she needed to be told about.

They got dried fruit from William's car. More hikers continued coming down the trail from Mount Sneffels.

Others were going up, planning to watch any fireworks they could see from the mountaintop, a wishful concept, Sophie thought.

"Is there any chance we passed them on the road? Maybe they hitchhiked down with someone else. We passed some other vehicles. They might not have noticed you driving by."

"I was keeping an eye out, but I suppose that's possible."

They arrived back at the cabin at five-thirty. Sophie opened the door and almost collapsed with relief. Amy stood at the kitchen counter with Tommy. They looked as if they'd just gotten home. Their packs lay on the floor in the living room. "Hi," Amy said. "Where were you guys?"

The question was perfectly natural.

"Searching for you," William answered. "We must have passed you going down. Did you get a ride?"

Amy nodded. "With some friends, actually. I hope you're not mad they were kids. We were glad they happened along."

Sophie was sure, suddenly positive, that Amy was lying. No. No, it must be her imagination. After all, what could Amy have done?

"Are you exhausted?" Sophie asked.

Amy shook her head. "I've climbed it before."

"How about the Californian?" William asked with a smile.

"I've got a kink or two." Tommy nudged Amy. "Walk me home?"

"Sure."

William picked up the packs to move them out of the way. He straightened up. "Didn't you drink any water?"

A moment's silence.

"Not enough," Tommy said quickly.

It grew strangely quiet as he collected his pack, and he and Amy left the cabin to walk down the road.

"Do you think they're lying?" said Sophie.

"Yes."

"Does she often lie to you?"

"No."

Sophie frowned. "But where would they have gone?"

"I bet they went four-wheeling over Imogene Pass. They probably walked back down to the junction of Camp Bird and the Imogene Pass road and met their friends."

"You think so?"

William opened Amy's pack and looked inside. "She didn't climb Mount Sneffels on less than a quart of water, which is all she drank."

"I'm surprised that's even enough to go four-wheeling." Sophie recalled the secret she was keeping from William—and from Amy. The secret she'd *decided* to keep. She now felt stupid for thinking she even had a choice in the matter. Clearly Amy needed both her parents. "What do we do?"

"Nothing."

Sophie considered this.

"It will be more painful for her. Besides, I trust her in general. I want her to believe that I trust her, not that I doubt her."

Because once in the past, Amy had been doubted, once she'd been threatened and told to keep the truth to herself.

"This is what I meant," Sophie said, "about the other shoe dropping. You know why she did this, don't you?"

"I don't believe for a minute that she lied to me today because I lied to her for fourteen years. Stick to music, Sophie."

"What's that supposed to mean?"

"You don't have to psychoanalyze her. This is normal teenage stuff. Crystal said girls are more deceitful than boys."

"The Company Woman would know about that," Sophie muttered. But she didn't want to snipe at William, and she liked Crystal. "Amy likes him a lot, I think." Because after he'd called her again, she seemed to have forgotten any thought of never wanting a boyfriend.

The phone rang ten minutes later, and William answered it. "You're walking?" He raised his eyebrows at Sophie. "When are you going to be home?" A longer pause. "How about twenty minutes after the fireworks end?" Another pause. "Okay. Why don't you come home now instead?" More. "Then we'll see you when the fireworks end."

"Amy?" Sophie asked as he hung up.

"She wanted to go to a party after the fireworks."

"You probably wish you had back the daughter she was before I showed up."

"I think it's more a matter of before Tommy Travis showed up." His hands rested on her waist, one at each side.

Then he hugged her, and the embrace brought a lump to her throat. He was her friend, her best friend, in some ways her only friend.

He knew her well enough to understand her strengths, her weaknesses and exactly what drove her.

AM I IN LOVE WITH HIM?

She was. He had proven to her long ago that he was good inside. She still believed that, and she knew, largely from knowing William, that goodness came both from inclination and from strength.

Nor did he compare to other lovers.

With other lovers, a breaking point always came. Sometimes, during lovemaking, they lost focus on her, and lust took over. Suddenly she wasn't there, except as breasts, a face, and particularly as a pair of open legs, as what lay between. It did not excite her, this change in men. What excited her was presence, a man being present, as William always was, never exploiting her.

They made love and then lay with their heads on the pillows, looking into each other's eyes.

"I love you," she said.

"And you know I love you, Sophie."

She didn't know. He seemed to make decisions from another point in himself rather than from love or being in love. He was in bed with her now, she suspected, because she was Amy's natural mother and therefore the person he believed he should be intimate with.

But he wasn't promised to her, and he felt that the only promise she could keep was to her music.

She said, "I think I'm going up to Paonia sometime soon. Fiona called. I just—I'm just going to meet with another musician. As a courtesy." *Don't do it, Sophie. Don't pretend to yourself for even one moment that it's possible for you to work with Peter Haight. You're choosing Amy, remember?*

William seemed curious. "A potential band member?"

"No. I'm not doing that again. Just somebody I might—I don't know—record with. Locally. I suppose. I just want to look into it." It felt like a lie and she supposed it was. But her confusion eclipsed guilt.

He stroked her cheek with his hand.

Sophie kissed his hand, believing in the tenderness of his touch, believing it was really love, deep love, maybe a love that didn't depend on marriage or happily-ever-after, didn't need those things.

She couldn't—and *wouldn't*—go on tour with Peter Haight.

But maybe, if she did decide to go, William wouldn't be threatened by it, by any of it. He'd never wanted her to give up her career. Nor had he ever agreed that her career and being his wife and Amy's mother had to be mutually exclusive.

Were they?

Would it make a difference if she really could do it all? Or would she still see condemnation of her selfishness in William's eyes?

He knew her and he understood her, and more than anyone else, he'd felt the impact of her choices, of her ability to love her art more than she loved other people.

CHAPTER FIFTEEN

AMY WISHED there was someone she could talk to about the fact that her dad was not her biological father, that her biological father was a rapist. She knew she could talk to Sophie about it again, but she had seen Sophie overcome with shaking and trembling on the subject of rape more than once, had seen her confront the man Amy now knew to be her biological father.

So he's a jerk. That doesn't mean that, I, by nature of my genes, am a bad person like he is.

She considered telling Tommy the truth, but she found herself too ashamed. Besides, it was private, Sophie's private business and her own, as well.

The whole world seemed to have changed since she'd found out about Patrick Wray. That was his name, Sophie had told her. He was intelligent and a good musician, a music teacher.

But he raped my mom.

It was a Tuesday afternoon, and Tommy hadn't called, so Amy walked out to the training barn. Her father was working with a Rottweiler from Germany, one he'd trained and sold that was now back to have his training refreshed.

Sophie watched the Rottie climb over a tall stepladder with a dumbbell in his mouth.

Her dad rewarded him with tug-of-war play and

smiled at Amy as he heeled the dog back to a kennel. Amy trailed behind him.

"Everything okay?" he asked.

"Except that I'm the offspring of a disgusting person."

William glanced at her as he secured the kennel. Then he leaned against the nearby wall of the barn.

Amy could tell he was thinking. Trying to think of a way to make it all right. It couldn't be.

"Sometimes my father seems pretty disgusting to me, too," he said at last. *Don't ask me to explain.* Before she could, he said, "The fact is, I'm your father. Legally and in every way that matters now." William leveled his gaze on her. "I will protect you no matter what."

Suddenly, nothing between them was different from what it had been before. He *was* her father, the person who watched out for her, who had quit his job because her truth had been shot down. In some fundamental way, he stood between her and any harm from her strange beginnings.

"Okay," she said. "What's the problem with Grandpa? Why did you say that about him?"

He debated the wisdom of giving even a partial truth. But maybe it would help Amy accept herself as he had to accept himself. "He's unfaithful to Grandma. It's worse than that. I'll tell you someday."

The face of the girl who knew things looked young and shocked. "That's awful."

"You're right." He reached for her and hugged her, and it was the same as ever.

Except that— "I wish I had your genes instead," she said.

"But then you wouldn't be yourself," he replied. "And I wouldn't change a thing about you, Amy

Ludlow. I like being the father of the highly unusual person you are."

SOPHIE HAD BEEN INTRODUCED to Peter Haight before, but it had been a brief meeting. For this one, he'd wanted her to bring all her instruments. He'd called her on her cell phone on the morning of the sixth, and they'd made plans for her to drive to Paonia the following day. She had told neither William nor Amy the name of the musician she was meeting. She brought Loki and Cinders with her but not Spinner, and that seemed significant to her.

Almost as though she was trying to put her life back the way it had been before Amy had spoken to her on Main Street.

But I don't want that, she told herself again as she drove north on that Thursday morning.

Because she and William hadn't spent a night apart for weeks. She didn't mind sleeping alone, but she craved him, as though he was a substance to which she'd become addicted.

And now she couldn't imagine not talking with her daughter in the morning, not practicing Bharata Natya together.

Even attempting to imagine life without Amy filled her with guilt.

For years, men had told her that her inability to give herself to relationships was a result not of belonging so thoroughly to her music but simply of fear. Fear of imprisonment. Fear of losing her freedom.

Her present circumstance seemed to prove them wrong.

William certainly wasn't imprisoning her. On the contrary, he seemed almost indifferent to whether she stayed or left. Which was why she was so moved when he revealed some trace of deep feeling for her. Like that morning, the look in his eyes when he'd told her to drive carefully.

With him, she didn't fear being consumed by the relationship. Sometimes, she was more afraid that he would become distant from her, that he was ambivalent about her presence in his life.

Yet he was her best friend, and she respected him.

The drive to Paonia took two hours, and she spent another hour looking for the property where Peter Haight was living in a yurt.

It was a hot day, and when she saw the yurt, she discovered that it was adjacent to a small adobe house. Peter Haight stepped out of the yurt, tall and slightly wild-haired. He waved.

She turned off the engine, climbed out, and said, "Do you like dogs? I brought mine. I can tie them so they'll lie under the truck."

"No, they can come in the studio with us." He indicated the adobe building.

On the phone, she'd told him frankly that she doubted she could do the tour with him, that obligations to her family were too great.

He helped carry her instruments inside. Rather than embarking on any discussion of plans, he got her some water and water for her dogs, and they took out their instruments and started playing together.

Immediately, Sophie knew that they'd hit on something unique, something marketable.

I have to do this. I have to do this tour.

But if she did, Amy would never trust her again.

And William …

Fifteen years had passed, and Sophie still remembered her emotions when he'd accused her of abandoning Amy, when he'd told her she was selfish. Yes, he'd been hurt and angry and very nasty. Cruel.

Yes, William was complicated. She couldn't help noticing how much dog training carried over into his personal life. He was as utterly consistent with people as he was with dogs.

Except on those rare instances when the strong emotions came through.

She didn't want to let Amy down. She didn't want to hurt her daughter in any way. Her commitment to Amy seemed to have infused her with a certain simple decency that she'd lacked before.

So she played all day with Peter Haight, they worked on two songs together, a new one of hers and a collaboration, and finally she explained to him that she'd recently been reunited with the daughter she'd relinquished at birth and that she could not possibly go on tour with him.

He didn't try to dissuade her from her choice but said he was disappointed, that he truly wanted to do a CD with her, along with a tour. The CD she could do. But she couldn't leave Amy to go on tour. They both admitted, however, that a tour would be the best promotion for the CD.

It was 10:00 p.m. when she drove into Ouray.

She had called William from the road to tell him when she'd be home. He'd mentioned that Amy had walked down to the movie theater with Tommy.

Sophie drove slowly, keeping an eye out for tourists who thought nothing of spontaneously jay-walking across Main Street. At the south end of town, the movie seemed to have just let out, and she saw Amy and Tommy crossing the street. She tried to get their attention, but they didn't see her. Tommy led Amy around to the passenger side of a red Jeep.

The full impact of this did not hit Sophie for another block.

Amy was riding in Tommy's car with him.

Sophie no longer particularly feared for Amy. Tommy seemed like any other adolescent with a girlfriend. But Amy had lied. She had apparently lied to William on the Fourth of July.

She had definitely lied tonight.

As she carried her violin and guitar into the house, the dogs following, William came in through the side door from the training barn and the kennels. She told him what she'd just seen. "I'm not going to pretend I didn't see that, William."

"No," he agreed. "I can't pretend that."

Sophie noticed that he had turned her "I" to his "I." Not "we." Was it her imagination? She dismissed it. "What should we do? Do we ground her? Have you ever grounded her?"

"No."

"Now, will you admit that there's a correlation between her lying and our lying?"

"No. I think she probably lied because she wanted to ride in his car. Or because he wanted her to ride in his car."

"Haven't other boys wanted her to ride in their cars? She's very pretty."

"The school's small here, Sophie. She's known most of the guys for years. She says she doesn't want to date them because it would be like dating a brother or something. So this guy shows up from California, and he likes her. It's more interesting."

Sophie frowned. "So what do we do? How do we keep her from doing it again? Lying, I mean."

"Natural consequences. She lies when she's with Tommy, so she can't go out with Tommy. They can come here."

"She'll just tell us she's going out with friends, then

go and meet him, instead." She watched William's face for a moment before remarking, "Dogs don't lie, do they?"

His head snapped up, his gaze fiery on hers. "I don't treat my daughter like she's a dog."

My daughter.

Sophie opened her mouth to say, *She's my daughter, too.* But she almost felt she didn't have the right.

It was half an hour before they heard Amy's and Tommy's voices outside. They couldn't make out what the two were saying to each other, but when Amy stepped into the cabin, she was alone.

Sophie sank down on the couch, her hands clasped together, fingers knit. She'd suggested William take the lead in this conversation.

Amy shut the door. "What's the matter with you guys?"

William studied her for a moment. "We're upset because your mom just drove home through Ouray and saw you getting into Tommy's Jeep."

Amy flushed, then moved into the kitchen, as though to create space between herself and her parents. She said nothing, just leaned against the counter, then turned and took down a glass from the cabinet, opened the refrigerator and grabbed the milk.

"Could you please explain?" William asked.

"Well, actually, we did walk to the movie together. But he forgot his money, so he like *ran* home to get it, and he drove back to the theater."

Sophie had to hand it to her. If it was a lie—and how could they really know?—it was credible.

"How long was he gone?"

She shrugged. "Twenty minutes, half an hour. We just missed the previews."

"And then he drove you back here?"

"Just to his house. We walked from there."

Sophie and William looked at each other. William said, "Okay. But nothing's changed. We don't want you riding in his car. If that kind of thing happens again, call home. Agreed?"

"Sure." Amy seemed vaguely disgusted—as though she had no respect for him or Sophie or their rules.

"Do you think that's unfair?" Sophie asked.

"At some point, I'll be old enough to drive myself. Will you let me get into the cars of other sixteen-year-olds who are driving? Or will you expect their parents to let them ride with me instead?"

"Who says you'll be getting a license at sixteen?" asked William, who seemed to have picked up on her tone and was trumping it.

"Oh, great." Amy rolled her eyes. "Whatever. I'm going to bed."

When she'd climbed up to her bedroom, William and Sophie looked at each other again.

"Why is she lying?" Sophie repeated.

"She wants to ride in his car with him, and she knows I won't let her." Same answer from William. "It's pretty obvious."

"But still." Sophie paused. "I suppose she realizes she can't persuade us to change our minds, so she thought she'd do it anyway." *Us. We.* She wanted to hear William say it even once.

William made a quiet sound like a laugh. "I'm sure you're right."

"What do you mean?"

He shrugged. "I don't give in to her often."

"You do sometimes?"

"Of course."

"This situation with Tommy and his car is going to keep happening," Sophie told him.

He shook his head.

"Why?" she asked.

"I told you. The next time she wants to go out with him, I'll tell her she can't."

Sophie spoke in a low voice. "You don't consider me a partner, do you, in raising her?"

He was opening his violin case, removing a bow. He didn't look up, but he did go still.

Finally, Sophie said, "I suppose it's only to be expected, after fourteen years. But I'm your lover and her mother. When do I get a say in her life?"

He said softly, "Now." But he still didn't look at her as he lifted the violin.

SHE WAS PLAYING her violin up in the loft the following day when William came in.

She finished the song and glanced at him.

"That's nice," he said. "Did you write it?"

Her mouth would not keep its truth. "Peter Haight and I wrote it yesterday."

William didn't blink. "You were playing music with Peter Haight yesterday? That's who you went to Paonia to see?"

She nodded. "Fiona called and said he wanted to get together with me. He had an idea about a tour, but obviously I can't do that."

William studied her. "So why did you go up there?"

"Are you kidding?"

He shrugged, shaking his head. "Okay. Silly question." His eyes rested on her violin.

"What?" she said.

"Nothing."

"Why don't you just say it?" she demanded. "Just get it over with. I know what you're thinking."

"How could you?"

She looked at him and saw in the depth of his brown eyes a maturity and wisdom she was unaccustomed to finding in men. It made her want to be more thoughtful. It also made her unsure. "I'm sorry. I assumed that you were thinking this is an opportunity I can't resist, and I'll pack up and go."

He shook his head again.

"Then why don't you *tell* me what you're thinking."

"I'm thinking that..." He paused, gathering his thoughts. "That it's a pity you've never believed you could do both."

"I can't talk about this," she said, suddenly close to tears. "You have no idea. You have no idea how exhausting it is to tour, to have a career in full swing. There's no space for another person. There's no room for love."

"Oh, get real, Sophie. Other musicians do it."

"It's a seedy life! It's no life for Amy. And you train—" She stopped, realizing that she shouldn't assume partnership with him, not really. "It's not good for Amy."

William looked at her for some time. "You should do what you want with your life," he said. "You want to be a mother to Amy but not as much as you want to be playing and writing music. If you need to go do this, I'll help you explain it to Amy. I'll even defend your choice."

Sophie stood up, setting her violin in its case. She stood before him and exclaimed, "Don't *ever* say that again, William Ludlow. I gave her *life.* There is a bond between us that is unbreakable, and she is the one thing in my life that is more important than playing and writing music. But what I do is who I am. Don't ever say I abandoned her. I have never forgotten you said that, and I never want to hear it again. I abandoned *you.*"

He ran his tongue along his teeth. "I'm sorry for saying that. I was nineteen and in love with you."

His honest words made her impotent, made her outburst petty.

"You just want to keep raising her alone, don't you?" Sophie said. "You don't want my input."

He didn't answer immediately. When he did, his tone was measured and aloof. "First, I haven't raised her alone. My mother's helped. Sometimes my father helped. Other people have helped. Girlfriends—not just Crystal. Second—sure, I'm happy to have your input."

"But not with me as an equal."

He closed his eyes as though asking for patience.

"Where is she now, by the way?" Sophie asked.

"She's in the training barn taking Tala over jumps." He waited before speaking again. "In some ways, I think pursuing your career is the best example anyone could give her. Bypassing the opportunity of a lifetime in order to take care of her might send the wrong message. My mother's remained married to my father all these years, despite his absence and infidelities. I'm not sure either is a good example."

"It *is* a good example. What I'm doing, anyhow. Leaving before was not. I left because I'd been raped, because I wasn't sure I could love her. But now I know I can. I am a mother, and that *has* to come before my career. It's the most dignifying thing in my life. If you don't want me here, we can figure out something different. I can sleep out in the gypsy wagon for now."

He laughed. "Where did that idea come from? That I don't want you here?"

She was appalled at herself. She'd been so certain she knew what she wanted—not marriage. Did she want it now? "I can get married," she said. "I can figure out how to make it work for me."

William studied her. He had grown very used to her face and found her more beautiful than he had Crystal. He loved her slim nose and full lips. He loved her fair skin and the few freckles across her nose and her dark eyes and her breasts, her body, all of her against him. He could make love to her any moment of any day. But she wasn't his. She had taught him the lesson that humans are free and cannot be owned, that the soul is always its own. He hadn't liked learning that. "Sophie, I know you. Your love for music is beautiful."

Her eyes were wet.

"Oh, Sophie." He sighed and reached for her, but she shook him off.

Sophie felt her eyes go hot, felt tears threaten again. *This is stupid. Why do I feel this way?*

"Just give us both a little time, Sophie. You're not certain. And you have good reason to want all the things you want."

I am certain! her heart cried. *All I want is to be with my daughter.*

But she wasn't certain. When had she ever been?

The potential for certainty might have been there long ago, before Patrick Wray had raped her.

"Like I told you, if you want to go on tour with Peter Haight," William said, "I'll help you explain to Amy. And I think her reaction might be quite different from what you expect."

"You want me to go?"

William couldn't speak. *No, I don't want you to go!* He shook his head. "But…maybe you should."

Sophie didn't understand her own feelings. When she'd left relationships in the past, it had been with a huge feeling of relief, like taking a breath of fresh air after having been submerged in water.

William had just granted her freedom, had just

blessed her freedom, but his words gave her no similar feeling of relief.

He was encouraging her to go on tour with Peter Haight. Yet she felt no euphoria.

Well, one thing was for sure. He was wrong about Amy, that she could walk away from Amy and he or both of them could explain it and make it all right. Amy was no longer an infant. She was fourteen, and she and Sophie had a relationship.

But what if she *could* take Amy on the road with her?

That wasn't what she wanted. She wanted the chance to play with Peter Haight. They had played together; he'd expressed interest in doing it again, fairly soon.

Would a man who loved her, who was in love with her, be encouraging her to leave?

William wasn't like other men. He had a core of realism. And it wasn't his nature to cling.

He knew her. He had seen the change in her the summer she came back to Ouray after she'd been raped. He'd seen her turn her back on him and Amy and set out in search of fame and fortune. William *knew* her, and William doubted. He doubted she could marry him. He must doubt that she could truly love…anyone.

But he doubts himself, too.

She didn't know what his childhood had been like, but occasionally he said something that gave a clue. *Oh, I've seen her yell.* His mother. At his father. *Oh, she complained.* About the infidelity. And one admission, like an island in the midst of her ignorance of his past: *He took Jonathan and me with him to Tahiti, and he was meeting a woman there. He didn't even bother to hide it from us.*

Sophie said, "I've decided not to go on tour with Peter, and I'm sticking by that decision."

He kept his eyes on her violin. He didn't answer. She couldn't guess what he was thinking.

"All right." With no other visible reaction, he turned and went back downstairs.

When the outside door closed behind him, Sophie realized she'd been holding her breath. Trembling, she wondered what had happened to her, to the Sophie Creed who was so independent, who *always* seized the chance to pursue her dreams?

But maybe a dream she'd never acknowledged, been afraid to acknowledge, was the dream of knowing her own daughter, being a mother to Amy.

Like that's all there is to it, Sophie. You're in love with him. That's what's happened.

Was William in love with her? She didn't know. It was possible that, after the choice she'd *made* fourteen years earlier, he never could be again.

Falling in love wasn't within anyone's control. If it was, she'd have *made* herself fall in love with any number of people in her life over the last decade.

And loving couldn't really be prevented, either.

If he truly loved her—or was, more precisely, *in love* with her—he wouldn't be able to stop himself.

She desperately wanted him to love her. And that was as surprising as knowing she'd fallen irrevocably in love with him.

AMY CHECKED the cabin, then peered outside and saw that Sophie's truck was gone. It was 8:00 p.m. Her father was in the training barn with an advanced obedience class.

She picked up the phone and dialed Tommy's number.

It wasn't that she was hiding from her parents. She would have called him if they'd been inside, too.

"Hello?" It was his grandmother.

"Hi, this is Amy Ludlow. Is Tommy there?"

"Of course, Amy. One moment."

Tommy answered. "Hi. Can you come?"

"Actually, he's not letting me out at all."

"What do you mean?"

"Exactly what I said. I asked if I could just walk to town for ice cream with you, and he said I'd been out at night too much lately." She'd already told Tommy that Sophie had seen her getting into his Jeep. One of Sophie's notebooks, in which she scrawled who knew what, lay on the kitchen counter. Idly, Amy flipped it open.

Oh. Songs.

"It's too bad," Tommy said. "I was really hoping to see you."

"You can come over here, if you want. My dad said that was okay."

"And do what?"

"Hang out."

Her eyes fell on the lyrics in Sophie's handwriting. *The chance that went by/ you and I/ three little people and a hill of beans…*

Amy didn't hear what Tommy said next as she tried to figure out if it was a song about a love triangle. But no…

Noble sacrifice/ buried dreams/ someone else will have to dig you out/ but you'll be gone/ there's only me/ to make the dreams reality….

Amy turned a page in the notebook. Tommy was saying he'd call her back if he could come over. Then he asked, "Would they let you come here? Then we could just go into town and they'd never know. My grandparents are going out to play bridge tonight."

"I'm sure they won't. They're suspicious. I think they know we didn't climb Sneffels."

"I wish you didn't have to sneak around."

She didn't know why the statement irritated her. She *didn't* have to sneak around. Tommy could come up to her parents' house, and they could hang out. Hell, her dad wouldn't even care if she took Tommy up to her bedroom. He and Sophie just wanted to know where she was and make sure she was safe.

But Tommy wanted to go to the party.

He also wanted other things from Amy, things she wasn't prepared to relinquish. Good grief, she couldn't even tell him the truth about what had happened to her mom, about who her natural father was. Nothing that had happened this summer made her feel like going all the way with Tommy Travis or anyone else. Not now, anyway.

If she couldn't go to the party, he'd find a girl who could.

It made her angry—that she wasn't allowed to go to the party.

She said, "Well, good night then." She stared at another page in the notebook. *"Withering," words and music by Sophie Creed and Peter Haight.*

Peter Haight? The folk singer?

She didn't know anything about Sophie doing music with Peter Haight.

But the lyrics were dated.

Her mother had written that song with Peter Haight the day before, when she'd gone to Paonia.

He was the one she'd gone to meet.

Did her dad know?

He must, Amy thought as she hung up the phone. But why hadn't her mom talked about it? And where was Sophie now?

"WE'RE LOOKING," said Amanda, "at going down to Argentina in the fall. Your dad and I want to work on installing clean wells."

"Will you take James?" Sophie asked. For the first time in her life, she dreaded her parents' going away. What if William asked her to move out? What if she learned he really didn't love her? *I need my mother.*

She had come to her parents' house to practice obedience with her mother and James. She had brought Spinner, who needed obedience as badly as James did.

Now she'd spent most of the evening wondering how to ask her mother if Amanda thought William really loved her.

"Oh, yes. We're going to take him. He's little, so we think he'll travel well."

Both dogs were on downs, faces turned to Sophie and Amanda, waiting to be told they could get up.

Sophie could tell that James's patience with the exercise was waning.

She debated whether to let it go until he got up on his own, so that her mother could correct him and thereby teach him the meaning of *Stay* or whether to release the dogs immediately. She chose the latter.

After she and Amanda had both said "Okay," the dogs got up, and Sophie took them out to the yard to run around.

She began talking, managing to explain about Peter Haight and about what William had said, not mentioning Amy's slight delinquency.

"It makes me uneasy," she admitted. "I'm honestly not sure William wants me around."

Amanda shook her head. "You could've fooled me. Watching the two of you at the wedding was nearly as romantic as seeing the bride and groom. William couldn't keep his eyes off you. Maybe he's just waiting to see what you'll do. Here you've had a wonderful offer, and he probably can't believe that you won't desert him—or that if you stay you won't regret your decision and resent him and Amy."

Sophie thought this over.

"So patience is the only solution?" she asked. "Time? Until he trusts me?" *Trusts me enough to let himself love me again?*

The phone rang, and Amanda answered it. "Hello, Amy. Certainly." She handed the phone to Sophie.

"Hello?"

"Hi, Mom. When are you coming home?"

"Very soon. Why?"

"Just wondering. You played music with Peter Haight yesterday. Dad said he wanted you to go on tour with him but that you've decided not to."

"Yes."

"I think you should," said Amy. "I think you're staying here because of me, and I think you should follow your dreams, that's all."

Sophie tried to understand what she was hearing, tried to understand why Amy would urge her to leave.

"But I wouldn't see you anymore."

"You'd see me sometimes. It wouldn't last forever. Maybe I could come with you. Not all the time. Just once in a while."

"Well, for now, I'm coming home," Sophie answered. "I'll see you soon, okay?"

CHAPTER SIXTEEN

WILLIAM LAY IN THE DARK beside Sophie and knew she wasn't asleep yet. He rolled over and held her, and when she snuggled against him, he inhaled her scent and wanted her again.

She kissed him with a kind of desperation. He knew she was in love with him. She had been long ago, too, and he with her.

He put his hands in her hair, kissing her, loving her, soothing her.

She wanted him to marry her, or to ask her to marry him.

He knew why he felt unwilling—or at least unready—to do this. There were many reasons. The first was that he didn't believe her *not* touring with Peter Haight was going to make anyone happy. That wasn't what he wanted from her, wasn't what he'd ever wanted. The second was that he doubted marriage itself was a happy institution. The third—the third he contemplated as little as possible.

That they would become engaged—or married—and she would leave again. Not leave on tour but *leave.*

There was another reason, too. There was no point in even looking at that reason, however, not with these other concerns so real.

With Crystal, it had been different. He still couldn't imagine telling her. He couldn't imagine her reaction.

Life didn't seem to have touched her in anyway that would allow her to understand.

But Sophie... He *could* imagine telling her. Still, why do it? Her future was music, fame, creation; it wasn't marriage to him and his.

When Sophie had arrived home from her parents' house, he'd listened to Amy admit that she'd looked through the songs Sophie had written, both alone and with Peter Haight. *Mom, don't give up this chance for me. You're a star. I want to hear the music you can make with Peter Haight.*

Sophie had said, *I've decided to stay here.*

He didn't want her to stay, not at the price of giving up the things she'd worked for. Because, to him, she was still—and would always be—a teenage girl telling him what had happened in a Porsche with a man who used to be her teacher. *He just kept telling me to do it. I kept saying I didn't want to.*

Pregnancy had almost cut short her dreams. And she'd gone after them anyhow. But changed. A change had been wrought in her that no one should have to experience. The summer before it happened, she'd been innocent. Her loss of innocence wasn't as simple as a loss of virginity. Something had been taken from her. Crystal, too, had gone through this. Sometimes he wondered if that was why he'd finally asked Crystal to marry him. That it had been like taking care of Sophie.

Except that Sophie could not be taken care of.

"William?"

"Mmm?"

"I love you."

He held her tight, her head against his throat.

Lying against him, Sophie reflected on her past relationships. She didn't like to think about any of the other men she'd been with. Now, none of them seemed safe, and she couldn't say why, except that it had been impossible for her to truly know them and even more impossible for them to know her.

Only William was safe. Because with William, the mysteries, the uncertainties, didn't matter. She'd known him so long, and it felt as though she'd known him even longer, since the oceans were formed.

"Will, why aren't you sure?"

William told her what he'd just considered—the three obstacles.

"So you want me to tour with Peter Haight," she said. "And you're not convinced marriage is a good thing anyway and you think I'm going to bail again. But you were going to marry Crystal."

"I had cold feet. I'm not sure I could've gone through with it."

"So you're never going to marry me."

William stroked her back, thinking about it, hungry for her, yearning for her. "I don't want—" His voice surprised him. Too quiet, and he could not speak more loudly. "I don't want to wreck things between us, Sophie."

"How?"

He just shook his head.

Sophie knew what was troubling him, what must be eating at him. The past. Not a mysterious unknown past but the past when she'd left William and Amy and gone in pursuit of a career in music. And he'd been left alone, bitter at her departure, with a newborn. It was possible that he hadn't forgiven her for leaving.

Even now.

And there was nothing she could do about that history except stay.

If he let her.

WILLIAM WAS UP FIRST in the morning, and when she came downstairs, he was on the phone. "Mrs. Simms, I know she did… But that was a special circumstance. She's not really a wedding singer. She's a folk singer, and—"

"I'll do it," said Sophie, walking down the stairs. "If you and Amy will back me up again." Maybe agreeing to play more weddings would help convince William that she was serious about remaining with him and Amy.

But maybe his telling this Mrs. Simms that I don't do weddings is another sign he wants me to leave.

But she knew William. William had been the one to ask her to move in. And he would ask her to move out if that was what he wanted.

William gave Sophie a rueful smile and said, "Mrs. Simms, she is interested. Let me give her the phone."

Sophie took the cordless from him. Mrs. Simms had been at Jodie and Micah's wedding and had been *so moved* by their family performance and she'd loved that one song that Sophie and William sang, that song about *believing*. Her granddaughter was getting married in Ridgway in August and hadn't done anything about music yet.

Sophie said, "I'll need to talk to whoever is hiring us."

"Well, I'm positive she'll want it. It'll be my gift to them. I did go ahead and ask Jodie what you charged, and she told me. Would you be willing to do it for that again?"

"Yes."

She would do it and grow used to singing at weddings and helping train dogs until William was as sure of her as Amy was.

But when she hung up the phone, William said,

"Why are you doing this? I know you want to play with Peter Haight."

"It's not a romantic thing, playing with Peter. You know that, don't you?"

"Yes, Sophie."

"And I love playing with you."

"I know you like playing with me, but Peter Haight is Peter Haight. Don't give up who you are for me and Amy or anyone else."

"I'm not. I'm expanding who I am."

"By singing at weddings? You hate weddings."

"The last one was my favorite ever." She looked long and hard at William. "Do you not trust me to stay with you?"

Sometimes he wasn't sure he trusted himself. He wasn't superstitious, but he could relate to Amy's fears of tainted genes, so to speak, more than she could ever have guessed. No surprise, really, that he'd opted to tell Amy her mother was dead. His life seemed wound around various deceits, not all of them his. It had occurred to him more than once that his father lived the life he did because of Moira's invasiveness; yet even if that was true, his father's response was still unsatisfactory, unacceptable, wrong. And it was part of him, that wrongness. The ongoing lie was part of him. "It's not that."

"What is it?"

"Many people can make a commitment and keep it. To be married, for instance. But it's not good if people decide to do something traditional for…for the wrong reasons."

Was he talking about his parents? Sophie was afraid to ask. She talked around it instead. "You think I'm staying with you because of Amy."

He shook his head.

"Or you're with me because of her?"

"No."

"So what are you talking about?"

"People can't always—or don't always—I'm not convinced it's a matter of *can't—*" *Was* that what he believed? Did he believe in free will? His mother's? His father's? His own?

Yes.

To think that, because one of his parents had made bad choices, some evil could lurk inside his blood was superstition, no more, no less.

And to believe it would be to let Amy down. Because then she could believe the same thing—that Patrick Wray's character dictated the kind of person she would be.

So tell Sophie. Tell her and then ask her to marry you.

He quailed at the thought.

"So. When's the wedding?" he asked, instead.

"The third weekend in August. I'll have to meet with the bride and groom, but it sounds like they do want us."

William nodded, still wishing she'd take advantage of what Peter Haight was offering, wishing she'd accept the rewards she'd earned.

What if he asked her to marry him on the condition that she agreed to tour with Peter Haight.

Yet that seemed too much like something he'd known his whole life.

A twisted kind of bribery.

The money to develop the botanical gardens, a grand piano, so many consolation gifts, so many types of appeasement, from his father to his mother.

William and his mother no longer spoke of it. Her stance never changed, and he knew it both pained her and shamed her if he brought it up, leaving him with feelings of guilt and a desperate need to protect her from all the hurt his father caused.

What would Sophie say, she of the normal family—adoptive but nonetheless healthy?

Amy came down just then. "I'm going to Tommy's."

Here we go, Sophie thought.

"No," William said.

"What?"

"I think you're planning to ride in his car. I think you lied to me when you said you were going to climb Mount Sneffels. If this guy won't go out with you unless you can get into his car, dump him."

Sophie watched, resigned to seeing William's method play out.

"What makes you think he won't go out with me unless I can ride in his car?" Amy demanded.

"Where did you go instead of Mount Sneffels?"

"*Nowhere.* You're one to accuse someone else of lying."

William saw Sophie turn away.

Amy had said the unanswerable. "He's a safe driver," she continued.

"There's no substitute for experience, and he's not old enough to make me comfortable."

"You'd feel better if he was twenty-three?"

William tried to remember if she'd always had such a smart mouth or if he'd only noticed it since her mother had come back into her life.

Amy shrugged. "Well, I'm going anyhow." She headed for the door.

"No, you're not."

"You can't stop me." She opened the door.

He stepped past her and shut it. "Go up to your room until you're ready to apologize."

"For *what?*"

"Because I feed you and clothe you and house you. I'm your father, and you're not a brat."

Amy turned abruptly and ran back upstairs. Her door's slamming reverberated through the house.

Sophie said, "Maybe we could get her a cell phone."

"After that?"

"Then we'd know where she is and who she's with."

"And you think she'd take no for an answer ever again?"

"I think she's only going to get older—and less and less likely to 'take no for an answer,' as you put it."

"You should let me handle this my way," he said.

"Why? Because you figure I'm not going to be here?"

He didn't answer.

It occurred to Sophie that perhaps she was experiencing some kind of karma. For all the lovers she'd been unwilling to marry. For all the years she'd spent away from William and Amy. For all the men she'd hurt. For hurting William.

For his protecting Amy from the same hurt. Clearly, that had been his intent in telling Amy that her mother was dead. And now Amy was lying to him.

If she asked him to marry her, what would be his reply?

It wouldn't help. If he wanted to marry her, he would ask.

Can I bear to stay in this relationship, loved but not loved enough for him to marry me? Loved less than Crystal?

Amy had urged her to go on tour with Peter.

So had William.

"If I went on tour," she said, "would you allow Amy to come with me sometimes?"

"Yes."

William thought, *She's going.* And he knew that this time Sophie wasn't leaving in pursuit of fame. She was fleeing a relationship in which she didn't feel herself to be an equal.

A proposal of marriage touched the tip of his tongue, like something he couldn't rid himself of. Yet he couldn't say it, because to say it to Sophie would require other revelations.

So tell her the bad part first. She's leaving. There's nothing to lose.

He said, "Want to take the dogs for a walk?"

"Amy will leave. And you asked her to apologize, which she hasn't done yet."

He hadn't forgotten, any more than he would forget he'd put a dog in a long down.

But it didn't seem important right now.

"I'll be back in a minute." He ran up the stairs and at the top rapped on Amy's door.

"What?"

"It's Dad."

"Come in."

She sat in the lotus position, looking both calmer and more mature than he'd expected.

He said, "You can go to Tommy's. You can ride in his car. Your mother and I are going for a walk."

Amy stared. "Why are you doing this?"

"I'm getting you a cell phone. Don't lie to us anymore. If you do and we find out, the cell phone and everything else goes, and I will make your life hell."

"I believe you."

He returned downstairs. Sophie had already gone outside.

They took Cinders, Loki and Sigurd and hiked up the gravel road, covering their faces when cars went past spitting gravel and dust.

"I want to tell you something I've never discussed with anyone outside my family."

She made a movement beside him.

"My father," he said, "for all intents and purposes, has two wives."

Sophie turned toward him. Her sunglasses hid the expression in her eyes but she looked baffled. "You mean—legally?"

"I don't know the law. He's married to my mother in this country. He has a woman in New Guinea as well, and they have seven children."

Sophie tried to absorb this, to see it, to believe it, to take in the reality that she knew William yet she'd never known this about his father. "Does your mother know?"

He shrugged. "I'm not sure how much she's aware of, but—my mother says he's not married to the other woman, that the other woman is not important to him. That she herself is his wife."

He watched Sophie playing it over, considering the angles.

"So," she said, "it's been going on for at least a little while."

"Almost twenty years."

"Does Amy know?"

He shook his head and repeated his conversation with Amy in the training barn, when he'd told her that her grandfather was unfaithful to her grandmother. "Strange. I never expected anything good out of that situation—for me, I mean. But it might have helped Amy. We have a parallel burden. Her situation's worse, but my father's behavior might help her live with her father's."

"Yes," Sophie agreed. "But tell me—have you met… these people? His other family?"

"Some of them. Not the younger kids. Jonathan gave me the most recent report."

"Your brother? Is he out there?"

"He's met my dad out there."

"You don't talk to your father about it?"

"Would you?"

Sophie considered. "Yes. I think I'd want to know them."

"You don't even want to know your own birth mother, Sophie."

"That's not exactly true. I just don't feel I *need* to know her. So what did your father say to your brother? He must have offered some explanation."

"Zero."

"Your brother's sure?"

"Apparently there's no mistaking the situation."

"This doesn't—" and she looked straight ahead up the road "—have anything to do with your not wanting to marry me, does it? I gather Crystal never knew."

"She didn't. And no, it doesn't have much to do with our future—yours and mine. Except that it's shaped who I am."

"Your mother knows," Sophie clarified. "Who told her?"

"I don't know. Maybe she found out on her own. She and I argued about it. She said it was nothing for me to worry about."

"Was it?"

"Oh, please. They'd have screaming fights. She'd end up sobbing, then insist he doesn't really understand what he's doing, that he operates 'outside our culture.'"

"So this isn't why you're having doubts about marrying me."

"No. Not exactly. But it's like an evil covering my family. A curse no one mentions. We're all tainted by it."

"Think about what you told Amy! Come on, William,

you're not your father, and his crime isn't yours." No more than Any was *her* biological father, no more than she was cursed by *his* crime. As William had been the first to point out. "I'll bet you've never so much as cheated on a lover."

True. "I've never talked to anyone about it before—anyone but my family," he repeated. "You *are* my best friend, Sophie."

Her smile was a slow dawning, familiar. And brief.

Sophie understood now. She saw how steeped in secrecy and deceit his childhood had been. How could he be expected to marry, have a family, have normal relationships? "How did you find out?"

"Oh, my dad took me and Jonathan with him to New Guinea. Our mom was doing a music workshop in Sydney. He introduces us to this woman, and Sophie, believe me, these people are *different* from us. And they've got this one-year-old kid who's half-white, and it becomes really obvious that my father is the dad. Jonathan and I are just totally baffled."

"Wait—this isn't the woman you knew who died of kuru, of that virus that was spread through mortuary cannibalism?"

"No, but she has practiced cannibalism, too, before my dad knew her. I haven't seen her for years."

Sophie had the unsettled feeling that they hadn't reached the bottom of it, that his father's Papua New Guinea had been no place for William and his younger brother.

He took her hand just as Sophie called to Loki, who had strayed across the road to sniff some weeds at the base of a boulder.

"Would you like," he said, "to be my wife?"

Sophie glanced up at him. He was asking now, and she hadn't expected it.

Married. You'll never be free again.

But she was sure now. She'd learned how to want the love he offered. Now, in the same step, she understood how to get married. "Yes."

"But I want to ask you a favor," he said and stopped walking. "The favor is you tour with Peter Haight this year."

"You want to wait a year to marry?"

"Not really. I want to marry you, Sophie, and I want you to go and do what you were born to do. Amy and I will come and join you when we can. And we'll be there when you can come to us."

"But I promised Amy I wouldn't go."

"Sophie, I heard Amy last night. She and I have talked about it. She believes that you love her and that it's dumb for you to give up your career for her. We want to support you, Sophie. Family members help each other. Amy and I want to help you."

"You really want to marry me?"

"Sophie, I've wanted to marry you for fifteen years. I want to do the growing-old-together thing with you."

"Together but apart. Touring with Peter Haight. You're really just looking for a way to keep me out of your hair," Sophie challenged.

"Anything for a little peace."

She grinned, half-laughing. "Then, there's only one issue left to settle."

"Hmm?"

"Who's going to play at our wedding?"

William sighed. "I don't want anyone mediocre. I wish I knew someone who had some influence with say, Peter Haight, or someone like that."

"I'm not sure he plays at weddings."

"Maybe that should be another condition."

Sophie laughed. "For whom?"

"For you. If you want to marry me, you've got to find someone to sing for us. Someone who can do that song…you know the one…I can't remember the title."

Sophie held his hand tighter and whispered, with truth, "Now, I believe."

"Shall we walk down to Tommy's house and interrupt Amy?"

"I'd like to know what they're up to anyhow," Sophie told him.

"Not as much as I would."

Tommy's red Jeep was in the driveway, and Tala barked and ran around the side of the house to greet Sigurd, Loki and Cinders.

Tommy and Amy were climbing a twelve-foot-high boulder beside the house.

"You brought your climbing shoes," William said when he saw her.

"No. Actually, we went back up to get them. I keep forgetting that they have this great bouldering place. See what I can do."

Sophie and William watched her pull herself up an overhang and over the top of the boulder, Tommy below her spotting.

"What are you guys doing here?" she called down.

William stole a look at Sophie and she at him.

"We were going to try and lure you away for a few minutes," said Sophie.

Amy hung over the side of the boulder and jumped down. "You can talk to me in front of Tommy." She trembled as she said it, and Sophie wondered if Amy feared they were angry with her or were going to deprive her of privileges.

Sophie saw the faint shake of William's head. He said, "Want to go down to Ouray for lunch? Both of you?"

Tommy said, "I have to go to work actually."

He had gotten a job at the hot springs pool. Sophie thought that either Amy would become a regular at the pool or Tommy would find another girl—more likely, other *girls.*

Amy said, "I'll go to lunch."

"Good. We'll go when you get home."

THEY SAT OUTSIDE on the patio of a historic hotel. William had ordered a bottle of wine, and Amy was drinking some sort of tea grown in Tibet.

Over the bread and wine, William said, "How would you feel if your mom and I finally got married?"

Amy had been sampling her tea and set it down abruptly. She shrugged. "Okay. I don't know why I'm surprised."

She drank some more tea, rather fast, and Sophie thought, *All of this has been much harder on her than she lets on.*

"Yeah, it's fine," she said.

She acted as if it was of no moment to her one way or the other.

"Obviously," she said to Sophie, "you're better than Crystal."

"Oh, thank you."

Amy said, "You should let me plan your wedding. You can pay me for it."

Sophie laughed. "Okay," she agreed. "It's a deal."

"Grandma is going to go nuts," Amy admitted frankly. "She doesn't like you much, Mom."

I'd better work on that, Sophie decided.

THAT AFTERNOON, when Amy had ridden her bicycle down to the pool and William was training dogs, Sophie visited the botanical gardens.

Moira greeted her more warmly than Sophie had expected. William's mother kissed her cheek, embraced her and said, "Come on. I'll walk through with you. Where's Amy?"

It was a better beginning than she'd hoped for from a woman who believed that Sophie had ruined her son's life.

"Amy's at the pool," Sophie said now.

Moira nodded. She showed Sophie the native plants, and together they hiked up behind the gardens to examine the trees, verdant after a summer of rain. When Sophie commented on this, Moira said, "Unfortunately, looks can be deceiving. The forests here are like tinder because of the long drought we had a few years ago. Trees don't recover from that. The Gambel oak doesn't recover, either." Thoughtfully, Moira said, "Amy seems to like having you in her life. How long are you planning to stay?"

Sophie didn't want to be the one to tell Moira that she and William were getting married. William had said he'd call his mother that night. "Well, I'll be in and out." She couldn't mention the tour with Peter Haight, either, not until she spoke with Peter again.

"She seems to be lying to William to a degree she never used to," Moira remarked.

Sophie didn't know what to say.

"*I've* been like a mother to her," Moira said. "She's been like my daughter."

"Yes."

"I'm concerned about her. She used to be more levelheaded. But suddenly there's this Tommy, so I suppose that's it."

"William thinks she's lying because— Well, I guess we think it's because she likes this guy and she's determined to get in his car with him. And I find it very frightening to have her riding in cars with kids who've only just learned to drive. Did you lie, growing up?" Sophie asked.

"Some. My parents were very strict. What about you?"

"I was—well, I was a pretty good kid."

"Until you got pregnant."

It stopped Sophie. She'd forgotten the long-ago recriminations that had fallen on her and William for "getting into trouble." Moira had blamed her exclusively. Then, even worse, she, Sophie, had left William with the baby. Would Moira ever learn the truth, that Amy wasn't her biological granddaughter? Would it matter to her? Sophie couldn't help thinking that perhaps it would.

Well, if Amy decided to tell people, that was up to her.

"Sometimes," Moira said, opening the door of the greenhouse where she raised exotic plants, "I wish I could give William his future back."

"What do you mean?"

"Oh, I don't know. Both of you had everything ahead of you. His father and I didn't want him to throw it away. We wouldn't trade anything in the world for Amy, of course. You just have hopes for your children. You don't like their options limited."

"Have you ever felt that your choices limited your options?" Sophie said before she could stop herself.

"You mean marriage and children? Or staying married?"

It was the first time Sophie had know Moira to admit to her that she'd perhaps considered *not* staying married.

"Well, it's lasted," Moira said, clearly meaning her marriage to Bill Ludlow. "You decide, really, every day, to be married. It's not a one-time thing."

Did Moira decide to be married—or not—as she

faced the daily reality of her spouse's other partner? Was accepting that situation part of her vision of marriage?

"Do you think Amy and I are obstructing William's future right now?" Sophie asked. *Just say it all, Moira,* she thought. *Say everything that's on your mind.*

"Well, Crystal really could have opened doors for him. With his law enforcement background, going to Washington with her... Well—" Moira shrugged extravagantly. "And Amy would've done better in a more urban environment. Better educational opportunities."

Sophie didn't bother telling Moira that she couldn't imagine William living in the city again and that he probably couldn't picture living there either. It wasn't fair for her to ask William's mother her true feelings without letting her know that Sophie was going to marry her son.

So Sophie said instead, "You know that song we sang at Jodie and Micah's wedding?"

"Oh, yes. Your famous song," Moira allowed in a disinterested voice.

"I wrote that song for William a long time ago."

His mother suddenly spun around. "And then you *left,* Sophie Creed. I can't believe you'd brush aside the pain you caused by mentioning a silly love song you wrote when you were eighteen."

Sophie was afraid that if she stayed—or if she left—she would cry. It was important that Moira Ludlow not see that. She would find those tears as silly as Sophie's only Grammy-nominated song.

Her one-hit wonder.

The wedding song.

"Thank you for the tour," she said quickly, blinking

too much. "Oh, gosh. I'm going to be late. I promised William I'd help him with the dogs. We'll see you soon."

It was awkward, and Moira had to know she was crying.

But Sophie didn't see her future mother-in-law's reaction, because even now Moira made no move toward her.

She just said, "Well, don't make him keep his clients waiting."

CHAPTER SEVENTEEN

THE FACT THAT her fiancé's mother was a beastly woman who disliked her was not going to stop Sophie from marrying him. She told William about the conversation, and William said, "Sophie, it's a good song. Everyone likes that song. It's a classic. 'Moon River' is a silly song if 'Now, I Believe' is. I apologize for her. I'm sorry she made you cry."

And that was it.

Amy, home from the pool late that afternoon and learning that William planned to call his mother to tell her about the engagement, said, "Oh, put her on speaker phone. This should be good."

"Okay, but I'm telling her she's on speaker phone."

Sophie said, "She's going to insist that you're ruining your life."

"My mother is a very adaptable person." He dialed her number. As promised, he told Moira she was on the speaker phone, then said, "I have some really great news. I'm very happy because Sophie and I are getting married."

A second's pause. "Well, that's wonderful, William! Oh, I'm so happy. Is Amy there?"

"Hi, Grandma."

"Amy, are you happy?"

"I'm completely satisfied."

"That sounds qualified."

"It's not."

"Well, congratulations, William," came Moira's voice through the phone. "I'm not going to congratulate you, Sophie, because you don't congratulate the bride-to-be, but I do think you've made a good choice in William, if I do say so."

William and Amy both rolled their eyes, and Amy buried her face in a pillow on the couch.

"I think so, too," Sophie agreed.

"Well, let's hope this wedding comes off, William," his mother said. "Try not to get cold feet this time. It's rather soon after Crystal, you know."

William said, "We just wanted to tell you the good news. We're about to have dinner," he lied without a blush, "so we'll talk to you later."

"All right. Well, I hope you're happy, sweetie," she said doubtfully.

As William hung up, Amy said, "Gosh, Dad, I hope you're happy in spite of making a choice Grandma obviously thinks is dreadful."

He laughed. "But that you and I think is really good."

"Exactly!" Amy sprang up from the couch, ran across the living room and hugged and kissed her mother.

THEY DECIDED to be married at the winter solstice.

Sophie contacted Peter Haight and told him she'd be able to tour with him. He came to Ouray regularly. They played music in the cabin, and Peter liked incorporating William's violin and voice and Amy's clarinet into some of the songs. They recorded in Paonia and in Durango and in one of the churches in Ouray whose acoustics Peter particularly liked. The CD would come out the following spring, and the tour would follow. In the meantime, she and Peter were performing at smaller venues in Colorado, New Mexico and Utah. They recorded a live version of "Now, I Believe," rewritten to a theme of world peace at a festival protesting the war.

William's father returned from Papua New Guinea in September, and Sophie and William asked him and Moira over for dinner with Sophie's parents. Because Peter was in town, they invited him, as well, and Tommy came, too.

Sophie's parents showed none of Moira's misgivings at the prospect of Sophie's and William's wedding. They'd been very pleased, happy for their daughter, delighted by Amy's enthusiasm about the upcoming wedding.

Sophie and William made lasagna for dinner. Amy sauteed asparagus and pine nuts.

As Sophie set out the salad and everyone began filling their plates, then sitting casually around the living room and kitchen, wherever each was comfortable, Dan Creed asked William's father, "What have you been doing in New Guinea?"

"I'm creating a dictionary of five local dialects of a very small region, complete with language tapes."

"That sounds like quite an endeavor. Who's your publisher?"

Bill named the university press, and there was no hint of the other part of his life in New Guinea, another woman, another family. Sophie had told her mother about the situation, simply because she didn't think keeping it to herself was necessarily for the best. Veil upon veil of secrecy was oppressive. She had seen its weight on William.

Moira sat on the edge of the couch, smiling serenely, behaving as always, giving no clue that her home life was anything out of the ordinary.

"Sophie," Moira said, "have you ever considered looking for your biological family?"

Sophie tried not to see this as another not-so-subtle attempt to persuade her to leave Ouray, William and Amy. "No. If my birth mother wanted to meet me, I'd do it, because I know what it would mean to her. But my parents are my parents." She smiled at Dan and Amanda.

"How did you adopt Sophie?" Moira turned to them.

Sophie could not believe that William's mother was asking these personal questions at a dinner that was not just family. She had never even mentioned to Peter, for instance, that she was adopted.

"We adopted her through an international adoption agency. She was just a few hours old. It was planned for some time."

"See, Grandma," Amy said, "blood doesn't matter. Like Dad was with me when I was born, and he's my dad."

"Well, he's also your biological father," said Moira.

Peter sat with his elbows resting on his knees, looking intrigued by the bizarre family interactions. Sophie wondered if he was writing lyrics in his head.

Amy's face froze slightly. Her head tilted up. Sophie instantly remembered the Amy she had first come to know, the Amy who spoke of *knowing* things, the Amy who said she felt like Cassandra and like a Delphic sibyl, her sense of inner precognition was that strong. Sophie remembered when Amy, some years ago, had not told the truth, had been frightened into maintaining a lie. She thought of Amy's more recent lies. Little lies.

But surely Amy wasn't going to tell this assembly that Sophie had been raped. *Not even my parents know, Amy.*

Yet she would say nothing to stop Amy speaking. *It's*

her right. Amy was aware that none of her grandparents knew that William wasn't her biological father.

Sophie stared down at her hands.

The silence lasted.

Moira said, "Isn't he?" Just the conclusion to her sentence. Not a question. A reaffirmation of blood.

Peter finished his plate and said, "Tommy, I was wondering if you'd take me for a ride in that Jeep of yours. I've been thinking of getting one."

Sophie gave him a grateful smile.

When the two were gone, Sophie looked at Amy. "Did you want to say something?"

"I always want to say things, but this is a family bent on concealing key truths."

Her four grandparents gazed at her in surprise.

Sophie eyed William. He nodded, agreeing.

"This is difficult," Sophie said. "William has known always." She could not say it in front of all these people. But why not? It wasn't her sin, it wasn't her shame. An appalling thing had been done to her. And it had changed her. If there was healing, it was in the joy of knowing her daughter and the certainty of William's fundamental *normalcy,* that he did not use her sexually, that he loved the entire person she was. "Soon after I left high school, I had a date with one of my former teachers. He raped me. Amy is the—really wonderful—result."

Dan Creed gaped. Shock and sorrow distorted her mother's face.

These people care. My parents love me, and they're not only horrified that this happened; they're upset that I never told them, that I suffered alone.

"Oh, darling," said her mother.

Sophie did not look at the Ludlows, but she heard and felt Moira stand and take her plate to the kitchen. "I would think," she said, "that you might at least have told *us,* William. Though I suppose you wanted to keep it a secret, Sophie."

"We both did," William replied. He moved, abandoning his food, which James promptly leaped up to the couch to devour. William ignored the dog and sat between his daughter and his fiancée. "And none of us is unhappy with the outcome." He smiled at Amy. "Now that Amy's allowed to ride in Tommy's car."

"Ha ha," she said.

Moira said, "Well, of course it doesn't make any difference. We still love you, Amy."

"I should hope so," Sophie snapped, unable to stop herself. Moira's being hurtful to her was one thing, but she wasn't going to let her wound Amy. "William *is* her father—" she looked at Dan "—as much as you are mine."

"Well, the marriage makes a lot more sense to me now," Moira said.

Sophie lifted her eyes toward the ceiling and rose from her place to start the dishes.

"Want to help me plan the wedding, Grandma?" asked Amy.

How wonderful you are, Sophie thought. *My peacemaker.*

THE MONTHS UNTIL THE WEDDING passed swiftly. Sophie and Amy went to Santa Fe together to buy dresses. The gown was a low-cut satin that Amy said looked like a gypsy dress or something an Indian princess would wear. She was to be the maid of honor and she wore a dress in a similar style in peach satin.

At eleven-thirty on the morning of December twenty-first, Amy was out in the training barn grooming dogs. William had spent the night before at his parents' house, so as not to see the bride before the wedding.

Amanda had come over to help Sophie and Amy dress, and Fiona was there, too.

After her shower, Sophie came out to the training barn in her bathrobe and asked, "What are you doing? Why are you bathing dogs?"

"I'm nervous, and grooming dogs always calms my nerves. Want a turn?"

"Grooming or being groomed?"

Amy gave a tiny grin. Loki stood on a grooming table, clearly not thrilled by the blow-dryer she was using. "I'm almost done. What time is it? Are you ready for me to do your hair?"

"Yes."

"Okay, you're after Loki."

Amy arranged her mother's hair in an elegant coronet with a center part, ringlets of her curls escaping. "You *do* look like a gypsy, Mom."

They drove to the church in the Creeds' car, and Sophie, Amy and Amanda all went into a room off the vestibule to wait.

Standing in the room with her daughter and her mother, Sophie reflected how she'd never imagined herself really getting married, let alone in a traditional church wedding.

She heard feet coming in and out of the church, heard William's voice and thought of the two weddings at which they'd sung together. The hope she'd believed could never be hers was with her this day.

Her mother went out to sit down. Then Sophie heard the first strains of music, and it wasn't Peter's guitar. It was a piano.

Amy went first. William's brother, Jonathan, was there to meet her, to walk down the aisle with her.

Sophie followed, taking her father's arm, smiling at him and seeing tears in his eyes.

Her own swept to the corner of the church where the musicians were playing the wedding march.

Moira at the piano.

Peter Haight on guitar.

The Wayfairers standing behind them, waiting.

Lalasa's eyes shone on Sophie's, not with an expression of resentment or jealousy, but with the tenderness of the friend Sophie remembered, a friend she now knew would love to spend some time sharing Bharata Natya with Amy, a friend who shared in generosity and love.

Her eyes said to Sophie, *I'm so happy for you. I wanted this for you.*

Beside the minister stood William, handsome in black tuxedo, Jonathan beside him. And fanning out in a row beside them, like four more attendants, Sigurd, Tala, Cinders and Loki.

As Sophie reached the front of the church, Amy nodded at the dogs, and they all lay down.

Sophie's eyes flooded. She lifted her gaze to William and saw his tears as well. She believed not just that he was hers and always had been. She believed in happily ever after.

"Do you, Sophia Tomaira Creed, take...?"

The ring.

Where was the ring?

From the back of the church came a small black dog carrying in his mouth a satin pillow with rings sewn on.

James came to the front of the church and sat before William, who took the rings from him.

"Thank you, James. Good boy."

James shook the pillow vigorously, grabbed it in his paws and ripped it in half. Stuffing spilled over the red carpet. He picked up some and brought it to the mother of the bride.

As they slid the rings onto each other's fingers, the Wayfairers played the opening chords to a song they'd played more often than any other.

And William sang to her, and she to him, *"Now, I believe...."*

COMING NEXT MONTH

#1338 NOT WITHOUT CAUSE • Kay David
The Operatives
Meredith Santera is the leader of the Operatives, putting the needs of others in front of her own. Which means that she chose the job over a relationship with Jack Haden. Now her job is putting her in contact with Jack once again. But this time they're on opposite sides.

#1339 SWEET MERCY • Jean Brashear
Once, Gamble Smith had everything—and then the love of his life decided, against medical advice, to have his child. Now he is a man lost in grief. Jezebel Hart can heal him. But she carries a secret she wants to share--one she knows Gamble isn't ready to hear, one that could destroy what the two of them have together.

#1340 BACK TO EDEN • Melinda Curtis
A Little Secret
On the eve of Missy's wedding to another man, Cole tried to convince her to go away with him. When he couldn't, he left, sure that she'd come to her senses eventually. He never glanced back and saw the result of their last night together.

#1341 EVERYTHING TO PROVE • Nadia Nichols
Going Back
Libby Wilson gave up a prestigious residency position to return to her Alaskan roots in search of her father. Now she desperately needs Carson Dodge's help. But Carson is recovering from a serious accident. Can he possibly be the man Libby needs him to be? They both have everything to prove....

#1342 UNEXPECTED COMPLICATION • Amy Knupp
9 Months Later
Carey Langford's going to have a baby. Too bad the father's a louse, and she has to do this alone. Fortunately, she has the support of her best friend, Devin Colyer. If only Devin could accept the child's paternity and admit his true feelings for Carey....

#1343 OVER HIS HEAD • Carolyn McSparren
Single Father
Tim Wainwright may be a professional educator, but since his wife died, he hasn't a clue how to handle his own children. Ironically, even Tim's new neighbor, Nancy Mayfield—a vet tech who prefers animals to people—seems to understand his kids better than he does.

HSRCNM0306